Angel oj ᴅᴇᴀᴛɴ

Michael Christopher Carter

Golden Hill Publishing

Contents

Angel of Death

Prologue

"Why have you come to see me? Why do you think you're here in my office today?"

Bloodshot eyes tear away from their occupation with the skirt hem tufting between chewed fingers. Peering up from the chair opposite, they meet the doctor's gaze for the first time and dart again to the safety of the fraying fabric.

"I don't mean to sound insensitive, but it is important. I could tell you why I think you're here, but that wouldn't be much use, I might be wrong."

The fidgeting slows but the scrutiny remains.

"Come on, Becca. Or do you prefer Rebecca, or Bex?"

"Becca. Just Becca."

He nods, knowing he'll have to try a less forward approach. "Okay, Becca. Is there anything you want to ask me?"

Stubby remains of fingernails press into her thigh and she rocks in jerky movements.

"You look exhausted."

Becca stops. Eyes tightening, her stare rises from her lap to the doctor's eyes.

He smiles. He's hit a nerve in the bullseye of his competence. "I might be able to give you some medicine to help you sleep, but I'll need to ask you some more questions first."

"NOOOO!" Leaping from her seat, arms outstretched, fingers like claws, her impetus to run to the door fails her and wobbling on the spot, Becca gives in and slumps back onto her chair. "No. I don't want something to make me sleep."

"Are you sure? You are showing a lot of signs that you haven't had enough: You have deep dark bags under your eyes and your skin looks pale and dry. You're unable to keep still; you seem very agitated."

"I haven't slept properly for two weeks. I can't."

"Why? No wonder you're not feeling great. It's imperative you get enough rest. Tell me about your bedtime routine. What do you do just before bed?"

Becca scowls from across the space between their chairs. "I can't go to sleep. I just can't, it's not safe. I thought you knew that?"

"As I explained. What I know is less important than what you know, or what you believe. Does that make sense?"

Taking a deep breath, Becca engages with the floor for a minute before she looks up again. Sighing, she hisses, "I've killed people."

Eyes, keen to move from the shocking news, train on his patient with practised resolve. Swallowing for the fourth time, he eases words from his mouth. "Really? Tell me about that then, Becca."

"Lots of people. I've killed lots. It was an accident at first, but then..." She coaxes the blur of her hands into her pockets, transferring their shaking to her body and head, swaying to control the motion like a skipper on rough seas turning the bow of his boat into a wave.

Breaking the silence, Doctor Fenton asks, "So that's why you haven't slept? Because you feel guilty?"

Becca nods. "I didn't mean it. I didn't mean to kill them. But I had to be sure, you see? I had to know, didn't I?"

The doctor's mouth opens. His lips meet a couple of times and his eyes narrow as if in thought, but there are no thoughts; none that make sense of his patient's confession.

"He'd wanted to die, he said. He told me he wanted to die, but I don't know if that makes it all right?" Her voice vibrates with the juddering of her body. "I don't know. I don't know." The words fall from her lips, bouncing like debris making no advancement on the listening ears. "It doesn't, does it? I wouldn't feel like this if it was a good thing, I'd done, would I? And now I can't sleep, can I? I can never sleep ever again. Never."

Protocol clicks a switch in Doctor Fenton's mind. Sleep. He knows a thing or two about that and falls into more well-rehearsed phrases. "I'm sure if you get a good night's rest, you'll feel a lot better. Will you trust me?"

"No!" Becca slams skeletal fingers into her thigh. "No. I can't. Why are you saying that? You can't have been listening. Nobody listens."

7

"Sorry. I am listening. Go on, tell me, why can't you sleep?"

The thin digits rub skin from her reddening leg. A tear plops onto her hand, then another. Why should she say? Doesn't he already know? Hasn't he been told why she's here?

"Becca? Becca? Tell me. I want to help. Tell me why you can't go to sleep?"

Raising her face, tears already dry, the swaying slows to still and Becca reaches the eye of her storm. Narrowing pupils fix on her tormentor's as a raptor, and with the same deftness, words like talons rip at the doctor's expertise felling him into scurrying surrender. "Because if I do, someone will die!"

Chapter One

The sun had squeezed its brightness through the small gaps in the venetian blinds for a while. Becca stared at the ceiling. Getting up and doing something would be good for her, she knew, but still her legs were reluctant to move.

Throwing back a slender arm, she yawed, then jumped from her bed at the sound of last night's coffee splattering to the floor as her long fingers caught the edge of the mug.

"Botheration!" she hissed as she stood over the slopping mess deliberating how best to tackle it.

The communal kitchen was downstairs and she would rather not make an appearance in her nightie and with no make-up, although she favoured only lip-stick anyway, confident her features were fine without adornment.

Carlos might be there and she didn't trust his Mediterranean hands to keep to themselves under the temptation of a near-naked nymphet in his midst.

Toilet paper it would have to be. Returning from her en-suite with a full roll, she wound off a wad and dabbed at the spillage. The melamine of the bedside table repelled the worst of its attack, but the carpet had already done a sterling job of soaking the coffee within the depths of its fibres; a child clutching a forbidden fragile object in an expensive shop, Becca, the frustrated mother fearful too forceful an intervention might result in further damage.

She'd shower and dress, then come back with the right product for the job. It had already soaked in, so there was no rush.

Pulling the blind chord, Becca allowed the day inside for the first time. It was bright. A glance at her phone revealed the time was nearly twelve and there were three missed calls from her mum. She'd have to wait until after she was clean. She couldn't handle whatever she had to tell her right now.

Two beautiful people smiled at her from the confines of a silver frame she'd got for Christmas. One was herself, the other was Callum. Striding to the unit upon which the frame rested, she gently lay the picture face down.

Why couldn't she just get rid of it? Isn't that what most exes did? Burn old photos in a 'boyfriend bonfire' or something? She would. But not now. Not today.

The shower was good. When they'd built the purpose-made student flats near Cardiff central station, powerful showers must have been on the architect's notes. It was much better than her mum and dad's one back home in Pembrokeshire.

Sliding back the door, Becca wrapped a towel around her and allowed her hair to fall at her shoulders in soggy strands. Staring into space, a shake of her head revealed it to be nearly dry and she noticed the goose bumps all over her arms.

Another three missed calls, and the time was half-past two. "Come on Becca! This course-work won't do itself."

Cardiff was the perfect spot. 'Juxtaposition' was her theme for this term, and with the tall buildings of the city centre backed by rolling hills, and parks full of astounding nature, photographing the contrast would be easy.

But Becca was a people person. Not so much the company of other people, but the human form and facial expressions held her biggest fascination.

Who could she photograph today? Probably no-one. It was late to organise something. She could wander around and see if any strangers took her fancy.

Sighing, she flipped open her MacBook and messaged the world of Facebook

Models wanted for second year photography student project. DM me for details'

Maybe old people in a playground, or suited business types in a wooded park; or perhaps one sad face in amongst a crowd of laughing, joyful ones. Yes, she mused. That seemed a good idea.

Today she could research locations. Being out in the city would provide inspiration, she hoped. She couldn't just stay here, she'd go mad.

Pulling skinny jeans over long legs, she buttoned a blouse over her bra-less breasts and set to leave. Skipping down the two flights of stairs rather than use the lift, she reached the front door and threw it open. The bang on the outside wall announced to the world that Becca Tate was here.

Construction workers still building student accommodation a few doors down looked up.

"Hello gorgeous. When are we going on that date?"

Becca's hand, flew to indignant hips. "I have not once said I'll go on a date with you. I'm still getting over my boyfriend."

"I know. Like I've said before. He's a fool to have left you. I'll show you a good time, girl."

"Maybe I don't want a 'good time.' Maybe I have more sophisticated tastes."

"Okay, Miss high and mighty. Just sayin' your ex-boyfriend must have been a fool."

Where the fierce loyalty came from, Becca didn't like to examine too closely. Without a word, she turned her back and strolled from their view

"Sorry, babes. Come back," the builder cooed.

Shut up, shut up! Becca fumed. Callum was definitely no fool. So where did that leave her?

Wanting to be away from the arduous workman, Becca couldn't move. Deciding whether to walk past the building crew, continue down the road, or cross over to the other side forced indecision glitching like a badly coded CGI character.

The door to her apartment block beckoned. No! Don't give into this. You have to get out. Willing her suitor to remain silent, she knew if he troubled her again, she'd have no choice but to return to the comfort and security of her nest.

Eyes closed to block out distractions, Becca focussed on putting one foot in front of the other. She could do this.

Beeeeeep! Screech!

Wind rushed past her face.

"Bloody hell! That was close!" she heard a stranger's voice. Opening her eyes, she shuddered discovering her sightless steps had taken her into the road.

A car and a lorry waited with tut-tutting drivers shaking heads holding ashen faces in place with a tentative grip. They forgave her because she was pretty.

As she stepped onto the opposite kerb, one called out. "You all right, love? I almost bleedin' killed you. Becca had no words, but she was most definitely not all right.

They would later assume perhaps that she was wearing ear buds and had become lost in the music. Or that she was drunk, or on drugs.

In truth, Becca didn't really know what was wrong with her.

Inspiration, that's what she'd come out to find. The Swiss church on the bay, with the ultra-modern millennium centre opera house in view. Old and New: that was juxtaposition, but boring and obvious; maybe more 'contrast.'

Juxtaposition was more a beautiful girl on a university course she loved, studying her passion in a city she adored, but feeling like she wouldn't have cared if the car or lorry had hit her and ended her short life.

She didn't want to die. She wasn't suicidal. It was just she had an apathy for life. And she certainly wouldn't have liked the pain. Juddering at the thought of broken bones and her lovely face. She owed it to her creator to look after that. Why, she was glad the car's brakes had been as good as they had proven to be.

Gladness lifted her enough for the real Becca to poke her head through the clouds.

Swinging her camera bag off her shower, she removed it, along with the lens caps, and hooked it around her neck. She was going to photograph something. *Anything* just to release those creative juices that had won her such acclaim for years.

Snapping away at everything and nothing, the viewfinder took her away from herself.

Pigeons walking, the dirty window of a launderette. Broken cars whizzing through the streets on the back of a huge lorry. She'd probably delete most of them, but one or two might end up a masterpiece.

Her phone pinged. Would it be a response to her Facebook plea for model volunteers? What would she ask them to do? Ideas raced for inclusion. Coming out with her camera had definitely been a good idea.

It was her mum,

'Rebecca. Please call me back. It's important.'
Closing her eyes, she felt sick. She needed a bit longer, camera in hand, before she phoned her mum back.

With fresh panic, Becca scoured her environment for inspiration. Breathing harder and faster, the buildings melted and merged with one another, colours of parked cars and buses swirled around her. The nausea grew unbearable. And then she was down.

Chapter Two

"**A**h, there she is. How are you? Do you know where you are? You fainted."

Becca opened her eyes shooting their gaze in every direction like searchlights. "My camera! Where's my camera?"

"I'll look into it. But it's more important that we take care of you first."

"No! I must have my camera!" Tears pooled in Becca's dark eyes, overflowing hopelessness down her cheeks. "I must have it. I need it."

"Okay. Don't worry. I'm sure it's fine. You just rest, I'll go and find out and I'll come back and speak to you." Swishing back the curtain and rustling it back closed again left Becca alone but for the noises of a busy A and E department inches away.

"My camera," she whispered to herself before crying out, "And my phone." She had to call her mum. Why was she here? What happened? Scrunching her forehead, she recalled the beeping of car horns. Had she been hit?

There was pain in her arms, but a quick pat down revealed being hit by a car was unlikely. Blowing relief through circle lips, she shuffled her weight down the bed. Rattling to her movement, bed was overstating it. She was lying on a trolley.

Swish the curtain flew back. "One camera!" Dangling it from its strap, removing himself from its responsibility. "It looks a good one. Are you a photographer?"

Becca smiled. She didn't even have to think about it, photography was her saviour. She didn't know what else she'd have done when Callum left. "I'm a student. Second year."

"Here in Cardiff?" It seemed a stupid question but Becca nodded. "And where is home?"

"Pembrokeshire!"

"Oh, it's lovely there. When are you going home next?"

Why was he so interested? Was he planning on asking her out? Did he understand nothing of term times? "Not until Easter, I suppose," she croaked, praying there would be no need to go home sooner.

"Can you go home a bit earlier? Or is there anyone local who could look after you for a bit?"

Callum. How could he have left her when she needed him? She should rename him 'Callus.' "I suppose I can go home anytime, if you think I need to, but it would cause problems with my coursework."

The doctor nodded. "I understand you'd like to avoid it; keep your independence. No-one likes admitting defeat."

Becca stared. "Why? What's wrong with me?"

"Not very much, I'm pleased to say. But I see this all the time; students putting themselves under pressure and not eating properly. Would you say you're under a lot of stress? How are your studies going?"

The tears that pooled this time stung more than the last. Shaking her head, she rasped "No. Uni is fine. I'm doing well."

"Something else? Are you worried about anything else?"

Her mum's text message flew to the front of her mind and then the face that was never far away. She tipped her head in rapid rods. "My... My boyfriend..."

"Well. He's mad if you ask me. Pretty girl like you. Some boys don't know they're born."

Becca's eyes sparkled behind dew at the compliment, but then clouded over as she had to admit, "There's no-one else to look after me."

Half-expecting him to offer to do it himself, Becca was dismayed at his next suggestion. "I'm reluctant to let you go home just yet. I'd like to see you eat and drink something."

"I'm not hungry."

Hands up to placate, he said, "I know. But food really is the best thing after an episode of fainting. You were out cold for some time. We were worried about you. While you were unconscious, we took some blood and ran a few other tests that all checked out. It all points, I'm afraid, to you not eating enough. Some good home cooking should see you right, and then you can catch up with your studies, no problem.

I can write you a sick note if need be. I don't mind."

"If I agree to go home, can I leave hospital?"

Pressing thin lips together, the young doctor hooked thumbs in jeans pockets and smiled, medical cowboy. He just needed a Stetson. "I'd like to see you eat and drink, but after that, yes."

"Thank you. Oh," she flicked her long dark hair from her face. "Have you seen my phone?"

The doctor frowned. "Lost that too?"

Well, I hardly lost it. I fainted. She nodded slowly.

"I'll go and have a look for that as well!"

Despite hospital etiquette, the swishing curtain offered little sound insulation and zero privacy. Becca could clearly hear the disappointing enquiries after her missing phone. Hissing and slamming the bed, she swung her legs round. She knew she had to eat; she hadn't done for... well, she couldn't remember. But if she'd lost her appetite, her first meal couldn't be hospital toast under medical scrutiny. Standing up and steadying herself, she vowed to stop at Starbucks on the way out. A skinny cappuccino and a salad. That would be better.

Moving the curtain without sliding the rings at the top, Becca could see the doctor disappear into another cubicle. Clutching her camera, she ducked under the folded back curtain and followed signs to the exit. As the door opened, she stepped outside, holding her breath until she passed the smokers in wheelchairs, cigarette in one hand, drip stand in the other.

Air burst from her lungs after a safe distance, and she began to feel dizzy again. "Sit down," she ordered herself.

Taking a breath, the dizziness remained. Focus. Pulling her Canon out of its bag, there was nothing drawing her eyes. Sighing, she flicked through the images on the small screen from her memory card. Whizzing through hundreds of photos at the flick of her finger; there was the human body project she'd done last term. And there was the ice-skating for her birthday. That had been fun. And there was Callum

Pressing the off button would be the most sensible thing she could do. Her finger hovered over it but she knew she was going to scroll on. She knew what would happen; it had happened before, but she couldn't stop. Reaching a trembling finger, she touched his smile. He was happy. *They* were happy. The ache gripped her heart, squeezing in hot fingers, nails digging in spiteful pinches, goading her to continue with one beat, begging her for relief with next. Her eyes blurring with a fiery moistness was the only small mercy. But she didn't even need the pictures anymore, her mind battling ahead with its own tortuous agenda.

Sucking in a croaking sob, she flicked from one picture to the next, willing the tiny man from the screen to become real once more. To hold him once more. What had she done to make him leave her? She feared she would never know. How could you go from this—she pressed the screen hard until the LCD blurred and she knew it would break if she pushed further—to not being here? The smiles must all have been lies, but why? She felt betrayed. They could have worked it out, couldn't they? If he'd only said how he was feeling? Weren't they worth being honest?

Scrolling the other way brought back the sixth form ball. That had been two years ago, and she'd felt like the luckiest girl alive. Other relationships suffering, torn apart as they set off for different ends of the country while she and Callum had picked the same Uni and got in. It was like the heavens approved, and why wouldn't they?

It had always been them. Always. There had never been a contingency plan and there had never needed to be. Or so she'd thought. Had she been boring? Spending too much time actually studying not partying? Isn't that what he wanted? She'd never been the extroverted type and was always proud to be content to just be. Were they so very different after all?

Her scrolling had carried on without her and the image her eyes rested upon next broke her heart even more. Her gran beamed full of life from the little screen. "I'm so proud of you, Becca, going to university. You've always taken brilliant photos." She told the same story every time. "Remember when we went to Cwm Yr Eglwys beach? I had a good camera, your dad an even better one, and you had that little cheapy we got you for Christmas. How old were you? Six? And we all took pictures of the waterfall and yours were works of art! You've always had the gift. I'm so, so proud."

Closing her eyes, quivering lips held back her cries. Would she be well enough to see her graduate next year? She'd love the ceremony and seeing her collect her certificate with robes and mortar board hat. Smiling, she could picture her now. "That's my granddaughter up there. Always had a flair," she'd tell everyone, wouldn't she.

Becca didn't want to fast-forward to more recent photos because her gran had aged so much. Invincible whilst she grew up, the family's rock had started to show the undeniable signs of mortality.

Placing her camera in her bag and strapping it back in, Becca stood. Giddy, she flopped back to sitting again. She had to get away or the doctor might see her and insist she stay here.

The taxi rank at the end of the road had two cars waiting, *Tacsi* illuminated for hire. "Come on, Becca," she hissed under her breath. "Only a few more feet and you can be on your way home."

Stumbling to the first cab, the window whirred down, "Where to, love?"

"Vere Street. Arafan House?"

"I know it. Hop in. Any luggage? Do you want to put that bag in the boot?"

"No. I'll keep it with me thanks."

22

As she strapped herself in, the driver nodded in the mirror. "Student are you?"

Becca nodded. She supposed it was possible she might be visiting another student in Cardiff's brand new halls without being one herself.

"What are you studying?"

In answer, Becca held up her camera bag to which the driver nodded again, this time with an added smile. "Photography?"

Becca forced her lips to curve in confirmation.

"I take a decent picture even if I do say so myself. Nature mainly. I likes to get out in the morning, catch a sunrise, birds singing, that sort of thing. Is that what you like?"

Staring through the window, Becca sighed. "I guess. Look. Sorry. Do you mind? I'm not feeling too great."

"Right you are. Nuff said. I won't say another word. Not another word will pass these lips."

Without looking. Becca could tell that swallowing down words was a struggle and she feared a Tourette's explosion if he held on much longer. "Nice, these new flats, aren't they?"

Becca ignored him. If he was interested, there were plenty of pictures online. That's how she and Callum had chosen. Damn! Why had this cretin made her think of him again? She just wanted to get home.

"Oops! Sorry. You want me to be quiet. Sorry. They look nice, though. From the outside..." glancing Becca's blank look, he added another "Sorry," for good measure before wrestling with another barrage of questions. 'What did she want to do with her photography? Did she think she'd work abroad, you know, with Brexit and everything? Will it affect her grant?' She shrugged a couple of times when ignoring him didn't seem to work.

Counting out the exact change from her purse into her hand, as soon as the cab stopped outside her accommodation block, she threw open the door and thrust the coins at him. "Thank you," she muttered as she scurried up the steps and disappeared inside.

Stabbing at the lift buttons didn't light them any brighter, nor did the elevator hurry down to her in heed of her distress. Jiggling on the spot, when the ping sounded to announce the arriving carriage, she cursed, "Come on!" as the doors took their usual sweet time to open. *'Lift going up. Doors closing.'*

Creaking torturously, the new cables would only get slower as they aged. *Ping. 'Third floor. Doors opening. Doors closing. Lift going down.'* Fumbling her key card from her bag as she shuffled along the corridor, as soon as she reached her door, she swiped, waited drumming her fingers as it buzzed, and then slunk inside.

She hadn't stopped at Starbucks. She hadn't had her salad and skinny latte, and now she was too tired to eat anything. Glancing at this morning's coffee stain, she clenched her fists. She hadn't bought anything to remove the stain either. Damn! That would be there forever. Stuffing her camera bag in the wardrobe, she slid to the bathroom and wriggled out of her clothes letting them fall into a heap on the floor. Forcing out a wee and then glugging a few handfuls of water from the tap, she hauled her nightie on and leapt for the bed.

Peeling open the duvet then throwing it over her head in a well-practised manoeuvre left her shivering in her self-filled tent, longing for her boyfriend's warm embrace. Hugging a pillow to her, pretending the downy case cloaked Callum's chest, she vowed to at least dream of him. He couldn't stop her doing that.

Chapter Three

The image from that Christmas flooded in Becca's mind like staring at the sun then walking into a darkened room. Falling like space invaders, one smiling face of her gran would reach the end of her peripheral awareness to be replaced by more from above

Throwing her head from side to side, sleep clawed at her, gripping tightly then shoving her back to the world of thirst and hunger. "No, no, no," she mumbled, kicking her legs to join her shaking head. Then the final palm of unconsciousness flattened over her mouth and nose suffocating any resistance. A gentle snore released the victorious hand of slumber as the Sandman nodded his satisfaction.

Lips quivered as her dreams began as they always did; with Callum. She could almost feel his arms around her as she nestled into his firm chest. But then, as every night, he was gone leaving her shivering in despair.

Somewhere within, the night-watchman knew a diversion was needed. Whispering into her sleeping ear, her psyche set off on a new journey. One without Callum.

Smiling, she walked into the familiar room, the tick-tock, tick-tock only mantle clocks of a particular age resound; like they can't believe how many seconds they've marked with no word of thanks or anything to show for their diligence, but resolved knowing without it, they'd be nothing. To Becca, and she supposed to so many grandchildren of any age, it was a sound of comfort; of security that some things never change. But it was a lie. Everything changes and even the clock knew it wouldn't last forever.

Approaching the grey covered head, no movement was visible but she always did sleep like an exhibit from Madame Tussauds "What are you doing up so late, Gran? You'll wake up terribly stiff. Come on, I'll help you."

Something of the stillness unnerved her. Stepping quietly towards the back of the chair, its flecked green marl much darker at the back where the material had not been pressed and rubbed by a decade of resting arms.

It was the third generation. Every ten years, she had told Becca, she ordered a replacement from the same department store in the same colour. She laughed how she liked to keep things the same. "The only thing that's changed about my chair is the price!" which seemed to treble every decade meaning her next replacement would likely be several thousand pounds.

Edging around the side, past her gran's legs, ravaged by a hundred minor injuries on everything from banging against the corner of a coffee table, to a fast-moving moth. The slightest touch seemed to damage her papery skin

"Gran?" Becca whispered. Reaching out trembling fingers, she called out slightly louder "Gran?!"

With a gaping wheeze, Becca's gran sucked in air and opened her eyes.

"Becca. You came. I told your mum not to bother you. 'She'll be too busy with her studies,' I told her. The first Tate to go to university. You mustn't get in the way of that." She sighed a twinkling smile. "I am pleased to see you though. I always am. I'm so proud of you, you know, Becca? You've always had the gift. Always had an eye for a photograph. Do you remember the waterfall at Cwm Yr Eglwys beach?"

She didn't finish the usual story about Becca's uncanny ability even with shoddy equipment. Instead, her eyes moistened and she held out a bony hand. "I'm glad you came, Becca. there was really no need, but I am pleased to see you."

Becca waited for the run of superlatives which always followed, but they didn't come. Eyes glaring, smile gently in place, her old hand fell from Becca's young grip and floated to rest on the faded fabric.

"Gran! Gran! Wake up! *GRAN!*" Becca held her beloved to her too late. Why had she let her babble on with how proud she was? Why hadn't she told her how proud *she* was of her? How she needed her? How she mustn't leave her? "Gran," she rasped. "I'm sorry."

Clutching her to her, wracking sobs shaking her to breaking gave way to numbness when she awoke squeezing a pillow in a tight embrace. "Gran?" she called out for the last time.

Releasing her grip, she replaced the pillow to its rightful place next to the one under her head, the small of her back pressing into her mattress, Becca stared at the ceiling. It was a dream. Just like any other. Just a nightmare.

Hunger failed to motivate her to take a step out of bed, and it was too early to get up anyway. Drinking little meant the gentle nagging from her bladder could probably be ignored too. Following the lines of her wallpaper in the half-light, she was sure it wouldn't be long before she'd succumb to sleep again. As her eyes blurred, she took the plunge and wiggled onto her side, arm punching between the two pillows with the other supporting her so her chest wouldn't press uncomfortably into the mattress.

Laughter. She'd know that infectious cackling anywhere. She could see her mum's back, and as she turned, a tray spun round to be thrust towards anyone who came within range.

"Becca! Shrimp vol-au-vent?"

Becca pushed the tray away even though shrimp vol-au-vents were her favourite. "Where's Gran?"

"She's just through there, holding court, as she always did."

Another raucous guffaw emanated from the dining room. Becca followed her ears, surprised as she turned the corner she couldn't see her. A group were huddled in the conservatory each holding a glass of wine and wearing dark clothes and faces to match.

"Where's Gran?" Becca's down-curved mouth and eyebrows inquired. Blank faces stared from her to a coffin resting on trestles that she wondered how she had missed.

"She's in a better place now, dear. Free from pain. She asked about you. You were always her favourite you know."

The cackling erupted again. Becca spun round to see her Gran, somehow in the green chair that lived in her lounge, not in Becca's house. Slapping the arms and laughing. "Don't tell them, Becca, love. Don't tell them. They won't understand like you do." *Bang, bang, bang*, she slapped the dusty green fabric. *Bang, bang, bang.*

Bang, bang, bang. Knock, knock. "Becca? Miss Tate. Are you in? I have your mum on the phone."

Becca's eyes sprung open and her mind stumbled the hundreds of miles from Pembrokeshire to Cardiff in seconds, then her legs struggled to get her to the door.

Fumbling it open, Becca stared at the woman in front of her.

"Hi. Becca? Becca Tate?"

Becca nodded. "Who are you?"

"Sorry. I'm Ffion. From the office. Your mum's been desperate to contact you. She's been really worried. You haven't answered your phone?"

Her line-mouth sighed. "That's right. I lost it."

Ffion looked unconvinced. "She's on my phone now. She phoned the university in desperation." Passing the cordless, she had the excuse of waiting for its return, giving the perfect opportunity to eavesdrop and she didn't even have to be subtle.

"Mum? Sorry. I was just reading your text when I fainted."

"Oh my goodness! Are you okay?"

"Well, I woke up in hospital. They ran tests and everything's fine."

"You don't eat enough. Ever since Callum... Well anyway. I'll feed you properly when you come home."

"Thing is. I need to keep up with my studies. I'll be home at Easter. You can fill me with hot-cross buns and chocolate eggs as much as you want then, I promise." She could promise nothing of the sort, but it was weeks away at least. Maybe she'd have an appetite by then.

"You can't mean it. You have to come home."

"Why?" Had she somehow spoken to the doctor?

"Oh, Becca. You don't know do you. I forgot you lost your phone. I've left you that many messages."

Her dream squeezed her chest like a vice so she could barely get her words out. "What don't I know?"

"I'm so sorry. It's been a shock to all of us but I know you were her favourite."

"Oh, my god, Gran? Is she okay?"

The sigh bought her mum time to speak. "No, love. She's not okay. She... She's dead."

Becca's fingers flew to her mouth. "When? When did she die?"

"Last night. In her chair. They'd let her out of hospital. That's why I was calling you before. She was desperate to see you."

"Oh my goodness. She did see me. Oh, mum. I dreamt of her last night. God, mum." Becca had no more words.

"Come home. The funeral's on Friday."

Becca nodded and handed the phone back to a softer faced Ffion. "She nodded yes, Mrs Tate. *Pause.* Yes. Yes, of course I'll look after her. You take care. Bye." Stepping inside, she thrust furtive arms around Becca, her shorter height placed her face between Becca's breasts and she pulled away. "Sorry. If you need anything... Can I get you something to eat?"

Becca stopped herself shaking her head. If she was going home, she needed to eat. She'd need the strength.

Shrugging at suggestions left Ffion guessing what she might persuade her to try. "I'll just grab what I can from the canteen." Smiling, she turned and walked away. "I'll see you in a minute."

As the door closed, Becca fell to her knees, spittle joining her gaping mouth in snotty strings. Clutching at the door handle, her face fell into the crook of her elbow. "Nooo!" she cried. "I said you should never leave me. I need you. You're my constant." Her fingers lost their grip on the door and she collapsed into a foetal heap on the floor.

Chapter Four

When the knocking came again, Becca stuffed her sobs and proceeded to cork them in with Danish pastries and diet cola with which Ffion had returned.

"I'll explain your absence to your professors. They'll understand. Don't worry about your work for now. Family is more important."

Brushing crumbs from her mouth and down her front, Becca finished swallowing and said, "Thank you." Then waving a pastry in front of her, she added, "And thanks for these as well. I was starving."

Ffion smiled. "Is there anything else you need, or shall I leave you to it?"

"I best shower and pack, but, thanks again."

"You know where to find me if you need me." It was a statement. Becca couldn't not know where the University reception was.

"I'll be fine."

With a final pinched eye smile, Ffion pulled the door shut. Sitting on the bed, Becca drummed her long fingers either side of her before flattening her palms and pushing herself up. Turning on the shower. She pressed the little red button on the tap that allowed it past the recommended 38° to 40°,42°, even up to a scalding 50°. The pain purged her of any other feeling and left her drowsy and numb. Flopping back on the bed, she'd sleep off her meal and pack when she awoke. There was no hurry now. If she'd answered her phone before, maybe she could have seen her one last time. That would have been worth rushing for. Putting the full-stop to the life which meant so much to her? That could wait.

"So, you dreamt your gran died, and then you found out the next day that she actually had."

"Exactly the same time I dreamt of her, in her chair when she had been in hospital." Becca drops her gaze. "She said she'd been waiting for me."

Dr Fenton steeples his fingers. Prodding his chin, he sighs. "And because of this, you think you killed her in your dream."

Becca says nothing.

"Because, I have to say, Becca, what is a far more likely explanation to my mind is that knowing your gran was unwell and possibly fearing you might miss your last opportunity to see her, it was natural, no, *expected*, I should say, that you might have such a dream. Staying in hospital yourself might have brought it all intolerably to mind. Under the circumstances, I'd have been surprised if you hadn't dreamt about her. It's a sad coincidence that she has... passed away, but don't feel bad about not seeing her. It's an image that's hard to shake off. Better to remember her vital and full of life. I think you did yourself a favour."

Sitting forward, he presses his lips before exhaling hard. "As for killing her? Absolutely not." Thrusting back in his chair, he allows his hands to unclasp and rest in his lap, a simpering smile plays on his lips to punctuate his point.

Becca nods enthusiastically. "Gosh, wow. That makes so much sense. That's because you're such a clever man of science, and I'm just a silly girl not coping with her emotions." Eyes glazing, she turns the force of her gaze on the doctor. "I am not a fool, doctor, I didn't just jump to this conclusion from nowhere. I thought the same as you; exactly the same; until it happened again.

The ceiling remained her biggest fascination. Tearing her eyes away to the rest of the room, as soon as she considered locating and filling her bag, it drew her attention like a bungee. Clenching her hand so tight her fingernails cut into her palm, she forced herself to sit up.

Opening her hands, the jagged feel of her nails made her examine them. Gone were the manicured talons, replaced now with chewed, rough edges. She hadn't even noticed their going.

Rolling over in her damp towel, Becca pulled at her bedside drawer and fumbled around between pairs of knickers and contraceptive pill packets to find her nail file. Her usual gel nails never needed filing apart from by Thu Le, her Vietnamese nail technician, meaning it could be anywhere.

Not finding it, she slumped onto the floor and thrust her hand under the cabinet. Patting the floor proved fruitless. On her knees, she flattened herself onto her chest and peered under the bed. Empty, but for her suitcase.

Giving up on filing her nails, she tried to chew carefully at the offending prongs, first in one direction, then the next, trimming too far without smoothing as she'd wanted, she stopped and flapped her hand as biting hard ripped the nail to the nerves.

Standing still, arms at her side, she sighed. "Come on, Becca. You're better than this." Hauling her case onto her bed, she flicked the catches and flung it open. The emptiness shocked her, and she stared. It was easily rectified, and would be as soon as she began to fill it. But she knew that would be difficult too.

Leaving the case open, she stepped over to her wardrobe and slid open the door. It was a far from sparse collection. What was the weather for the coming week? It was a very mild spring, but it could turn at any moment and it did tend to be windier on the steep hill overlooking the coast which was her family home. Picking through the outfits, there was everything she needed; summer mini-dresses, woollen dresses, jeans, leggings, blouses, T-shirts and jumpers, and shoes ranging from flip-flops to running shoes to formal. But nothing black.

Staggering back to the bed, she perched on the end. Focussing on nothing, she became aware her rough nail had found its way back to her teeth. Forcing it down, she slipped it under her thigh for safe-keeping. "I'll need something black," she said to galvanise herself into action.

Walking over to her clothes, she grabbed armfuls with no decision or care, yanking them from the hangers and tumbling them into her case. If she was going to take such a large bag, she may as well save herself the agony of choosing clothes by taking the lot.

A couple of hangers-on dangled from corners of hooks. Without taking in what they were, Becca pushed the wardrobe closed, shoving it the last couple of centimetres as the hinges clogged up with the draggling lingering garments.

Should she buy something here in Cardiff, or wait and grab a bargain in Fishguard. Pembrokeshire fashion was cheaper but Cardiff offered more choice. Did she want choice? Or did she want to hurry home? Plucking her keys from the dressing table/desk, she strode to the door. She realised, as she slammed it shut, she wanted neither.

She'd never been much of a shopper. Callum had shown more interest than her. 'This would look nice on you,' he'd say, or, 'Those lovely long legs of yours deserve this short skirt.' She'd got rid of most of those things since he'd decided to leave her, not just because they were painful but

38

because they were insulting. "If you liked my long legs so much, why aren't you here!" she hissed under her breath as she strolled down the corridor.

A light drizzle had sent the builders inside, she was grateful. It also meant she'd call an Uber rather than walk into town, and whilst she usually enjoyed the stroll, today she felt exhausted.

Within moments of confirming her order, an Uber cab pulled up and Becca hopped in beside the driver. He already knew where she was headed but she confirmed anyway, it seemed rude not to. "St David's Centre, please." The driver nodded silently, perhaps because conversation seemed unnecessary, perhaps in awe of Becca's beauty, or perhaps because she looked so close to the edge he feared the wrong word might tip her over it.

Chapter Five

St David's Centre buzzed with shoppers and lunchers and loiterers. A group of teenagers stared at her as she approached escalators of Queens Arcade and as she passed they muttered between themselves. Becca didn't care. She had always provoked jealousy from her peers, and today more than ever, their spite had no power. Like ash into a volcano, their ire was incinerated in Becca's own grief with no effect.

Passing the pharmacy, the smell of coffee roused her and she glanced over at a small chain outlet with tables arranged outside in the main thoroughfare.

Tempted, she could do with the energy and the calories, she lost her appetite when an elderly lady sitting outside began to laugh. It wasn't that it reminded her of her gran's. It was nothing like it. But in recognising its dissimilarity pulled her unavoidably to the forefront of her thoughts.

Knees buckling, she tottered to a chair and pulled it from under the table to sit. When a waiter approached, she could only point to the menu because no words could swim past the sorrow in her throat.

The first steaming sip of her extra-foam soya cappuccino burnt her lips and tongue and she placed it back on the saucer.

"Oh, sorry. Careful, it's really hot," he apologised as though Becca should be forgiven for not knowing the drinks coming from the steaming coffee machines fizzing and hissing on the counter would be hot. She nodded and thumbed the small handle, staring at the sputtering foam as it died a little with each bursting bubble.

How was she going to get by without her gran? Her mum and dad were great, but they were always busy with her little sister and her beauty pageants and child modelling. They said they were proud of her photography, but was that because it had set Sophie off on her 'career?'

She'd always been her gran's favourite, she knew that. She'd always been everyone else's favourite from every relative she could think of to every teacher and now every lecturer at uni. Because she was nice and conscientious and reliable.

Sophie was none of those things; pretty, blonde, and young, the real baby of the family who thought the world revolved around her; a notion her parents seemed determined to reinforce.

Becca knew her gran had worked hard. The eldest of thirteen, she'd been caring for her brothers and sisters from the age of six. And then she had her own children. When they flew the nest, she went into nursing and set the world alight with her graft and ingenuity. She always said she saw herself in Becca. 'Your legs are nearly as long and lovely as mine,' she'd joke, hauling up her crinoline skirt and placing her varicose veined, bruised but arguably slender and shapely calves next to hers.

She loved all her grandchildren, of course, but Becca knew her hard work and determination lit a fire in her gran's heart that never burnt out. "Why didn't I come home and see you?" she cried into her hands, turning the waiter away with wide eyes and eyebrows to match as he mouthed 'Okay.' She knew the answer. If she'd seen how ill her grandmother was, she'd have had to admit the inevitable. She spared herself that at least. Gained a few days of blissful ignorance. And her memories, untainted, could forever be of her vibrant healthy consort.

She knew it was true, and that in many ways she was fortunate to have been spared, but now, when everyone had begun to grieve, for her it all seemed like a nightmare she would wake from at any moment and when it did hit her, she wasn't sure how she'd cope.

She needed Callum. His strong arms around her. He'd always known what to say, she comforted herself, then slamming a fist on the table, she snarled, "No!" All you said was a pile of shit! Coffee spilled from the oversized mug onto an equally outlandish, plate-sized saucer which captured most of the spillage—perhaps that's why they have them, Becca mused as she pushed her chair back from the table too late to prevent determined drips falling and wetting her leg.

Tottering, unsure what to do, the waiter bustled through the door. "Can I get you another? Or would you like your bill."

Becca nodded leaving him unsure which request she was granting. "Another?"

"No. Thank you. I'll pay."

Following him to the till, she handed over a wad of too many notes. Frowning, he handed all-but-one back along with some coins. "Have a nice day," he smiled then called to the waiting line, "Next!"

The coffee, what little she'd ingested, had done nothing to perk up her mood, but the thought of sitting and letting her gran and Callum back into her thoughts wasn't an option. "Keep busy, Becca," she ordered herself. "Funeral clothes won't buy themselves."

The door for Primani was closer than the more expensive Debenhams. Walking straight to the womenswear as though on rails, Becca grabbed the first black item she saw; a long T-shirt with a band she'd never heard of on the front. Squinting at the label, it was a size ten. She always felt she should be an eight, but her height and robust shoulders usually necessitated a ten, sometimes even a twelve. Eyes jerking left and right, struggling to locate a mirror; an aspect of the shop that refused to lock in her mind despite repeated visits.

Holding the T-shirt to her bosom and letting it hang, she tilted her head from side to side as she debated its length and appropriateness. Wincing at the weight she'd lost but could ill-afford, an eight would probably be better, she decided, then changed her mind. Hanging loose gave a detachment. Rolling her shoulders, she imagined a tighter fit and shuddered. No. This was fine, and the way it hung off her helped it past her knees. Black tights, a jacket, maybe a scarf or some pearls would be fitting. Black, but party. She was sure it's what her gran would have wanted.

Queuing, she picked up a little packet of tissues by the till. It might be useful at the funeral. Looking down at the small folded white squares through the cellophane wrapper, her eyes moistened and she grabbed another, then another, struggling to the till when she was called without dropping them.

"Would you like a bag?"

"Yes, please," Becca plopped her items on the till noting what a stupid question it was and then disregarding her own criticism when a customer next to her unfolded a shopping bag from her purse.

"Twenty-eight pounds exactly," the short, overly-made-up face smiled at her, mouth curved into a smile wasn't joined by her eyes. Becca handed over the same notes she'd thrust at the waiter but this time had only two pound-coins in her change.

Swinging the bag, when the door swished open and she stood back in the corridor, she halted. "Well. That's that then." How else could she fill her time to put off what she had to do? "You'll have to face it, won't you?"

Reaching the doors, the rain had stopped. Should she walk home? That would give more time to think things she didn't want to. Best get a cab back again and finish her packing to keep occupied.

"Come back in an hour. I'll need to go to the station."

The man at the wheel lost colour from his face. Swallowing, he tilted his head. "You'll need to use the app. I can't know where I'll be. Use the app, someone will come." As Becca walked away, he gulped and leaned over to grab the door she had left. How should he rate her? She looked like she was going through enough. He'd give her the benefit of the doubt.

Throwing her new clothes in the case on top of the pile from her wardrobe and chucking a couple of books she'd started but not managed to continue with, she was ready to go in five minutes. "I should have just got him to wait!"

As the same car pulled up minutes later, the driver smiled. "That was a quick hour."

Becca smiled back. "Yes. I can't put this off anymore."

"Put what off?"

Words jumbled in her mouth and her mind stuttered deciding whether to tell. "Just something I have to do, that's all."

Nodding, he hopped out of the car and trotted round to her side, gallantly plucking her heavy case from the pavement and placing it in the boot. Trotting back, he joggled into a comfy position, yanked his seat-belt as it caught and clipped it into place. Revving, he joggled the gear lever and crunched it into position. It hadn't been this noisy earlier, had it? "Sorry. It's playing up," he grinned as he smashed it into gear and bunny hopped away.

Heart slowing as the journey settled into a normal pace, grateful the gears were now behaving after their talking to, or each set of lights would be a nightmare.

Looking through her purse, she was debating paying for her train ticket with cash, or should she use her card? She wasn't totally sure how much money was in her current account. She'd try. If it didn't go through, she'd offer part payment on card, the rest cash. She didn't like the idea of having no money on her at all. What if there was an emergency?

Relaxed in her decision, she leaned her elbow against the glass and her chin upon her hand. The rocking and jiggling of the car wobbled her eyes closed. Springing them open, embarrassed her Uber driver should see her asleep, she focussed her gaze.

The rear-view mirror seemed directed more to the back seat than to the road behind. This driver cared more about the inside of his car than the outside. Becca imagined herself glancing nervously at an intoxicated passenger who might be about to create a major cleaning headache.

In this traffic, it was a good ten minutes to the station. Eyebrows knitting in question at her fatigue, she nodded as she remembered she hadn't eaten since Ffion's offerings, nor had she absorbed her daily caffeine fix. She didn't want to. But she nodded off again.

Her location influenced her dream, and as she wobbled along on her dreamy bus, mountains loomed one side and the ocean the next. A dolphin zipped by on a surfboard, doffed his straw boater and tilted his sunglasses down his nose. "Welcome home, Becca," he said, before launching into typical dolphin cackles.

Eyes bulging, his sunglasses fell off. Unable to speak English when his message was of vital urgency, the dolphin pointed a triangular flipper forward. Becca frowned. What did he want?

Suddenly she was in Planes Trains and Automobiles. Laughing, knowing the other drivers were crazy or drunk or both, the couple driving past on the other carriageway mouthed and shouted clearly, "You're going the wrong way! Wrong way. *Wrong Way!*"

Chuckling, her Uber driver leaned across. How do they know which way we're going? "Thank you," he called. "But I think I know which way the train station is. I'm a professional!"

The mountains were dark and the ocean darker; then they morphed into tall buildings and a sea of cars. A shark swum through the throng, casting cars this way and that in its wake as it thrashed its tail in a frenzy. And then it was a bus.

There was no chance it would miss them. As the corner clipped the bumper of the Uber, it sent the car spinning, the driver's face thrust towards the steering wheel.

Squeeeel!

The screech of brakes woke her with a jolt as the bus of her dream flew past in front of them.

"You f...ing idiot!" the Uber driver shook his fist. "I thought we was gonna be toast then! Good job the brakes work better than the gears!"

It was frightening enough, but knowing what she'd seen in her head shook her.

"Sorry. So sorry," he nodded in the mirror again and again. Crinkling his lips, he clenched his fist and pressed it into his thigh as it plunged up and down to operate the clutch. He was going to get a bad rating from this girl, he could feel it.

Pulling smoothly outside the station taxi-rank, he smiled expectantly at Becca. As she pushed open her door, he shoved his open too but Becca was already striding off. "Miss, miss! Wait! You forgot your bag!"

Slugging it from the back, he raced along to catch her up, the little casters on the bottom rattled on the uneven ground. "Wait, miss!"

Becca stopped and turned. Pausing for him to catch her, she smiled and took the case from his hand. "Thank you. Sorry. I'm..." She was what? Having a nightmare? Predicting people's deaths, or imminent deaths? "I'm under a lot of stress," she plumped for. Now which way to the ticket office.

Chapter Six

She boarded the train even though she'd been warned it wouldn't be moving for twenty minutes. What else was she going to do? She'd managed to book a straight line with no changes, so she could get the sleep she craved for three and a bit hours, or she could hop off the train and grab something to eat. That was a better idea. Station prices were high, but buffets were more expensive.

Rotating a sorry selection of sandwiches and snacks in a vending machine, Becca settled on a scotch egg. How bad could that be? A kiosk sold fresher looking snacks at a premium, but their coffee smelled okay.

Buying a latte (they didn't do soya so her stomach would suffer later) afforded her legitimate use of a table and chair. A sign warned *Only food and drink purchased on these premises to be consumed at this picnic area.*

Picnic? Who came for a picnic in a railway station? And what did it mean, *on these premises?* The kiosk? The station? Becca decided she'd take her chances and unwrapped her scotch egg. In answer to the questioning leer from the barista, Becca took a mighty chomp devouring half the egg in one bite. As the dry crumbed meat mixed with the drier egg yolk, Becca couldn't swallow it. Gulping her coffee and burning her lips for the second time that day, she forced it down and gasped, leaning forward to get gravity involved in shifting the egg from her mouth.

The upward turn to the barista's pressed lips suggested he considered karma had been restored. Determined to sit for as long as she wanted, Becca wished her camera was more accessible, as the people bustling to and from trains looked like a missed opportunity. She was sure by the time she'd wrestled her camera from her case, and then out of its bag, she would have to hurry along to her own train so she couldn't risk it.

Instead, she sat back and allowed the nourishment of her food to reach her ravenous belly. Dainty bites and sips of her latte were finished just in time and the signalman nodded to Becca and pointed at her train. "A couple of minutes, okay?"

Becca nodded and smiled back. At least some of the staff were friendly. Slugging down the last of her coffee, Becca stood and edged through the crowd to her train. Hauling her case beside her, she sat and stared from her window.

The coffee kiosk was doing a brisk trade but even from here, Becca could see the spite in the gestures. With a wince, she realised too late, it was just the type of juxtaposition she could use for her project. Unfriendliness in hospitality. She didn't think the micro-expressions would carry across the platform, but when she got back... She'd managed to keep her reason for travelling from her mind, but with one careless thought, it was back, pounding in her head and her heart.

Taking a deep breath, Becca distracted herself looking at the other passengers as they bustled along the concourse. What were their reasons for getting on this train?

Probably, most of them would be going for a break as millions did every year to her beautiful county. She was lucky, Fishguard didn't attract the tourists the southern resorts did. And there was always plenty of space in the secret valley and the hills.

They did look happy, and whilst jealousy at their carefreeness could eat into her, Becca decided to embrace it and try to allow their joy into her.

A small family; mum, dad and toddler looked set to become larger as the roundness of the mum's tummy as well as the protective arm of the dad as he guided the guardian of his loins' fruit into the carriage gave the clues.

Smiling in their direction, their joy surely could lift her mood, but then it sank when she saw their eyes. They were fearful. Or was she projecting her own melancholy onto them? Was she so low she couldn't even witness happiness?

Reasons for their disquiet swirled in her mind. Was there a problem with the pregnancy? Perhaps this wasn't their first try. Maybe they'd been told to prepare for a baby that didn't meet their idea of perfection. Maybe the mum wasn't as healthy as she looked.

Shaking her head, Becca clenched her fists and flattened her palms a few times to dispel the tension. Closing her eyes to protect herself, and the little family, from her negativity, Becca shuffled down in her seat to rest. Disturbed briefly by the station whistle and the train chuffing from the platform, soon the rumble of the metal wheels rocked her to sleep.

Her mind fell to its default torment of her and Callum in happier times; this time, probably influenced by subconscious understanding of heading home, it took her to a previous homeward bound encounter; Christmas.

When she was little, she and Sophie used to love decorating the tree together, but as she'd grown older and busier, and because Sophie always persuaded Mum that she hated doing it, in the dream it had already been decorated when she first saw it. It suited her well enough, at least they couldn't squabble. And soon she'd be decorating her own tree in her own house with her man her mind meandered through the grim fairytale.

In the blink of an eye, the tree appeared parched in her mind's eye. Like one of those plants that for some reason tried to eke out its existence in the desert, but really it just looked like every other discarded conifer after twelfth night.

Around it, the room was black. *"Callum? Callum, are you there? I need you!"* she cried, but she knew he wasn't. From another room, her gran's laughter echoed. *"Gran, is Callum with you?"*

Voices. There were definitely other voices. It didn't sound especially like her boyfriend, but it was quite muffled, unmistakeably male she was sure.

Opening the door from the lounge, instead of the dining room, a long corridor extended. Flickering fluorescent tubes illuminated the way past people on rows of uncomfortable looking chairs and others in high-backed wheelchairs being pulled backwards into side rooms and other corridors.

Walking past them all, she joined a throng of mumbling stragglers at the bottom of the lift. There wouldn't be room for them all. Becca didn't even know where she was going, but squeezed around the crowd to the double doors marked 'stairs.'

Pushing them open, she walked through and trotted up the first flight as the Georgian-wired glass doors flapped back on their hinges a couple of times before staying closed.

Reaching the first floor, the signs indicated wards of no interest that she had little understanding of. What was she looking for?

Up another flight, there were two signs; one indicating the neo-natal unit, the other saying,

'No Admittance. Staff Only.'

Opting for the one that wouldn't get her in trouble, she pushed open the doors which responded more viciously than the ones two flights below and made their attempt to grab at her and crush her between their frames. Screeching their disappointment that she'd passed through unharmed, they waited for her inevitable return. They'd get her next time.

At the end of the corridor were another set of doors, glass with blue frames. As she approached, pictures of mothers and babies adorned every wall.

Before the doors, a smaller door stood ajar and beckoned her into a room declaring itself to be the visitors' room. Who was she visiting? She wasn't here to see her gran again, was she, because this was entirely the wrong place.

Before she could decide, the blue framed doors swished open. A man carried a car-seat and an intense look on his face, following on in a wheelchair pushed by a nurse was a red, puffy woman with ruddy cheeks and a smile of pure relief.

When they saw Becca, their eyes widened and they stopped and stared, the man squashing himself and his tiny charge against the wall, and the nurse wheeling the lady laden chair into an alcove they now shared with a little trolley.

More doors directly in front slid open and Becca stepped in.

"No! Please! Give me another chance!"

It was the pregnant lady from the train. In a chair beside her, fingers white in his wife's grip, sat the man. Turning to see what she was looking at, when he saw Becca, he jumped back in his seat. "Please! Just one more chance."

Becca had no idea what they were talking about, and although their words appeared to be considered, this being a dream, she probably didn't look her usual approachable self. She smiled. If it was in her power to give them the chance they begged for, she was beyond happy to allow it. Nodding, she cranked up the smile and they smiled back with such gratitude.

"Come on then," the doctor smiled. Let's give it another try."

The woman screamed and the man cried and the woman screamed more, then another scream; the unmistakable first breaths of an infant who can't believe what just happened to him.

"Here you are," the doctor said, handing the waxed blue bundle onto his mother's chest. "Perfect. Skin to skin contact. Babies love that."

Squinting, Becca wasn't sure who liked it most, the newborn baby, or the doctor who couldn't take his eyes off the milk-laden breasts of his patient.

Nurses bustled around wiping brows and cooing, "Isn't he beautiful," whilst popping a little hat onto his head.

Becca coughed getting the doctor's attention just as she intended. Grinning at her, he pulled down his face mask. *"Now that's a pair worth seeing. Much bigger than yours."*

"You said you liked me as I am; that I was perfect. Didn't you, Callum? Didn't you! Liar!"

"It's the end of the line, miss. This *is* where you wanted to get off, isn't it?"

The ocean through the window and the steep slopes of Carn Ingli mountain *'The Mount of Angels'* casting shade through the other and Becca was certain she was home. "Yes, thank you."

Grabbing her bag, Becca hauled it down the aisle walking backwards so she could tug it through the gaps between seats.

"Oh, after you. We'll take forever."

Spinning round, Becca met the smiling gaze of the father of the small family. Behind him, the mum, who had looked so sombre three hours ago, beamed at her, glowing in her incubation. Was it arriving in Pembrokeshire that had bucked their spirits, or had her dream been of more significance than just a dream? Had she seen and smoothed a path to their future happiness?

"Did you really think that? That you'd foreseen their future? And in so doing, they'd been reassured? Even though you said nothing to them?"

"Well, I was hardly going to say, 'Excuse me, I just dreamt of you and despite some earlier misgivings and your disquiet when you boarded the train, I'm pretty sure your baby is going to be just fine,' was I?"

Doctor Fenton shrugs and scribbles on his pad.

"I don't really think I thought anything at the time. I mean, nothing much had happened then."

"So, you think you may have given this dream greater meaning in retrospect when other things happened?"

"Yes. That's right."

"What things?"

"Well, I'm getting to that."

Chapter Seven

"**B**ecca! Oh, I'm so pleased you're here. It's a shame you couldn't see your gran when she was... Well, you know." Regarding her daughter up and down, Donna scrunched her lips. "Although, if she'd seen how thin you're looking, she would have worried herself sick."

The inappropriate irony lost on her scatty mother, Becca hadn't the fight to argue. "Some good'ol home cooking will soon sort me out," she said truthfully but fully aware the positive effect her words would have.

Beaming, Donna pinched her cheek. "Exactly. There's already some of your favourites waiting at home."

"Not... Not shrimp vol-au-vents, is it?"

Clapping her hands, Donna shrieked, "Yes! See. I remembered."

It was reference to a row where Sophie's favourite foods were always represented every Christmas but hers never were. 'Sophie's are just more Christmassy, that's all,' Donna had defended, but fajitas weren't Christmassy just because they used turkey instead of chicken. And she'd have been delighted with turkey and stuffing vol-au-vents anyway, but now wasn't the time to revisit Sophie being their favourite. "Thanks, Mum," she squeezed her eyes then reached across and patted her mum's arm and Donna smiled back.

"The car's a short way up here."

It was the only one in the carpark and Becca hadn't been away so long she'd have forgotten the family's yellow VW. Opening the door, Donna shoved Sophie's school bag and coat into the back so Becca could sit beside her in the front. "Sorry. Your sister's been a bit distracted, what with…"

Was she ever going to say the words?

"Yes. Since Gran died. I get it. I've been distracted myself." Distracted hardly described the worrying delusions she'd been having but talking about it was not an option. 'Oh, I know,' she would get before being discounted in the face of something banal like, 'Did I tell you we painted the fence?'

Gazing through the window, it was great seeing the sea again. Cardiff Bay was pretty, but the rugged beauty of the North Pembrokeshire coast was what filled Becca's cup.

As the Mount of Angels disappeared in the door mirror and Fishguard Bay grew larger with the gain in height up the improbable steepness to Strumble Head, Becca's spirits lifted, but then like a balloon getting ahead of itself, they popped on the spikey stalactites of her world crashing down as she remembered once again why she was home.

The view blurred by the ocean in her eyes, Becca carried on staring. As the car pulled into the Dorma bungalow's drive, Donna paused before taking off her seatbelt. Words of comfort may have been poised to spring from her lips, but they clung on before crawling back into the safety of her mouth and down her throat to her heart where they hunkered down for safety to fight another day. "Come on. Everybody's waiting."

Everybody? Becca noticed the street full of cars for the first time and realised they were here for her gran. "Why are they here now? The funeral's not for two days, is it? It's not been brought forward?"

Donna shook her head. "No, no. Just come in. It's a busy time."

Her mum bustled inside and Becca stumbled behind. Her home for eighteen years didn't feel like where she wanted to be. Sophie and her mum and dad had built a forcefield of a new Becca-less life since she left for uni. Nothing could stop them and their pageants without Becca's demands on their time.

As she stepped into the hallway, she walked into her dream. "Shrimp vol-au-vent?" Donna squawked to people out of sight then turning to her daughter she offered the same with the same manic smile.

Scooping a few from the plate, Becca walked through to the dining room. Her gran's laughter didn't precede her entry this time but she knew what to expect.

"I didn't want to upset you. I wasn't sure how you'd feel, but we're keeping a vigil." Placing the tray of hors douvres on the piano, Donna wiped her hands on her skirt. "Not that we think any evil spirits would want to get to Mum... Your gran, but, well. I just thought it'd be nice to have her home. She was born in Pontfaen just down the road, you know."

Of course she knew. Her gran loved being born in the secret valley. *'We even have a different New Year's Day—Hen Galan—still in the Julian calendar not the Gregorian one, so it's on January thirteenth. Even the Romans couldn't find us!'* she'd cackle.

Dark suits topped with faces she barely recognised doffed cups of tea and glasses of wine as she stepped into the room. Her heart ripped at the sight of the coffin. Collapsing into a chair, she hid her face. Grateful it wasn't an open casket like she'd seen in so many American films. She didn't think she could bear to, but wouldn't it be nice to see her just one more time?

Smoothing fabric between her fingers, she jumped up as she recognised the seat. "What's this doing here? Why is Gran's chair here?" Angry at the vultures, she swallowed it down. It was a good thing, wasn't it? It couldn't stay in the council house her gran had lived in for years. It should stay here in this house forever. If her spirit ever wanted to visit, it would have a place to sit.

"You okay?"

Squinting, Becca looked up. "Sophie. Hi. No, not really."

"You look awful."

Becca smiled. "You look well." The compliment more of an insult in the face of what was important. "Done much modelling lately?"

Sophie smiled and tilted her head. "A bit." Lowering to her haunches, she patted her sister's leg. "You could. Put on a bit of weight, maybe colour your hair. You don't look so bad."

"Thanks, Sophie. Means a lot." Becca squeezed her fist near her heart clutching her little sister's gorgeous sentiment where it wouldn't escape. Pushing herself up, she said, "I ought to circulate; speak to the guests."

"Yes. They don't get to see you enough... Just like Gran."

Becca paused in her step. Lips trembling, she closed her eyes and took the next few steps blind.

"Becca! Mind the vol-au-vents!"

The crash echoed as she walked into the tray her mother had brought into the dining room. Eyes pinging open at the clattering noise, she glared. "Give it a rest with the fucking vol-au-vents."

"Becca!"

"Fucking vol-au-vents!" Becca screeched again storming from the room.

"Sophie, be a love and pick these up."

"But I didn't spill them..." Becca heard her sister moaning as she stomped up the stairs. Flinging open her bedroom door, a shriek from inside made her pull it close again. "Rebecca? Sorry, didn't your mum tell you?"

Pushing open the door again, she took a step inside. Her great aunt Carrie stood in bra and panties looking remarkably pert for a woman in her seventies. "Tell me what?"

"Oh. I hope you don't mind, I've been using your room. I came up when Christine... You know?" she flopped on the bed and clutched the blanket to her. Kindred spirit. "I suppose she's in a better place, but she was more than a sister. No, seriously, she was more of a mum to me than my own mother."

Becca walked across the room and sat beside her aunt. "She was more of a mum to me too. No. That's unfair. Mum's great."

"I know how close you two were." Swallowing, she blinked away tears brushing the same away from Becca's cheeks. "You were her favourite. You're exactly like her, you see."

Leaning in, the pair hugged in an awkward but comforting squeeze. Pulling away, Aunt Carrie leaned forward, her ample aged bosom straining her bra, she plucked a stack of papers from a carrier bag beside the bed. "Here. Look at these."

In her hand were old sepia photos of people she didn't recognise in India. Flipping back and forth, she paused on each one. A typical group photo; a couple in the middle flanked by others to each side and leaning in from behind. British and Indian faces smiled out in caramel grins.

The next was just of the British couple pointing at the gates of a large house. But then they became much more interesting. A servant girl peering over the lip of a bucket she was filling with a coy smile and a light in her eyes; the same girl dancing; another servant, a strong male this time flexing muscles as he strained holding the lead of a huge dog.

"Your gran took these."

"Really? They're wonderful."

"She didn't rate them. But she loved all yours. There are, let me see..." Carrie counted on her fingers whilst looking up, "Six, no eight, of your photos hanging in her house... Her old house. She'd want you to have them."

Becca nodded, unable to speak.

"Remember the ponies?"

"Mm hm."

"They were her favourite. Taken on the mountain up there, weren't they?"

Becca smiled. "They're wild, but so tame. They virtually licked the camera!" Laughter tinkled the atmosphere until the suffocating cloud of grief stilled them. "Shall we go downstairs?" Looking down at herself, she grinned. "I'll get dressed first of course." The bells of mirth jangled again. "You are okay with me in your room, Rebecca?"

The name grated. What was she to say? 'No, you'll have to take the couch?' "It's fine. I'm not here much, I suppose I can't expect my room to be here when I come back."

"Well I did have to be here."

Becca held out her hand and took her aunt's. "I know. Sorry. I should have been here too."

Tilting her head, Carrie smiled. "Perhaps. But everything happens for a reason. I'm sure Christine is happier you remembering her fit and well. I envy you. And anyway. You can't change the past." Standing up, she tottered to the wardrobe. "This is for the funeral." She held up a black dress with a short jacket. She didn't add, 'What do you think?' What could anyone think? It looked like what you'd wear to mourn then never wear again.

"Mine looks very similar. Great minds think alike."

"Quite. Now, give me a hand with this while you're here." Becca helped her pull a grey woollen dress over her head. "And this."

"Isn't that..?"

"Yes. My sister's Krugerrand. Insisted I have it. She insisted people take a lot of things these last few months. Your mum's got her chair. That's special. She…"

"I know. I dreamt it. It happened like I was there. I wonder, perhaps on some level, I might have been. That seeing me, even on some other-worldly plain made her let go."

"Really? That's remarkable. I'm sure you're right. I've always held a lot of store in dreams. Not always, but often they mean something. Hindus do lots of dream interpretation. It's a big thing in India."

"So, you're half Indian, Mum's a quarter and I'm an eighth. That's right isn't it."

"Yes. Your gran's red hair was a surprise. There must be some strong genes from the Armstrong side of the family." Fingering the gold coin hanging on a chain around her neck, she smiled a watery smile. "Shall we go?"

Arm in arm they re-joined the vigil. Sensing the tension, Carrie skilfully guided Becca round the approaching tray of nibbles before the word vol-au-vent could be screamed again.

Sitting in her gran's chair, she gazed into the haze of the room seeing nothing. A metallic glint took her attention and she followed the shape of the coffin handle, very straight and functional, its brass colour the only nod to extravagance. There were two more handles visible and presumably the same on the other side. The wood looked attractive: polished, light. What was it? Oak? Pine? It was beautiful, whatever it was and it looked expensive, kind of. Becca had no idea how much they cost.

Your gran is in there.

Closing her eyes, she could almost see her, lying, arms crossed over her chest, a peaceful smile upon her face; it was easy to believe ripping open the coffin lid, she would wake with a smile.

Examining the image further, it changed. Suddenly black, Becca shrank at the thought of her body, emptied of vital organs, pumped full of formaldehyde, lifeless. No. her gran wasn't in there. It was just her earthly husk. Her gran was somewhere else.

"What time do you want to keep vigil? Becca?"

Drawing her focus, Becca looked at her dad. They were the first words she'd heard him say to her. "Keep vigil?"

"Yes. Someone has to stay with your gran, day and night."

"Why?"

"To keep her safe."

"Safe? She's dead. What you think; wolves are going to take her in the night?"

"Well someone's got to do it, and I know how close you two were."

"Exactly. I can't imagine anything worse. Nothing's going to happen to her and I would find it most disturbing. She doesn't need me."

Her dad rolled his eyes. "Just like she didn't need you all month when she was dying."

Standing, a vol-au-vent she didn't know she was holding fell to the floor.

"Becca. What is it with you and those pastries today?" her mum tut-tutted as she bent to scoop up the crumbs.

Scowling, Becca shook her head. "Oh, I don't know, maybe I'm preoccupied thinking about someone I really love having died. Why aren't you? Instead of jollying it up with nibbles and stupid vigils. Whose idea was this?"

"Becca. Have a bit of respect. That's no way to talk to your mother."

"I don't even have a room to stay in."

Carrie leaned forward and added, "I can sleep on the couch if it's a problem."

"No. Of course not, Aunt Carrie. I wouldn't hear of it. But it would have been nice to be asked." She glared at her mum.

"How? I've been trying to phone you for days."

Mouth opening and closing failed to fall on any words. She was right. How could she have asked? Shoulders slumping, she mumbled, "Sorry. You're right. Where am I going to sleep?"

"I've made you a lovely bed up in your dad's study. It's got your favourite flowery bedding on and everything."

"Thanks, Mum." Shuffling to the doorway, she turned. "I'm going to get my head down now, if that's okay?"

"Don't you want to spend some time with your gran?"

Squeezing tears down her cheek, she shook her head in rapid jerks. "No." As she disappeared into the hallway, Sophie's timbre reached her ears, "I'll do it," she volunteered. Squeezing her eyes, Becca's mouth crinkled. What a little trouper.

Pushing open the study door, it looked pretty. She hadn't just been cast aside with no thought. The bed felt cosy and she loved those yellow and blue cornflowers on the duvet and pillow cases.

Peeling back the cover, she plumped up the pillows and slipped inside. Reaching up, she flicked the switch above her head on the wall and plunged the room into darkness.

Eyes fluttering behind trembling lids soon sprang open. Tiny LED's on the printer and charging laptop blinked away filling the room with more and more light as Becca became accustomed to the darkness.

Huffing, she turned away from them and faced the back of the couch and the wall. The room glowed orange, then blue then a purple mix of them both, then every minute or so, complete darkness.

The hubbub of laughter and chatter; plates, knives, forks, glasses clinking grew. What did they all have to be so cheerful about? Sticking her fingers in her ears and screwing her eyes shut, Becca breathed into the dusty sofa-back and resolved to sleep.

Chapter Eight

Rolling over, her eyes opened. More light filled the room now. Not quite daylight, but the sun was on its way. Another day of people bustling around the house. But not now. Now it was silent.

Swinging her legs around, Becca stood and walked to the door. Pushing it open, the quiet was blissful. Stalling in her steps she wasn't sure if she wanted to go in the dining room or not. Before she decided her feet had tottered for her and she was half-way there.

Padding barefoot through the kitchen, she paused at the island and uncovered the pastries under the cloche and crammed a few fishy-flavoured entrees in her mouth. Wiping crumbs from her chin, she reached the pair of Georgian doors now closed.

The half-light of dawn glinted on the brass handles and the square plaque on top that must say her gran's name and some kind words. Maybe she could read those.

Timid steps reached the coffin and she placed a delicate palm on the cold metal. The urge to talk to her gran came and went without words.

"You couldn't keep away after all."

Heart thumping, Becca turned to see her sister sitting cross-legged on the green recliner chair. "Sophie! I almost jumped out of my skin." Impressed her little sister had actually followed through with her promise to keep vigil and it wasn't a ploy to curry favour.

"You okay?" Her sister's arms were around her. "I do worry about you, all alone down in Cardiff. I'll come and stay with you, you know? Just say the word."

Squeezing her sister's arm, she smiled. "Thanks. I'm okay."

"Are you sure? I mean after Callum…"

"Don't say it. I don't want to think about that. I'm struggling losing my lovely gran. I can't think about how Callum left me."

"But…"

"No, Sophie. I'm fine. I'd love him to be here, of course. He would be a great comfort. Always gave wonderful hugs, but he had other ideas. It's hard not to picture him without feeling it was all a crock of lies."

"No. He definitely loved you."

"Then why did he…"

"He had other things going on, I guess. Uni is stressful, you know that. He loved you, he just needed something you couldn't give him. Oh, no. That came out wrong."

Becca shook her head. "You're right. I hate that you're right. I'd have given him whatever he wanted; still would, but he didn't talk to me. Anyway… I'm here for Gran." Patting the wooden coffin, she looked at her sister. "Doesn't it feel weird to you? She's actually in there. If we opened this lid, our gran would be lying there."

"It doesn't seem real does it? I mean, she's always kind of just been there. I never dreamed she would die, did you?"

Becca knew she hadn't meant literally but couldn't help flinching at her nightmare. "No," she croaked.

"Do you reckon Mel will come?"

Pursed lips parted to say, but she sufficed with a shrug instead.

"I suppose it depends if she's sober enough. And if she can get a lift. I heard she lost her licence."

"That was ages ago. It was only for a year. I'm pretty sure she's got it back again now."

"Doesn't deserve to. She could have killed someone."

"Very sensible, Sophie. When did you get so grown-up?"

Smiling, Sophie asked, "Do you mind watching Gran for a bit? I'm pretty tired."

Reluctant, but not wanting to force her sister to lose any more sleep, she agreed. Sitting in the chair, she didn't keep vigil for long before the peace of the room took her away to her dreams; dreams she would very soon come to fear more than ever.

Chapter Nine

It was no surprise when she awoke to the first signs of morning: her mum clattering cups and boiling the kettle in the kitchen, that she could remember her dream. And the subject of her midnight ruminations was of little wonder either.

Grinding her teeth, she played it back over in her mind. Her cousin Mel was staggering in the street. Behind her, smoke rose from what remained of a car and a tree. It was a quiet country road, but if you can't avoid a stationary tree, what hope would a cyclist or a horse and rider have had?

She'd doubtless see her later. Should she be nice, or should she let her know how irresponsible she'd been? It would probably depend on whether anyone tried to force pastries down her today.

Sliding from the chair, she joined her mum in the kitchen. "Morning."

"Oh! You gave me a fright. I didn't expect you up." Realising the direction she'd come from she added, "Were you in with your gran?"

Becca felt a reluctance to confirm the fact in case she thought she'd complied with her parents' demands. Oh, come on. Don't be petty.

Gran was never petty, she was always very tolerant. "Yes. I took over from Sophie. She's growing up fast."

"Yes," her mum beamed. "Maybe she'll go off to uni like her big sister. I am proud of you, you know. I just worry. And sorry about your room. I didn't think I could put Aunt Carrie on the pull out."

"I don't mind. Honestly. The study was lovely. I was just in a bad place yesterday."

Her mum squeezed her shoulder. "Cuppa?"

Becca hadn't had anything made for her for a while. Not without leaving the house and going to Starbucks, anyway. "Yes. I'd love one, thanks."

Hugging mugs to their chests the pair nattered about the weather and kept one-another abreast of the mundane day-to-day. "What's the plan tomorrow?"

Donna tapped her cup handle then answered whilst staring through the front window. "The hearse is coming at ten and we'll follow in procession to the church. Webster's are carrying the coffin, although my uncles, Stan and Sidney, will be there. Obviously, they won't take any weight. One is eighty-seven, the other one's eighty-three. Then we'll wait at the front for Father Jenkins to conduct the service."

"I can't believe she's gone."

"I know. But she's still here," and Donna patted her heart, then croaked, "She'll always go on in here."

Back in bed after a draining day of more of the village paying their respects, Becca stared at the ceiling. Tomorrow was it. It would be hard, but hopefully she'd get closure and begin to move on. Whilst she'd tried to convince herself her gran would go on forever, of course she'd never really believed it.

Swallowing bile, her cousin not gracing them with her presence sickened her. They all expected her to arrive today because she wasn't really a morning person so starting her day in the right place was essential. She'd better not turn up late tomorrow, Becca picked at skin around her thumbnail with her index finger and hoped she'd sleep better tonight. Heaven knows she needed to.

Chapter Ten

The impending sense of dread prevented her managing any of the cinnamon toast her dad had cooked for everyone.

"Are you not going to eat that?" Sophie pointed her face at Becca's plate conveying in one glance that she really ought to because she was far too skinny, and that Sophie herself would be forced to consume her unwanted sustenance otherwise.

Picking a triangle up, she nibbled at a corner. As the taste hit her tongue the first swell of nausea rippled through her. Squeezing down past her epiglottis her stomach readied to the threat, defending itself with acrid bursts of bile to meet the incoming menace.

Shoving her plate towards her sister, cheeks billowing, Becca scraped back her chair and fled from the room. Sophie was devouring the second half of her breakfast before she reached the door.

Retching over the toilet bowel, a few spits sufficed to reassure her digestive system that she wasn't actually planning to eat anything. Collapsing against the bathroom door. How was she going to get through today?

Without returning to the kitchen, Becca slunk off to the study to retrieve her rumpled funeral uniform from its confines. As she shook the creases from it, she regretted having not hung it up, but without being in her room and seeing her wardrobe, the notion had escaped her.

Sighing as she tightened the belt and pulled on the jacket and slid on her shoes, she quietly exited the room and tottered along the hallway to the long mirror near the front door. Her mother always liked to check her appearance before leaving the house even if it were just to pop to the store for milk. Living in such a small village meant being seen in the wrong outfit could be talked about for years to come. That's what she thought, anyway, because that's what she would do herself. The rest of the village had no interest.

Regarding her reflection, she was ratified that the cheap material of her dress had shrugged off the creases inflicted whilst incarcerated in her suitcase and now happily clung to her slight frame. She really had lost rather a lot of weight. Perhaps when this was over her appetite might improve.

Confident of approval, she walked into the kitchen where the rest of the family still sat drinking coffee and chewing on the last crusts of cinnamon toast.

Seeing her in her black, her mum gasped. Hand flying to trembling lips, her dewy eyes took in her sombre daughter. "Oh, Becca. Are you okay?"

Nodding in quick jerks, she pried her eyes away from her mum's knowing the shared emotion would grow too strong. Walking past them all to the dining room, she slumped in her gran's chair and stared out at the room. As it blurred in her moist eyes, the coffin swirled in wood and brass hues filling her view, obliterating all other thoughts.

"You'll be fine, my love," her voice echoed ethereally around the room. "I couldn't stay forever, now could I? Remember me in good health, and how much I've always loved you, Becca. You've always been my favourite person in the whole world. I know you'll respect my memory."

Tears tracking Becca's cheeks plopped freely down her chin and onto lifeless hands in her lap. "I know, Gran. That's why I'll never get over you. Who else will love me like you did? I thought I'd found love with Callum, but we all remember how that ended, don't we."

"I still do love you; not *did* love you. I'll always be in your heart and looking over you."

Nodding, she would have to get over losing her because there was no choice.

"Have you been sitting in here the whole time, love?" Auntie Carrie stopped in front of her. "Only... they're here and," she struggled for words as she fingered a knuckle on her right hand with her left, "They'll need to take her."

Face crumpled, Becca stood and walked to the conservatory and stared at the rain running down the glass. Even the weather was miserable.

Hushed murmurs reverberated around the room as the undertakers organised themselves to move the coffin through the house. Screwing her eyes tight was no use, her ears heard every noise; every creak, every breath, she could picture it clearer than if she were looking straight at them. As they reached the front door and the sounds of them faded, Becca rested her flat palm on the cold of the window pane, its iciness matching her shattered heart.

"Come on, love. We're getting in the cars now."

Turning from the rain-smeared glass, Becca bowed her head and slunk to her mother's side. The house was empty apart from them. As they stepped from the front door, the row of cars acted to underline the end of an era. "Which car?"

Frowning, Donna nodded to the front car. "The first one, of course. With Sophie and your dad."

The stretched black Mercedes had three rows of seats. Beside the chauffeur remained empty and the two other rows were occupied by her mum and dad and then her and Sophie in the back. A smart suited man in top hat and tails carrying a staff walked in front of the cortege until the end of the street when he climbed into the passenger seat of the hearse before continuing the crawling pace . Picking up speed, the funeral procession of the two black cars and lots of others following behind, headed into the secret valley and on to Pontfaen church.

The tight roads were impassable as her gran's popularity filled them. Squeezing into the only gap (deliberately left for them) the hearse and the family cars pulled into the small churchyard of the tiny church with its stumpy steeple. It seemed unlikely all those who had come to mourn would fit inside.

Following the coffin and her two great-uncles, Becca sat at the front of the church within touching distance of the vicar.

Watching with dancing eyebrows as he wondered, among other things, about breaching fire safety laws, the vicar sighed as the doors closed for the final time and he could begin.

"Welcome, welcome, one and all to the funeral service of the much-loved member of this parish, Mrs Christine Austin, ne Armstrong. Christine was born on the first of May, nineteen thirty-nine right here in this village to Mrs Beryl Jones and Colonel Eifion Armstrong before being whisked away when she was only five years old to Kolkata, Calcutta at the time, of course, when her father's career in the army dictated.

"Spending her early years in India, in 1948 she returned home to our wonderful secret community here in Cwm Gwaun; that's the Gwaun Valley for those of you who have travelled here from England. Gwaun being the river and the reason Abergwaun gets its name. Aber meaning estuary, or where a river meets the sea. It's Fishguard in English. Anyway, I digress..."

Becca had heard all these details first hand, and how she'd married her childhood sweetheart, Jack Austin who she never got to meet, and so found herself drifting away to her own memories. There followed hymns, including one in Welsh mumbled by more than the visitors from across the big bridge. It was probably a joke from her Gran. She always said she could speak Welsh, but rarely gave any evidence but a smattering here and there and insisting on singing 'Happy Birthday' in two languages, sometimes three when she could remember the Hindustani she'd spoken in India.

As the congregation muttered through, taking longer to attempt to read the words than the singing gave time for, Becca imagined her gran laughing, looking down upon them and she smiled.

A Eulogy from her Uncle Stan covered the same things the vicar had opened with but with added anecdotes. Everyone was impressed remembering how she'd raised her siblings like a mother, then had her own children and then trained to become a nurse finishing at the very top of the profession as Matron of a major hospital.

Bang!

Stan stopped mid-sentence as all eyes turned to the door.

"Sorry, sorry. Carry on." Becca's cousin, Mel, stood at the font grinning. "Devilishly difficult to find," she shook her head. "Sorry, do carry on, please," she repeated, smoothing her skirt and taking the seat offered to her by an older male mourner.

Pin-hole pupils burnt into her and she mouthed sorry again before Stan carried on with his touching memories of his sister.

As he concluded in choked-voice difficulty, many of the congregation had tears streaming down their face. Becca surprised herself that something more pressing than expelling some of the grief she felt filled her thoughts... Rage.

How could she? How could she get here late and then show such disrespect? Why hadn't she come yesterday to avoid this, and why hadn't she waited quietly, or crept in without banging the door?

I know you'll respect my memory

Her gran's words floated through her head over and over like a ticker. *I know you'll respect my memory!* "I will, Gran," she hushed under her breath. "I will."

Chapter Eleven

The service finished with another hymn and then the organist played them out with a haunting rendition as the tears streamed down faces of emotion-piqued mourners shuffling in an orderly line from the church.

The wake was to be a cold buffet and drinks at the Gelli Fawr (large copse) Hotel a few hundred metres away, which meant everyone could walk in a sombre line.

Arm in arm with her mum and sister, they halted in their tracks at the sight of a gushing Mel as she bounded towards them. "Sorry I arrived late, but you know what I'm like with mornings!" she rolled her eyes and grinned.

"Yes, we do. That's why we expected you at Mum and Dad's yesterday so you could come with us."

Mel nodded along as though not adhering to that plan was all part of her chaotic charm. "I know. Mad, isn't it?" she laughed.

"What's mad? The fact you can't show respect for our grandmother?"

"Hold on, Bex, I'm here, aren't I?"

'Bex!' Becca seethed. "It's Becca, as you well know. And yes, you are here. We're supposed to be grateful you bothered at all, are we?"

"Rebecca, that's enough. Your gran wouldn't want you two to fight."

Wouldn't she, Dad? Becca wasn't so sure. Her gran was placid and kind, but if one thing gnarled her, it was disrespect. Well, as a colonel's wife, mother of four, virtual mother to thirteen and Matron of an entire hospital, it was the least she deserved.

The spread laid out on a long table in the function room at the hotel boasted the type of food that could be plated and walked around a room: sandwiches with the crusts off, sausage rolls and other savoury pastries along with fairy cakes and petits fours jiggled around the room to the background murmurs of 'Sorry for your loss,' and 'She was a lovely woman.'

Along with the food was the alcohol. The bar was well-stocked and everyone tucked in. Apart from Becca. She knew she was meant to be celebrating her life, but jollity just seemed wrong. And one other person who was doing more than tucking in was riling her—Mel.

Firmly in her sights, she strode over to her cousin. "Enjoying yourself, Mel?"

Pausing her glass between bar and lips, Mel frowned. "It's very nice, thank you. Gran would be pleased at the turn-out, don't you think?"

"I'm sure. I take it you're not planning on driving home?"

"Of course not! I can't afford to lose my licence; I've only just got it again."

"How long were you banned?"

"A year. They gave it back a month ago so I rewarded myself with that." She nodded towards the window. Past the other cars stood one Becca was sure hadn't been there when she got out of the limousine. It was red and expensive looking. "That's nice. What is it?"

"Porsche Cayman. It's so, so quick. A dream to drive. I've missed driving so much, I wanted to make it memorable."

"Work going well then?"

"Yep. I sold a huge Georgian place in Swansea the other week for nearly a million!"

"And you get commission on that?"

"Of course." She patted the side of her nose to suggest she wouldn't share how much but Becca suspected it wouldn't take much pressing and she was determined not to give her the satisfaction. "How's being a student working out?"

Becca nodded with her mouth down-turned. How was it going? "Stressful I think is the word."

"I can imagine. Especially after Kieron."

"Callum."

"Sorry, Callum."

"Well, I'll leave you to it. I need to circulate." She needed to get away from her show-off cousin. Hands trembling, she knew her passive aggression had hit home, but she couldn't shake the rage. Compliments from uncles, aunts and family friends brought her mood up, especially the constant reminders of how highly Christine had thought of her. "If she could prise you into the conversation, she would. Reminded her of herself, I think. How are you coping?" another aunt; a younger version of her gran, whose name she couldn't remember, asked her.

"It's too early to tell. She was old, but it's still a terrible shock. I thought she'd always be there, you know?"

Everybody did know and everyone offered similar platitudes. When it was all over, Becca would sigh with relief. She'd stay at home for the weekend but travel back to Cardiff at the earliest opportunity. Making the most of her photography would be a necessary distraction. She could take her camera out here, and probably would, but when inspiration struggled to stretch its head above the grief, a remit set by the exam board was a welcome template. She couldn't wait to get back.

One by one, people left until the last of the extended family came over and bade their farewells. "You'll have to come and see us again in happier circumstances. It's quite spectacular when it's not raining," Becca's dad invited with insincere handshakes. He hated visitors. They always wanted to do things when all he liked doing when he got home from work was watch football.

"It looks lovely now. The perfect resting place for our Christine. I'm going to miss her so much..."

"Where's Mel? She hasn't driven, has she? She's been drinking all afternoon but her car's not there!"

"I'm sure she won't have. Maybe someone drove it for her. Come on, let's get back to the house. We'll have to get a cab."

"No, no. I can give you a lift."

"Thanks, Brian,"

It was the first time Becca had heard the name. Moments later and they were in Uncle Brian's old Ford and being dropped back at their house.

"Thank goodness," Becca sighed seeing Mel's red sports car in the driveway. Walking into the house, it was surprisingly silent. Where was cousin Mel?

"Melanie, are you okay?" Donna called out. And then Becca's dad joined in too. "Where is she? Her car's here. Surely she can't be far."

Not caring where she might find her cousin, Becca tottered to the study to remove herself from the staid funeral attire and get into something more comfortable. The smell hit her first; the cheesy alcohol bile of drunken vomit. Then the sound of snoring, and finally, the sight.

Like a disgruntled bear, Becca flew for her cousin. "Mel, get up and clean this mess. I've got to sleep here!"

Eyes springing open, Mel sat bolt upright. "Sorry. I felt a bit unwell; must be the stress of the funeral, I suppose. I wasn't sure where I was meant to be sleeping and when I saw the pull-out bed all set up, I kind of assumed."

"Understandable. What I don't get is why you've been sick on the floor."

Peering through slit eyes, Mel surveyed the scene. "I don't think that was me."

"Oh, don't be ridiculous."

Sighing, Mel eased herself from the bed. "Where's a tissue?"

"Tissue? I think you'll need more than that!"

"Well, kitchen roll. Oh, you know what I mean." Mel slunk from the room leaving Becca staring at the mess. After a minute, she wondered, why she was standing guard. Backing out, she walked back to the kitchen.

"... it's a lovely car. Pretty good on fuel considering the performance, and really well built. Well it's the Germanic quality, isn't it?"

"Are you going to clean up your mess?"

"Oh, Hi, Bex. Yeah, yeah, in a minute. I was just telling your dad about my little Porsche."

"Who drove it here?"

"What do you mean?"

"I mean, you couldn't drive back to Swansea because of how much you'd had to drink, but your car is in the drive. Who drove it here?"

"Well, I did. Duh! It doesn't matter on these quiet country roads. It's the forgotten valley. You're hardly going to see a police car here, are you!"

"That's not the point. You could have killed someone."

"Oh, calm down. It's only a mile or so. And I'm here safe and sound. No-one died, did they."

"Well, apart from our grandmother. She wouldn't be impressed. And it's secret valley."

"What?"

"It's secret valley, not forgotten. You said forgotten."

With a face of 'whatever,' Mel sat at the table with a fresh coffee Donna passed her.

"And it's Becca, not Bex and Callum, not Keiron. For heaven's sake, do you know anything about this family!"

"Becca! That's enough. Your cousin's hurting too."

"Well at least she's in comfy clothes. I can't get changed because my room, or rather your study with a pull-out bed in, stinks of her sick."

"Oh dear, Mel. You feeling okay?"

"Bit better now, thank you, Donna." She turned to Becca. "Don't worry, cuz. I'll clear up in a minute. Just let me settle my nerves with this coffee."

"Sober up, more like."

"Becca!"

"Don't worry, Mel, dear. I'll clear up. Well, you won't know where anything is, will you."

"Oh, thank you, Auntie Donna. Are you sure? I was dreading it, to be honest. It really smells. I think it might have been one of those fishy things."

Striding down the hallway, before she reached the stairs, Becca just caught the tail end of, "... We'll have to have a word with that hotel. Maybe we should complain if you've had food poisoning..."

"Give me strength," Becca sighed.

"What are you doing?" Sophie demanded as her sister knocked and walked in her room.

"Can I crash on your beanbag or something? Mel's been sick all over the study."

"Ew! Yes, of course. But you'll have to let me stay with you in Cardiff in return. I'd love to come to the city. It's so dead here." The unfortunate word hung in the air.

"Don't knock it. Sometimes the fast pace in Cardiff is a bit in your face and I long to be back here in quiet old Fishguard." Well why do we hardly ever see you? Sophie didn't bother saying. "But, yeah. Of course. I'd love you to come down. That'd be great."

Wearing cutesie pyjamas and covered over with a blanket from the bottom of her sister's bed, Becca rolled in the pit of beans and turned to her sister. "You don't mind if I go straight to sleep, do you? I'll probably head back tomorrow."

"Aw, don't. I'd like to see a bit more of you."

"Thanks, but I've got loads of work on at uni. We'll see, okay?" Turning over, she shielded her eyes from the light with her fingers. It had been a draining day, and she was annoyed that the most memorable thing about it would forever be her stupid cousin.

It took a few moments to realise where she was; seeing it from a different angle to the night before, but the tree and the smoke from the smashed car looked the same. And now she recognised the car as Mel's red Porsche, it made perfect sense.

She hadn't learnt her lesson. At least it was only a tree she'd injured and not a human, although in the hundred years the gnarled oak had lived through everything from the first world war to the London Olympics, little had changed in the sleepy valley. In such calm surroundings, she bet it had never imagined such a violent demise, if trees imagined anything at all.

As Mel walked away clutching her head, something caught Becca's eye. There were two Mels! The one walking towards her and another, still in the car, slumped over the steering wheel. It was this Mel the director of her dream zoomed in on now.

The blast of the horn echoed around her head as she grew closer. Face caved in where her nose and teeth used to be, blood oozing from her ear as strands of golden hair clung to what was left of her cheek, the horn blasted a fanfare of death through the valley.

Ravens circled. When would they get their chance at the fleshy bits of dead human? How could they get past the metal armour that surrounded her? They'd sit nearby and wait.

The dream changed as dreams do and Becca became one of the Ravens. Flapping her mighty wings, nostrils on her dark grey beak smelled the stench of death in the air and she soared high into the sky; high above the secret valley, high above the mountain of angels, Carningli, and up into the clouds above the bay.

A dark shape below her caught her eye and she jolted her head sending wind past the wrong feathers and her body into a spin. Smiling with her beak, she realised what it was. She was so high, her silhouette cast a shadow on the clouds. Regaining control of her flight, she flew one way then another, the different directions causing different shadows.

Flying east, the shadow disappeared, west and she could see the full expanse of her wings, like an angel. A dark angel. From side to side, she formed a straight line, then a triangle then a paper dart. Flying west was her favourite. She wished she could do this all the time.

A call from below. She had to go. Was it breakfast? Flying straight through her own silhouette, a shudder shot down her spine as she re-entered the world of the blasting horn and disquiet in the valley.

Down and down, the horn grew louder, down and down and down.

"Becca! Wake up! It's cousin Mel!"

Chapter Twelve

T he horn blasted through the open bedroom window as Sophie stood over her. It was still like a dream and Becca wasn't certain until later, when the drudgery of normality convinced her, that it wasn't.

"She's had an accident. I can't believe it. Come on. Help us!"

Sophie rushed from the room in the assumption her sister would follow. Wriggling, it took a while for the beanbag to surrender its grip on her form. Rocking forward and falling back didn't let her go so she slid to the side and flopped onto her hands and knees. Aching, she pulled herself up gripping the radiator beside the door. Stretching away the cramps, she ran downstairs still in the cartoon pyjamas.

"What's happened?" she cried as she reached the kitchen but the room was empty. Retracing her steps, she got to the front door which she noticed was ajar. As soon as it opened, she could see it as well as hear it.

Gasping, she couldn't believe the scene. The grey and black plumes of smoke she'd witnessed in her dreams swirled skywards; and from where they were originating, she knew the old oak was the source.

Rummaging for shoes in the box by the door, Becca squeezed into her sister's vans and raced off downhill, reaching the corner into the Gwaun Valley in minutes. As she rounded the bend, the horn grew louder still and the smoke choked her. Straining to see through the haze, the figures of her mum, dad and Sophie could be made out standing a few hundred metres away.

Out of breath, Becca slowed to a walk in stunned silence. It was the same as her dream but for one thing: there was no second Mel walking away from the scene; only the dead Mel slumped over the wheel of her Porsche.

Knees buckling, Becca fell to the floor. "How...?" How what? How did she dream the exact nature of two family members dying in the space of a few days? Creaking sobs scratched in and out of her as she crouched on all fours, her groans merging with the car horn like a birthing cow.

She'd had the dream twice for Mel, hadn't she. Why hadn't she warned her? Face creasing from the blow of guilt. The first dream she'd almost felt it's what she deserved; for having scant regard for others' safety as she sped around drunk. Is that why she hadn't said anything? And then her antics at the funeral had made her so angry. But this? She wouldn't wish this on her worst enemy, and her cousin wasn't that, despite the distaste she'd had for her lifestyle.

Hauling herself up, she trod to her huddled family, along with Mel's car, the sirens of police, fire and ambulance crews echoing through the valley moving ever closer were deafening.

Turning away from the wreckage, face grubby with unwiped tears that had tracked through foundation and sweat, Donna screeched at her daughter over the cacophony, "I said she was welcome to stay a few days but she said she'd leave first thing because of *you!* Because you don't like her, she felt she couldn't stay and now look!" Pointing at the crumpled red metal as though Becca might have been unaware, she screeched again, "Look! Look what's happened."

"You're blaming me?" The words fell with no force from Becca's lips. Was it her fault? She could have warned her. She could have been nicer to her. But Mel must have known not to drive; that alcohol would still be in her system for hours more, so it couldn't really be her fault, could it?

"I don't know. Mel's been going through a lot lately. Charles left her when they found out she couldn't have children. She took Mum's death badly. She said you were upset with her and she didn't feel welcome."

"Well, she did interrupt Gran's funeral, drank too much and then drove home and then proceeded to puke on my bed!"

"I know all that, but she didn't deserve this, did she?"

"No! I'm not saying she did, but I didn't just make her unwelcome for no reason. If I'd known how she was going through such a hard time, maybe I could have acted differently, but how could I? No-one ever tells me anything."

"No? Well we never see you. And we all know how fragile you've been after Callum, and we get it. Really we do. But the world doesn't revolve around you. And if someone doesn't behave just as you want them to, show a bit of tolerance because you just don't know..." Turning away, she clutched into Becca's dad's chest whilst he stroked her hair and the sobs rocked her. Sophie never took her eyes from the car.

"Make way, please," the authoritative timbre of the firemen ordered as they rushed through with hoses and cutting equipment. "Can you stand back please? The police will want to take statements if you're witnesses? Do you know the driver?" They all nodded.

Unwelcome, Becca slunk away and walked back to the house. She didn't need to see the burnt remains of her cousin as they cut her from the wreckage. What she'd seen already would stay with her for the rest of her life. Two deaths in a week. Two deaths she'd seen exactly in her dreams. She couldn't help but worry she was responsible, but that was foolish, wasn't it? How could she be?

Chapter Thirteen

Rushing into the study, Becca was relieved the mess had been efficiently cleared, and then felt guilty for being uptight. It was the last thing she'd remember of her cousin. They'd spent some happy times on family holidays. They'd never been close, but family is family.

Throwing on clothes, she wondered if she should go upstairs and grab her funeral clothes. Shaking her head, she thought she had no choice. She'd need them again soon.

Trailing her case into the hallway, she scuttled up the stairs to her sister's room. Finding the clothes where she'd left them folded near the beanbag on the floor, she scooped them up and raced out of the room again. Almost reaching the top of the stairs, she was halted abruptly.

"Rebecca. Where are you off to in such a hurry?"

Aunt Carrie. Halting at once, Becca knew she couldn't bolt. She couldn't not tell her aunt what had happened, and she couldn't break such awful news and run away. "You'll need to sit down. Something terrible has happened."

Retreating back to her room—Becca's room, she sat on her great-niece's bed clasping her hands in her lap. Her face had no colour. Gulping, she prepared herself as much as she could for whatever she was about to hear.

"Did you hear the horn?" she indicated she hadn't with a tremble of her head. "There was a horn; really loud. It was Mel's car... She crashed it."

Wrinkled hands flew trembling fingers to her lined mouth as she wheezed in a sharp breath. "Oh my goodness. Is she okay?"

What words could she say? Holding her aunt's gaze, she shook her head until she was certain the message had reached its target.

"Oh." Gulping, she sighed. "Was she drunk?"

"I think so. Well, she still had yesterday's alcohol in her system, I expect."

"She'd only just had her licence returned. Oh, dear, dear, dear. Why? Why did she rush off?"

Becca stared at the floor. Tears stinging her eyes, she looked up when her aunt's hand guided her face to look at her. "It's all my fault. She left early because of me. I wasn't very nice to her."

"You were cross because of how she was disrespectful to Christine. You can't blame yourself. She was running away from the truth, not from you."

"But she's had such a hard time. I didn't know. If I'd known..."

Searching for words of comfort, Carrie settled on repeating, "You mustn't blame yourself," and stroking Becca's hair. "You've got such lovely hair, Becca." Standing, she announced, "Come

99

on. Let's go and make some breakfast. Your mum and dad will need it."

How could she think of food at a time like this? It's what her generation did, Becca supposed. It would be a distraction, and she needed that. "Okay. Come on."

"Oh, there you are. I couldn't believe you ran off like that, young lady."

"Why not, Dad? It's not like there was anything I could do."

"No. You've done enough."

"Rob. That's unfair. Your daughter is blaming herself. She doesn't need you making her feel worse. What's happened is a tragic accident. It won't do any good and won't bring Melanie back apportioning blame. Mel chose to drive. She should have known not to. The stress she's been under, this could have happened any time. I mean, she arrived drunk at the church which presumably means she drove all the way from Swansea under the influence."

"She bought a bottle of vodka at the corner shop. That's why she was late. She couldn't stomach the funeral sober."

"Well, it's not Becca's fault and it's dangerous and unfair to blame her."

Surprising everyone, Rob took his telling off to heart. Turning to his daughter, he looked down at his shoes. "Sorry, love. It's just a shock and I lashed out. Of course it's not your fault."

"I'm sorry too. It's just too much to take, isn't it. How much tragedy can one family stand?"

Donna covered her face with her hands and Rob moved in to hold her. Becca stretched her arms around the two of them. Apologies fresh in her mind, she wanted to believe she wasn't responsible, but couldn't rid herself of the nagging notion that somehow her dreams had influenced events. Screwing her eyes, she pressed in tighter to her parents' embrace. Biting her lip she sighed. You're being ridiculous.

Chapter Fourteen

Beams of light lined the sky pointing at the valley where emergency services still worked clearing away the remains of metal and wood where the life of her cousin had ended so abruptly.

How could she have seen it so clearly in her dreams? Before she even understood what she was seeing the universe conspired to bring her clear sight of upcoming death. She could do without it, thank you very much. Witnessing such horror once was more than she could cope with. Closing her eyes, she sprung them open, unwilling to risk drifting away to sleep, despite it being unlikely so early in the day. "I'm going for a walk."

"Want company?" Becca looked at her sister. unsure for a moment. "Thanks, Sophie, but I just need to be alone for a while, I think. Is that okay?

"Of course. I don't really fancy walking, I just wanted to make sure you were okay."

"I will be."

"The police will want to talk to you," Donna warned.

"I know, but I'm sure it won't be today, and if it is, we don't know when. They won't expect me to wait around. I need to get away for a bit. I don't suppose I'll be that long." She was sure she would be long, but she couldn't be doing with arguing.

The light shining its ethereal searchlights into the valley emanated from one spot: the mount of angels, Carningli. She hadn't climbed to the summit for years, but Becca knew that's where she headed now.

Walking past the turning that would return her to her cousins place of death, Becca continued past the mountain and onto the next road that sign-posted Pentre Ifan burial chamber, beyond which she knew rose Carningli Mountain.

The path was steep. Already hundreds of feet above the beaches of Fishguard Bay, the open heather moorland was giddying in its vastness. Pockets of white moved in the distance as sheep grazed the hillside.

Alongside the wild mountain ponies herded near the capstone of the five-thousand-year-old monument, Becca was surprised to see a small number of cattle; some large, and some obviously young calves. Were they wild too? Or perhaps more likely, one of the villagers was dabbling in animal husbandry, utilising the communal ground. Un-phased she walked past without disturbing them.

Reaching a jumble of bluestone, Becca remembered the peak was a steep climb from here over the jagged rocks; exhilarating, but as her shoes failed to grip a couple of times, she realised climbing without telling anyone perhaps wasn't sensible.

Vowing to be careful, she hauled herself along a path carved out by thousand of hooves before her own trainer-clad feet had arrived.

Whilst narrow, the route showed the most direct path. The sheep could be relied upon not to waste valuable energy

So steep, thighs burning, the highest point wasn't visible until she was upon it, but as she pushed on, clambering on all fours, hands clutching at clumps of grass for traction, suddenly the rocks that marked the summit were in view. Breathless, she struggled upwards to reach it, desperate to be on top of her world and rise above the emotions dragging her down.

Touching them for the first time with open palms, they beckoned her to climb that little bit further. Fingers finding fissures in the route to squeeze into, Becca used her last strength to clamber on top of the tallest rock. Gasping, it really was another world.

As free as a raven, she could see for fifty miles in every direction. Directly south, the equal height summits of Foel Eryr and Carn Sian either side of the Preseli high point, Foel Cwmcerwyn, rolled on to other summits in the range fading to flat before ramping up to the larger mountain ranges of the Brecon Beacon National Park heading up the Swansea valleys.

North was the ocean stretching to infinity, grey on one side and with a glance right she could see Cadair Idris and Snowdonia in the far distance. An insignificant pebble on the mountainside, Becca's troubles seemed to fade away. How could she, little Becca Tate from Fishguard, possibly have any influence? I mean, just look at it all.

Laughter rumbled in her belly and vibrated her lips. As the sound tinkled in the air she realised how rare a sound it had become. Attempts to coax more out failed as the weight of the world slid back down her throat in a sodden lump.

Determined to wrest herself from the grip of misery that was blighting her life, Becca threw open her arms and screamed, yelling no words, just to unblock the bung of emotion. Screeching and screaming, she shrieked until she was hoarse knowing no-one but the wind and the skylarks would hear her.

Sea breeze rushed clouds in from the coast spoiling her view. Closing her eyes against the disappointment, Becca tottered on the rocks and steadied herself from tumbling a thousand feet into the ocean bubbling and fizzing on Newport Parrog below. Her mind made allowances for loss of sight, and recognising the importance of maintaining balance, kept her upright.

Smiling, she'd overcome her surroundings and was queen of her existence. Confirming her control, the sun shone warmth on her back like a reassuring caress from her creator.

Opening her eyes with a sense of unimaginable power, the sight confronting her almost toppled her from her exalted perch.

Faithful to her dream, the silhouette of raven wings shadowed on the clouds, but it wasn't the open appendages of a mighty bird, but her own outstretched arms.

A sudden fear knotted in her. Who would she find dead as she fell through the clouds this time? Like a dark angel, she had to strive to keep her power at bay.

"It makes sense to stay here, doesn't it? The inquest won't take long. Everyone knows what happened. Stay here, please?"

Becca shook her head. "I need distance. You don't know what it means to me to get behind my camera."

"Why not photograph around here? You always used to love that. Remember those ponies? Mum loved those."

"I know, I know. But after everything, I need instruction to get my creative juices flowing."

"I'll instruct you!"

"Mum! If I'm going to be told what to do, I might as well be getting good grades for it. No, I have to get back to Cardiff. I'll see you in a week, presuming Mel's funeral..." saying the words hit her. How could it be real? She'd seen her for the first time in years a few days ago, and now she'd never see her again. "Her funeral will be in Swansea, won't it? Uncle Clive and

Lorraine will have to come back from Tasmania for that."

"They're coming day after tomorrow. You should stick around to see them."

"It makes sense, but I barely know them and their daughter's funeral isn't the time for a reunion."

"Yes, well. Maybe you're right. I'm just enjoying having you home, that's all."

"I'll be home soon, and I'll be less stressed if I can catch up with some of my coursework."

Hugging, Becca wasn't completely sure leaving was the right thing, but it was hard to control her emotions in her family home. Better to be in control of them in her own space in Cardiff than to let them out carelessly. She didn't know where they would take her.

"Say goodbye to Dad and your sister."

"Of course." Becca backed out of the room and knocked on the study door which had returned to its usual purpose after Carrie went back home.

"Come in," Rob's voice called from behind the door. As it pushed open and Becca walked in, he nodded, mouth turned down in disappointment. "You off then?"

"Afraid so. I need to get back."

"Well, look after yourself." Putting long arms around her, he pulled her into him and kissed the top of her head. "See you at the funeral," he gave a watery smile. Becca nodded and left for her final goodbye. "I thought you might stay here until after."

"I need to go, and there's no point going to Swansea from here. It'll be quicker from Cardiff anyway."

"I suppose. Well, it's been... eventful."

"Yeah. I hope when I come back at Easter we can just get on with eating hot-cross buns and chocolate."

"All for our lord and saviour."

Becca chuckled. "That too, of course. You know how Jesus loved a good chocolate egg!"

"You haven't left anything behind?"

"Well, there's nothing in here, but you can check my room, if you like."

"Okay. I'll see you in a minute."

Bag in hand, she received her final cwtch from her family before backing out of the door.

"Why don't you let me give you a lift? You can't want to carry that heavy bag to the station."

"Dad, it's on wheels and it's downhill all the way. I'll be fine. The walk will do me good."

Turning back after glancing at his wife, Rob said, "Okay, if you're sure."

As she reached the bottom of the path, Donna called out, "Make sure you eat up. You're looking far too thin, young lady."

"I know. I'll try. Bye."

She was glad to be away. With each step and each trundle of the little wheels on her case she was further from torment. Without constant reminders, she might be able to pretend nothing had happened. At least until the funeral.

Clouds scudding the sky took on sinister forms; one began with a face followed by shoulders; her gran's shoulders as she sat upright in her chair smiling down at her.

Attention taken by another in the form of a car, smaller clouds behind puffing from its exhaust as it zoomed through the sky. Was that them in heaven, or was she seeing things? Certain it was the latter, Becca forced her eyes from them and concentrated instead on her feet as they trotted one, two, one, two down the hill to the railway station.

Around a bend and past a few more shops brought her destination in sight. The Irish sea glistened as ripples raced to the shore, sunlight reflecting in a million different directions.

Checking her purse for the umpteenth time to confirm her ticket was still tucked safely inside, she waited on the platform and watched the numbers tick by on the digital display.

Behind the station building, the looming whiteness of the huge ferry pulled into dock with the apparent effortless ease a modern car slips into a space at the supermarket with its automatic parking. Becca wondered if the ship benefitted from such luxury or if it were down to a skilful and harassed captain on the bridge winding wheels and pushing buttons to bring the leviathan to a seamless standstill.

The train would arrive soon to whisk her, and those who wanted away from the natural delights of Pembrokeshire, off to the thrills of the city whilst those arriving might be off to sail away to distant lands; or Ireland anyway.

Staring at the hulking sight, an urge to be away from her life completely, to leave the station and board the boat to cross the sea and forget everything gripped her, but it faded just as fast when she remembered that with nothing but scenery to occupy her, she would think things she shouldn't; thoughts that would drag her to places she couldn't bear to be.

Cardiff and university, taking those pictures she needed to take, that stood a far greater chance to distract her, and hopefully add to her grades.

The single engine and carriage combination arrived with only a handful of passengers. Stena Line weren't going to be making enough profit to justify sailing the rough seas today. Waiting for the remainders to pick up their phones and purses and carriers and holdalls as they realise their rail journey has come to an end, each smiled as they glanced the azure ocean skirting the long harbour wall to roll into the beach as they stepped onto the platform.

Sidestepping a man with a large rucksack, Becca took a seat with a table by the door. Sitting waiting for the train to move, she wished she had something to read. More and more bodies filled the small carriage until finally, the guards closed the doors giving instructions for where to sit, which as soon as they backed from the train were whole-heartedly ignored. The whistle blew and the unmistakable surge as the metal tube allowed power to its wheels hauling Becca on her way.

Leaving the ocean, the railway headed inland past the heights of the Preseli Mountain and through valleys to Carmarthen from where it turned abruptly south to hug the coastline again. Across the choppy waves and high up on a hill, the turrets and crenulations of Llansteffan castle silhouetted again against the sunny sky, dark and brooding in contrast to the bright golden sand of the beach below, Becca looked away. She was seeing juxtaposition everywhere she looked but it all seemed so obvious. And was it really so dark? Was her disquiet clouding her creativity?

Taking out her camera, she wouldn't get the perfect shot from the train, but perhaps movement against a backdrop of something that had stood perfectly still for a thousand years was interesting too? Pausing after two or three shots when normally she'd take twenty, Becca replaced the lens caps and lowered the camera back into its bag. She wasn't in the mood.

Staring through the window, she hadn't noticed how full the train had become. Running from Pembrokeshire hardly seemed worth it, but now at Burry Port having passed Llanelli and heading for Wales's second city, Swansea, there was barely a spare seat.

The young man who had opted to sit next to her instead of taking one of the seats elsewhere sat rigid, arms straight beside him, he made very sure not to touch Becca.

She wanted to sleep the rest of the journey. When photography deserted her, it was the only respite from her grinding thoughts. But the man wasn't going to let that happen.

"You a photographer then?" His face flushed at the obvious question and he attempted to joke it off. "Don't tell me, you're a brain surgeon!"

"Student. At Cardiff."

"Really?" What was so surprising? Didn't she look the typical student? "Interesting course?" Becca nodded. "I never went to uni. I had to get out there and work, you know? Couldn't sit around. I needed to make money."

The impression of go-getting entrepreneur missed its mark. "I don't do a lot of sitting around. I'm busy all the time, and then I have to write virtual novels about what I've photographed. It's exhausting. If you're confused because I seem to have taken some time off, it's not because I have nothing to do, in fact I'm dreadfully behind. My grandmother died last week and I had to go home for the funeral, and then my cousin died crashing her car into a tree the next day."

Gulping, the lad opened his mouth to speak and then closed it and opened it again. Face burning, arms straighter than ever, he said, "I'm sorry. I didn't mean to imply that you spent time sitting around, and of course I didn't know what you've been going through. But if there's anything I can do..."

He was. He was using her vulnerability to hit on her! "There is something you could do,"

Becca coiled a strand of hair around her long finger and bit her lip unsure if what she was about to ask might be too naughty. "If you wouldn't mind... Could you sit somewhere else, I really want some peace before I have to deal with Cardiff crowds."

The redness took on a sinister quality with the sheen of sweat that burst forth around puffy dark eyes. "Sure. I was only trying to be nice."

No you weren't. You were trying it on. "Thank you, that's most understanding," Becca stretched her legs onto his seat as he was still vacating it and before he could say anything else, she shut her eyes. Minutes later, she opened them to see where he had gone, and scowled as her gaze immediately met his. "It's really creepy watching someone sleep."

"Leave the young lady alone, there's a good chap," a large rugby playing type leaned over. "She's not interested, so take the hint."

"I never said she was interested. I was only trying to be nice."

"Take the hint. I won't ask you nicely again." The large man sat back, confident he wouldn't need to. Smiling at Becca, he acknowledged her 'Thank you,' and turned his attention to his phone to give her privacy. The young man stared out of the window, moist eyes looking like he might cry. Becca closed her eyelids and allowed the rumble of steel on steel to rock her to sleep.

"Wakey wakey," it was the nice man again. "The train's stopped at Cardiff now. That young

113

lad has scarpered so you've got nothing to worry about. You want me to call you a taxi?"

"You better not say, 'You're a taxi!'" Becca grinned and the man laughed hard as though he'd never heard the joke, or perhaps grateful it had been used in a real-life situation. "Anyway," Becca cut through the mirth. "I'll be fine. I think I may walk."

"Okay, well take care. Pretty girl like you." Unwilling to spell out what that meant, he repeated. "Take care."

Becca hooked her camera over her shoulder and wheeled her big bag along the road. The walk wasn't the issue, but the pavement click-clacked the wheels which echoed back from the high station walls in an irritating way that the soft trees of the Secret Valley and the sea hadn't done on the glass smooth tarmac. Stopping at the taxi rank, she leaned in the window. Giving instructions home, she added, "Could you give me a lift in with this bag?"

Keen to help the pretty damsel in distress, the driver hopped out and demonstrated his strength with a jerk of the heavy case into the boot. "And that one?"

"Oh, no. I always keep my camera with me." Hearing the footsteps of him walking round the taxi, by the time he reached the drivers door, Becca had her eyes screwed shut in pretence of sleep. Earlier small talk had irritated her. Now she just wanted to get back to her flat and rest.

As the taxi pulled up outside, Becca thrust the right money at the driver and waited for him to remove her case. With the smallest gesture of goodbye, she wondered while it ticked over outside, was he being a gentleman and seeing her safely inside before pulling away, or was he just confirming where she lived, fancying his chances a different day?

Walking in the city with Callum, she'd never had this problem. What was she supposed to do? She didn't want another relationship; she wasn't sure she ever would again, but being accosted every time she dared to step outside was more than she was willing to take.

As the door closed behind her, she leaned against it. Lips trembling, her knees followed and she fell to the floor. Hammering the carpet with clenched fists, she bit into the floor and screamed. This was why she had to get away. At home, she bottled it up, she didn't know why. Perhaps she didn't trust them with her emotions. Now on her own they flooded out of her and she feared, perversely, that she needed them after all.

Chapter Fifteen

Falling onto all fours, Becca crawled to her bed. Pulling back the covers, she climbed in, and fully clothed, pulled the duvet over her head.

Her gran sitting in her green chair, laughing hysterically flashed with images of Mel's mangled sports car, then Mel staggering from the wreckage, face caved, blood streaking her cheeks and neck.

Then she soared above the clouds, raven wings casting their dark feathered shadow on the scudding clouds below. The wings remained, but as she watched, the hook-beaked protuberance of her pointy carrion face morphed into her own flat features.

In her silhouette, her body, arms and legs shaped sharply, the only part of the savage bird that remained where the wings.

Flap, flap, Becca heard them, and as she glanced behind she could see them. Beating in time with her heart, holding her in the sky with effortless ease. Eyes falling to her clothes, she saw their blackness and she knew she was a dark angel; an angel of death.

When Becca woke, she didn't know if it was night or day, or even if it was Monday or Tuesday. She wouldn't have been entirely shocked if it had been later than that, or even if she'd missed her cousin's funeral, or even Easter.

Still without her phone, she had no other clock to tell the time by. Switching on the TV, she saw the news and the time and date in the corner of the screen. She'd slept for thirteen hours.

What was she going to do? She knew what she should be doing, and usually it coincided happily with what she wanted to do. It had always been her escape. The world looked different through the viewfinder: better; like she had some control over it.

Perhaps that was the problem. Without inspiration, she didn't feel in control. "Just go out and enjoy yourself," she said out loud to the room.

Without showering, she debated washing and at least changing her underwear that she'd worn since yesterday morning and slept in as well. Sitting astride the toilet, she tried pulling the gusset of her knickers towards her nose, they weren't that stretchy but she got within three feet and the smell didn't render her unconscious. They'd do for now. Maybe a grungy look would garner less attention from local Lotharios.

Happy with her reasoning, she slipped her trainers back on and grabbed her camera.

Reaching the door, she wondered how full the battery was so ran round to the other side of the bed where she always had a couple on charge. Slipping one into her bag, she was ready to go again.

She couldn't see the builders as she pulled closed the door, but banging and sawing noise confirmed their presence. Either they couldn't see her, or her less than coifed appearance was having the desired effect when no cat-calling greeted her arrival to the outside world of Cardiff city central.

Relived, she allowed her attention to drift to the bustle of the city. Pedestrians straining their gaze up and down the road in attempts to navigate the busy road without walking down to the crossing; drivers staring ahead, some very severe, others smiling and tapping the steering wheel in time to the radio, others still, lost in plumes of smoke or vape mist.

Taking it all in, a man caught her attention sat at a cafe opposite her looking pensive as he tapped his lip with a finger and glanced at his watch. It wasn't contrast as she needed for her Uni work, but his expressive features held Becca's attention.

Swinging her camera round, she snapped thirty photos in a minute, pulse raising as buses and cars whizzing past added to the tension.

Adjusting the shutter speed, Becca whipped her little bendy tripod from her bag. Keeping the camera completely still, she focused on the man, his stagnant hang-dog expression captured against the vibrant blur of rushing traffic thrilled her.

A quick review of the shots on the camera's screen made her grin. It was perfect. And it was contrast. Of course, it was. She'd found the perfect image to include in her juxtaposition project without thinking. That's what she'd do. Spend the day walking around the city photographing people. With hundreds of pictures, some others might end up being perfect too. And she'd enjoy herself. God knows she needed that.

Walking with a grin on her face, her cheeks ached, so unaccustomed to the gesture had they become. Hair swinging in opposite time to the camera bag, she felt like an advert for shampoo, then remembering her un-showered appearance, pursed her lips, mouth curving to one side. She could be a before shot.

A couple sat on a bench outside a shoe shop. Becca stopped. What told her they were together? They weren't touching. What clues were there? There was a symmetry to them. He had his legs crossed one way and her the opposite. A second after she smoothed her hair behind her ear, he scratched his ear on the opposite side.

Leaning to her, confirming their togetherness, he whispered in her ear and pointed into the distance. She frowned and peered over her large sunglasses. For a heart cramping moment,

Becca thought they were looking at her, angry at her intrusive stare, but following their gaze she saw an aeroplane had taken off from Barry and was heading over them, its trajectory suggesting a westward journey, perhaps to Ireland but more likely off to New York, or further.

Becca's first thought was of how wonderful that would be. As busy as Cardiff was, and as much as she loved her country's capital, New York must be so exciting. All the iconic sights and tourists reacting to them, residents proud but irritated at the added crowds.

Picturing herself on the plane, a cold judder shook her. Arms rigid, she gripped the armrests and stared ahead as a panicked stewardess pulled a mask over her face and gestured frantically at the doors.

The air was solid with tension as passengers all around had a tentative grip on their panic, but one word that it was needed and they'd stampede like a spooked herd, crushing all in their path.

Jolting from the feeling of falling, Becca gasped with relief as the jet banked higher and levelled off and looked as stable as could be as it flew into the distance.

It couldn't be a precognition, could it. She had no plans to travel. Ashen faced, she shuffled to the next bench and sat down. It wasn't practical to fear every thought she had. A couple of prophetic dreams under very specific and unusual circumstances were all she had experienced. Losing her gran was hard. Grief did the strangest things, but she couldn't afford to panic like this every day.

Top lip flaring, Becca shook her head as the new buildings constructed of shiny glass and curves stood opposite the Victorian straight and proper architecture of a hundred years hence. It was what probably represented 'juxtaposition' on Wikipedia and was not the sort of obvious non-art that Becca hoped would get her a first in her degree.

Scouring the street for inspiration, the familiar surge of panic rumbled through her. Batting it back down, Becca stood and took a deep breath. Enjoy yourself, remember? That's how to do the best work.

Another shorter breath moved her on. A dress in a shop window drew her gaze. The headless manikin wore it well with a slant-shouldered pose and complimentary bag and shoes on display in the ensemble. Becca liked the dress, but more so the abstract display. It was very her. She couldn't see the price. Another intentional part of the presentation to force the potential buyer inside to inquire.

It wasn't the same aim, but Becca wanted a similar effect with her pictures. Some people might take it all in in a single glance, but those, with interest piqued, who dared to look a little closer would get so much more from them. Cheeks reddening, she felt pretentious, but being different was what excited her.

She'd learned, or rather she'd been born with the gift, to make a scene the best it can be by where to position the objects, how close to get and what to include. A simple pebble in a rippling stream can look as beautiful as the loftiest mountain. As can a simple, everyday person exude equal, if not superior, beauty to the most glamorous Hollywood idol.

Stepping away from the window display, satisfied her mojo had been fuelled, the next sight to greet her confirmed it. In the entrance of a bank, representing wealth and happy to show it in its glossy façade, was the exact opposite. A human so down on his luck he had been reduced to sleeping in a doorway.

Becca wondered, does the bank have significance? Was it a heartless lending decision that sent him on his downward spiral?

Like a wildlife photographer, Becca dare not breath as she removed her camera from its bag and unclipped the lens caps. Slowly, she brought the viewfinder to her eye and clicked. Damn! Why did these digital cameras have to be so noisy? She was sure there was a function to turn off the fake camera shutter sounds, but she didn't have the time to go into and decipher the menu. Not while her quarry sat hunched metres away from her.

As the man didn't react to the clunks and whirrs, Becca felt braver and moved closer. Hood covering his head, hunched over his knees, she was sure he must be drunk to be so unaware.

Bony, grimy fingers poked from the sleeve of his thick looking coat; dirt so imbedded only came from being out here a long time. Twisting the focus as she grew closer, she wondered if she had time to fit the macro lens and get some really interesting shots.

"Leave him in peace." A girl on the arm of a rugged tall hoody-wearing boyfriend commented as she strolled past. "Bloody journalists."

"She might be going to help him. You know, highlight the homeless problem?" Becca heard the boyfriend argue. The girl's response was a distant mumble, but it resulted in the locked arms unlocking. Becca grinned as the chunky arm of the boy slid from the girl's waist, then shoulder as she slipped his apology off like an uncooperative child.

Guilt at her covert cowardice made Becca step forward. "Ahem," she coughed. "Is it okay if I take a few photos?" As she said the words, it struck as so disrespectful. She didn't enjoy her own photo taken, and the occasions which demanded it were fraught with frequent checking and re-checking her make-up, and how she looked in the mirror to attempt to look her best; although she was rarely happy with any photos, she was in. She didn't hate them all, but she didn't recall one she actually liked. It was unlikely that being so far from his best, this man would welcome the moment being kept for posterity, but instead of screaming at the audacity, he shrugged.

"I'm sorry, I don't know what that means. Are you okay with it? Would you rather I didn't? I've taken a few already, but I can delete them if you'd like?"

The man shrugged again. "Don't care..."

"How about I snap you and then show the pictures to you? Make sure you're okay with them?"

The suddenness with which he lunged forward made Becca gasp. "I already told you, I don't f...ing care! I don't want to be alive. The last thing I'm going to give a stuff about when I'm dead is whether you took my f...ing picture, isn't it?"

"You don't mean that!" Becca hissed, hands on haughty hips. "I mean, if you wanted to be dead, it's not difficult." Standing up to her full height, she surveyed the area. "I can see a dozen ways you could kill yourself right here. Any one of these buses that pass feet away from you would do the trick, for starters; then there are plenty of really high things you could jump from; plenty."

She lowered to her haunches and leaned in to stare in his face. "I don't believe you want to die at all. I think you just like to whinge about it to make people like me feel guilty for taking your picture."

He hid his face in his hands. "Just leave me alone. You don't know me. You don't know the first thing about me. I don't want to be alive. I think about it all the time. Do you think I want to live like this!" He swung his arms from side to side encompassing everything he owned. "It's not living at all. I'd rather be dead."

"Like I say, why aren't you then. Come on, I'll help you to the road."

"I'm scared. I'm scared of the pain if I get it wrong. Knowing my luck, I won't die, I'll just cause myself agonising injuries and I can't stand any more pain. I've suffered enough."

"Oh come on. There must be painless ways. Most of your homeless buddies seem off their face on drugs. You can smell the bloody weed as you walk by."

"You can't die from taking weed."

"You fucking can if you take mine..." Becca laughed.

"What are you talking about?"

"Sorry. It's an old joke."

"I'm glad my imminent death is so amusing to you."

"No. It's not. You don't know the half of it. This week, my best friend, the woman I admired most in the whole world left me. My wonderful, beautiful, clever, funny gran died." Becca looked at the ground before staring him in the eye again. "Then at the funeral, my childhood friend, big success story, Porsche driving cousin crashed into a tree and died too. The funeral's next week. So don't talk to me about death. I've had enough of it."

"I'm sorry for your loss, but that makes me scared too."

"What?"

"It's not just the pain, it's what happens after. I welcome a blanket of nothingness. I'd wrap that baby round me and disappear into oblivion without another thought, but what if it's not that? What if that's not *The END*? If we're judged by our life and I end up somewhere worse that here?"

"Why? What have you done that's so terrible?"

He stared at his hands. Holding them in front of him, they trembled so violently he plunged them into his pockets just to steady them. "Leave me alone. Why are you even talking to me? I didn't ask you for anything? My life is shit enough without you coming and judging me for it."

Lips pressing together, Becca tried to remember what she'd said. In the face of the distress she'd caused, the words jumbled together, rolling round her mind like little spikey balls making her wince with every recollection as they bounced around. "Sorry. It's not you. I've... I've had a bad week and when you said you wanted to die and I so wished the people in my life were still here it made me angry. But you're right. I don't know you and I had no right to take it out on you." Gulping down a wad of grief, she leaned in to touch him. "My god. I am so sorry."

"Okay. I don't care. Just leave me alone." Pulling his hood more over his face, he shuffled further into the doorway.

"Okay," Becca returned. "Good luck." With what? Turning his life around? Finding a good way to die? It was a useless platitude and she wished she could take it back. "Anyway... I'll be off." The idea of taking more photos squeezed guilt into a painful shudder. She had enjoyed it, but it was spoiled now and she barely recognised herself. It was time to cut herself some slack.

Walking back towards the university, she rehearsed in her mind what she might say to her tutor. She needed more time. She wasn't coping and she needed to acknowledge that; find out what her options were. Forcing herself through a course wasn't going to get her anywhere.

Without her phone, she didn't even have her tutor's phone numbers. She'd have to get another cheap pay-as-you go handset. It was very isolating not being able to be contacted. Stopping, she looked up and down the street. There were phone shops everywhere, but now she wanted one, she couldn't remember where. Squinting up the road, she was sure she saw a well-known logo and headed towards it.

Inside, rows of phones looked the same as one-another. Advised of her low, low, budget, the sales assistant deployed his advice. "What are you mainly going to use it for? This one's only £100 and it's pretty good. The camera's not bad. It's not fast. You won't be able to play many games, and the memory is pretty low. But if the main thing you want to do is make and answer phone calls and texts, you could do a lot worse."

"I think I might have to. I wasn't planning on spending that much. I don't have that much."

The salesman's face dropped. "Okay. How much were you thinking?"

The one hundred pounds made her say "No more than fifty pounds," but shaking her head, she decided to risk making a fool of herself by being honest. "But really, I was wondering what I could get for a tenner?"

"Ha!" he grinned, but then it slipped. "Oh, you're serious."

"I just don't want to be uncontactable."

"Incommunicado."

"Exactly."

Eyebrows threatening to leave his face, the assistant turned and walked away. Fearing her and her ten pounds had been abandoned, Becca was relieved when he returned holding a box. "Nothing for a tenner, but we've got this for twenty-five."

Placing the box in front of her, the tiny screen and large buttons looked like he'd dug it up from 1989. The target customer must be a stubborn elderly person afraid of technology, so making it look like a house phone might soothe them. But every old person Becca knew had shiny black screens and used them all the time. Her gran always made her laugh after every 'Okay Google' inquiry, she'd say 'please' and 'thank you.' 'Well, she's so helpful. I don't want to upset her,' she'd grin.

"It's er, very reliable. The battery lasts for weeks."

"Is there really nothing better? I mean, I've still got to pay for the calls."

Becca left the shop with a contract for less than she had planned to spend on pay-as-you-go vouchers and a phone that boasted more technology than she'd heard of. Okay, the specifications were apparently woeful compared to the flagship models, and okay, so she couldn't pronounce the Chinese manufacturer, but it looked good, and it hadn't cost her anything up front.

She'd spent her budget on a case to protect her new equipment. Callum would be proud. He always had the top-of-the-range iPhone and she'd have his sim-only cast-offs and top them up when she needed. Clenching her phone in her hand, she cursed herself for letting him invade her thoughts again.

Marching to Uni, she had a clear mission to fill her contacts with relevant lecturers and try to buy some time to get her work back to enjoyable. On the way, she'd phone her mum and find out exactly when and where Mel's funeral was and book that time off too.

"Hello?" the uncertain voice answered.

"Mum, it's me."

"Oh, thank goodness. I was getting worried about you. Is this your new number? Hang on, let me write it down so I can pass it around."

She knew she meant to her sister and dad, but it felt like an invasion. "I'm going to book time off now, so I wanted the details of Mel's service…"

Details freshly written down, Becca arrived at the reception desk.

"Hello, Miss Tate. How was the funeral?" Ffion peered through the bullet-proof glass of the reception desk. Becca wasn't sure if it was actually bullet-proof, it seemed unlikely, but it was very thick. Why it was there at all? How angry could some students get?

"It was hard. And there's another one next week."

Eyes wide, Ffion, gasped. "Really? You poor thing. Who... whose funeral?"

"My cousin. She crashed her car on the way home, well barely a hundred yards from my mum and dad's house. Killed instantly." Biting down on the words, she stopped herself admitting the prophetic dreams she'd had.

"Oh, my goodness. Of course you can have time off. Hang on. I've got a form somewhere. You should speak to Janet, Mrs Barker. It might be worth you taking another year. I've seen students do it under exceptional circumstances, and I would say this qualifies."

"Oh, I'm sure I don't need another year!" But as she objected, her mind un-knotted. Another year might be exactly what she did need. "But give me Janet's number. I'll arrange to have a chat."

Chapter Sixteen

"**Y**ou really have had a lot to cope with, haven't you, cariad." Janet Barker nodded as she sat on the corner of her desk addressing who had been a vital, vibrant student, and now stared at her, fiddling fingers agitating the hem of a pocket and gaunt face creased in grief. "What I don't want to do is hang another year onto your time here when I know you're capable of catching up. I'd say, keep it in reserve; yes you can definitely have an extra year if you need it, but agree that maybe you won't.

"You are a very talented photographer. What you've produced already shows me what you're capable of. A lot of your grade is down to me and where that's the case, you've got no worries. You've surpassed requirements as far as I'm concerned. I usually let students get on with things, make mistakes and learn from them. But in your situation, I can steer you more in the right direction and tell you what's needed and what, not so much.

"I'm assuming you won't be up for the presentations later this month, and that's fine; certainly not worth staying on for. You might not get your absolute best grade, but I'm

131

confident you'll be happy with what you do get, and next year you can move onto bigger and better things.

"If you don't manage; and I don't want you to stress over this at all, take it easy and walk it next year. You're young. You have, god willing, all the time in the world."

Sitting back and not talking for ten seconds told Becca she had finished. Appreciating the support, she felt a little guilty at her irritation at her incessant verbalisation of every thought. "Thank you. I hope that helps me feel less stressed."

"Mmm hmm. Have you seen a doctor?"

"Well, yes. I fainted and ended up in Accident and Emergency. I hadn't been eating enough, but I'm okay now."

Janet nodded, but her eyes slit in her disbelief. "Make sure you do, eh? Keep your strength up." Standing to leave the room, she smiled. "Bring me any work you complete, but no hurry, ok? Now, I need to go home for my tea, or," She said looking at her watch, "Maybe I'll grab a bite in the city. Care to join me?"

What? I think I'd go deaf. "No, thank you. I just want to get some rest."

Nodding and walking in tandem, Janet steered her student from the studio/classroom and strode along the corridor. Becca paced her own walk so there'd be no chance of catching her up for more chats.

Rather than relieved, she felt deflated. What would she do with herself without the pressures of her coursework? It was what had defined her for months. But a sudden hunger gave her a sense that perhaps a weight had lifted, and directly from her appetite.

"So that's a starter of garlic bread with cheese, and a twelve inch ocean with extra anchovies. Are you expecting someone to join you? Should I leave this place setting?"

"No, no. I'm hungry, that's all."

"And, why not? We can always box up what you don't eat and you can have it at home can't you."

Why the waitress might want her to feel greedy about her order, she could only put down to jealousy, her own proportions suggesting she would love to eat a huge pizza without worrying about her figure. Becca had long since made the decision not to care what other people thought of her. She was a good person and if people wanted to judge her differently on an aspect of her appearance or a particular mannerism, that was their problem.

The waitress walked away tapping the pad and mouthing the contents to herself, an actress learning her lines. What was her story, Becca wondered? No-one set out to be a pizza waitress. It was a stop-gap; extra money to get somewhere else. She'd done bar-work and a bit of waitressing herself in the pubs back home in the summer and a few little cafes in Cardiff to supplement her student loans. Was this girl a student? Becca looked for more clues.

133

She looked tired; defeated, bags under her eyes told of late nights. Apart from her interest in her order pad why else did she put Becca in mind of an actress? She didn't have an appearance that would send casting directors wild, but her face was animated so as to show what she was thinking; or perhaps only what she wanted you to think she was thinking.

Becca wanted to photograph her, capture undetectable micro-expressions, erased before the observer could take them in. Only in a still image could the true self in all its flaws and beauty be witnessed.

And then one day, and no-one knew when, that truth would be all that remained. The animated life she gazed upon now would be erased just like Christine and Mel. What would be the demise of this girl? Would she, like her gran, achieve a full satisfying life leaving grateful mourners and admirers behind, or would she, like Mel, be wiped from the face of the planet before she'd properly found herself?

Eyes flitting from the waitress to a family celebrating a birthday a few tables away, Becca wondered the same of them. They wouldn't exist like that forever. One of them would die before the others, and it might not be the obvious older ones, and they'd leave a massive hole that try as they would, they'd never fill. Tears would come, wrenched from the pit of their stomach to flow behind closed doors and into pillows late at night. And just when they'd think they'd cried their last tear, a hand would raise from beyond

134

the grave to remind them and the sand would blow from the hole to be filled again.

Becca sneered. Why weren't we better prepared? Everyone loses someone. It's the only certain thing. Yet even when we're convinced they're in a better place, we hurt. We hurt so much.

Was it just this generation? Her gran had been virtual mother to her siblings and not all of them made it to adulthood. No-one made a fuss. The very reason her great-grandparents had had so many children in the first place was because they knew they wouldn't all survive. Nowadays we're spoiled. We expect to live a long healthy life with no worries and we damn well expect our children to be happy and healthy.

How did they cope? Staring at the multi-generational family, Becca could barely deal with their future loss, and no-one had died.

"One garlic bread with cheese. Can I get you anything else? Another drink?"

Becca forced her eyes back onto the waitress smiling down at her, pen and pad in hand in case she said she'd like something. Her finger gripped the pen so hard, it bent backwards at the joint whitening the tip. Glassy eyes failed to conceal her agitation 'Do you want something, or what?' they screamed as she stood, simpering smile crinkling sourly.

"No. Thank you." Couldn't she see she hadn't even started the first one?

Relieved to be allowed to leave, as she parted, she called back, "Let me know if you need anything."

"Yes, I will. I know how restaurants work. I'm not retarded."

"Ha ha. Okay then." Her eye-roll was detectable even from the back of her head. Becca ignored her and picked up a burning hot cheesy bread. Pressing the burning past her lips, "Fuh, fuh-fuh fuh," she said to cool the burning bite. 'You must have a mouth made from asbestos,' her gran always joked as she ate and drank before anyone else would consider taking a mouthful.

She liked food hot if it was meant to be hot. Hot food had to be piping and cold food must be ice-cold. No luke-warm, room temperature fodder for her.

As it burned, Becca swallowed it down, just more of life's pain to endure with strength and force of will. Staring at the waitress as she gulped it down, her demise had a sudden and urgent interest. Picking up another segment of bread, she bit it half-way down the slice knowing the size would make it burn more with no defence. Holding the waitress in her gaze as she watched her walk away, she projected her hatred; for her and for the unfairness of life directly at her.

Reaching the end of the room, about to walk through the left door sign-posted 'in,' she seemingly detected Becca's gaze, spun around and stared back. As their wills collided across

136

the floor, the poor waitress's was no match for Becca's force of nature. Tripping on her own feet, the tray went flying into the air, glasses, some empty, some half full with ice-cube dregs spilled over her in a fountain of humiliation. Becca just stared like Carrie White wreaking revenge, but for what? And she wasn't responsible. Not in a supernatural way. She'd asked for Becca's disdain as soon as she passed judgement on her meal choice. But it was an accident, plain and simple.

In the ensuing chaos as other waitresses carrying equally laden trays of hot pizzas side-stepped the stricken girl whilst others rushed over to help her up and to clear up the mess, the most prominent thought in Becca's head was her pizza had better not be getting cold.

Inquiring after its readiness from a waiter hurrying past, he appeared relieved he had an excuse not to involve himself with the mess and promised to find out where it was. Returning with a pizza platter, he placed it carefully in front of his new customer. "Sorry about that."

"Is she okay?"

"I think so, but they're sending her home. She'd nearly finished her shift anyway."

"Well, I hope she's all right."

Chapter Seventeen

Despite the waitress's absence and how she therefore wouldn't see she'd been wrong about her needing to take it home, Becca determined to finish every mouthful of her pizza, and just for devilment she ordered a hot chocolate cookie for pudding.

Full from the biggest meal she'd eaten for as long as she could remember, Becca strolled further into the city, a box containing most of the cookie protruding from her bag. Every couple or group of people walking towards her, or she passed sitting on benches or in cafes, Becca had the same morbid thoughts: wondering who would die first. Stopping, she leaned against some railings at the end of an arcade. "It's probably perfectly normal," she assured herself. "You've had an impossible week that would turn anyone insane. And being judged by that girl who knew nothing about you, well, who wouldn't be annoyed. Get through Mel's funeral and things will start to look better, I promise."

"Are you okay?" One of a group of lads approaching from behind asked her, crinkling his forehead and his lips as he examined her ears for a Bluetooth earpiece to explain her talking to nobody.

"Yes. I will be. Just had a difficult week, that's all."

"Wanna come to a party with us?"

She didn't, but she didn't want to go back and just sleep in her flat alone as she counted down the days until they put her cousin in the ground. "Where?"

"Not far. Park Place, just off campus?"

Remembering her two-day old clothes, she wondered if they'd be put off if they caught a whiff, but she didn't care. "Okay, then yes. Thank you."

The freshmen walked with their queen, loyal subjects taking turns at being court jester. "Did you play any good pranks when you were a fresher?"

Becca paused in her step, wide eyes shone no warmth. "Listen, guys. I'll come to your party because I haven't anything better to do, and I'll probably get really drunk, but I can't be doing talking about childish pranks, okay?"

"Maybe we don't want you at our party if you're going to be miserable?"

"Suit yourself." Becca turned around to walk away.

"He's only joking! Please come with us."

"No need to sound so desperate," his friend shushed in his ear.

"Make up your mind. I won't be messed about."

"We'd be delighted, wouldn't we, Jake?"

"Yeah. Sorry. I was just joking."

Becca shook her head and rejoined them in their stroll to the party. Rounding the corner at the end of the street, they were greeted with the *wob, wob, wob*, of drum and bass. Could she really be bothered? It was better than being alone.

"Who's the lovely lady, Jakey?" the front door opened and the bassy rhythm echoed into the street.

Jake flushed red. "She's er…"

"Becca."

"Well, come on in, Bex. Make yourself at home."

"It's Becca, not Bex."

"Oooh, sorry!" Turning to Jake, he winked. "Pulled yourself a feisty one here, haven't you."

Jake's mouth opened and closed. Becca considered correcting him, that Jake had definitely not 'pulled,' but then she thought better of it. "Come on, Jake," she curled her hair around her finger and bit her lip. "You promised me a good time. Don't disappoint me." Crooking her arm for him to escort her inside, he bounded to her and did his duty.

"Nice one, mate. Well done."

The hallway was crammed with people squeezing in two directions, some to the kitchen for more drinks, others upstairs to the bathroom and maybe somewhere quiet to get close, but hindered by a passionate couple who hadn't sought solace, and instead exhibited their affection on the bottom step. The first four out of five buttons on her blouse were undone, breasts spilling from an ill-fitting bra, one hand pressing the cranium surrounding the lips she was working further into her face, the other probing clumsily at his rigid fly.

"Show some self-respect!" Becca sneered, bending over into the girl's face. Facial gyrating paused while she regarded the freshly-arrived spoil-sport and then increased velocity and volume threatening to suck the very life from her gratified cohort.

Clenching her jaw, Becca strode past them to the kitchen. She needed a few drinks if she was going to stand the company of this uncouth crowd. Bottles huddled on the counter with beakers dotted around. Some were empty, others half full of drinks, none were in the nice stack of newness she would hope for. Picking the cleanest looking one, she convinced herself it was unused and accidentally discarded.

Unscrewing the vodka, she poured in a good double-measure and topped it up with a little orange juice. Throwing it back, she repeated the action a few more times, on the final occasion she substituted gin. A need to sit somewhere still and quiet compelled her to shove between two couples occupying a grubby sofa. Nursing her drink, she surveyed the crowd.

Bodies jigged and jostled around her. She remembered her own first taste of freedom. She'd never been hedonistic, and anyhow had arrived with Callum, but it had seemed so overwhelming being away from home; so grown up.

The silly children falling over themselves looked anything but. She tried to smile, to find their exuberant enthusiasm endearing, but it rankled. Didn't they know how serious life was? Were these really the people they wanted to be with? Likely they were just going along with what was expected. They'd party hard this first year and next year would hit them like a fist of regret and they'd be crying, 'Why didn't I do more work last year?' and they'd knuckle down or as so many do, give up.

The pain as she ground her teeth stoked her anger further. What a waste of resources. Parents, taxpayers all putting their faith into the future generation, and they pissed their student loans away and gave up unemployed with no hope or intention of ever paying it back. How much time and money thrown into the gutter of wasted opportunity so they could give it a go?

Becca had never, and never would, give something a go. She only did things she wanted and she gave it her all. Go hard or go home. That's why she knew she'd be a success. She'd known Callum was the one for her and had never had any doubt. That's what made it so hard to swallow that she hadn't appreciated there were two sides to a relationship, and unless both sides weren't quitters the outcome couldn't be guaranteed. And Callum, unfortunately, had been a quitter.

She would learn. Rely on herself and sure things; like Uni. It would return what she put in in spades and set her on a life-path of success. She couldn't waste anymore tears on what had turned out to be a bad choice.

Turning to the couple on her right, their lewdness made her sick. Were they quitters? This time next year would they still be eating each other? Were they in love or lust? Their vibrant probing of one-another didn't seem the pairing of two great minds ready to take on the world and win. They looked like a ten thousand pound debt just waiting to be signed off for the next poor sucker.

Writing them off as quitters she wondered what would become of them. Plenty of people aspired to careers that didn't require a degree and god bless them. If everyone wanted the same thing, the world would be full of people after the same job and lots and lots of misery. Shaking off a nagging doubt that it was, she reminded herself of a friend back in Pembrokeshire who had declined going to university to stay behind cleaning pubs.

Becca had scoffed, but the same friend now managed a hotel and was well up the ladder of her career and gaining on the job training that would result in a degree that was relevant to her career and all paid for by the company she worked for when she herself was basically still at school and racking up years of debt.

Others were happy to stay cleaning or working in a factory or picking up litter and that was good. Becca knew if she was that person, she'd be the best litter-picker-upper they'd ever see. She'd take a pride in her work. Streets she cleaned would win awards for being the pleasantest in the country. She knew it.

And when the end came, obviously a long way off and unpleasant to think about, but when it did she'd look back as her gran had done and she'd feel complete and proud. What would these idiots do?

Having no aspirations and being content was better than failing wasn't it? It didn't waste other people's resources for a start, but psychologically, beginning a career as a failure must be the worst, which was why so many people didn't cope.

She wondered about TV talent shows, the winners and almost winners who believed a long showbiz career awaited them but in reality, the vast majority were dropped back into mediocrity. That mediocrity must taste all the more bitter for viewing it from above.

Pained faces on NHS deathbeds, scruffy mourners leaving their dull houses and decrying their pathetic lives at pointless funerals. Becca swallowed the last of her triple-gin and the bile that had risen to her mouth and closed her eyes.

Laughter and music and indecipherable rhubarb floated on the air, only the sharpest of words squeezing between the soft cushion of the lothario next to her's posterior and the back of the couch penetrating her mind, and when they did, they wrested her from slumber.

Growling against them, Becca pulled her hood up and prodded some of her hair into her ears, a girl across the room stared at her. Closing her eyes was adequate defence.

Bom, bom, bom, ting, ting ting, the muffled sounds lulled her to a calmer place but from nowhere the pizza girl flew into her thoughts and riled her again. Did she look like eating a starter and twelve-inch cheese feast was a regular occurrence? And what if she did? What business was it of hers? Ought she to complain? What if she upset someone a little more fragile with her careless remarks? And judging people on superficial appearance or momentary behaviour was stupid. Sighing, she realised, isn't that exactly what she was doing now? Forcing the girl from her mind, she conceded maybe she was just having a bad day. She was having a lot of those lately.

Sharp pain as a stiletto heel impaled her foot through her trainer, Becca yanked it back. "Oi! Careful!"

"Oh, I'm so sorry. Bit the worse for wear, I'm afraid. Here, squeeze up, I need to sit down."

Becca stared imploring her to get lost. When she steadfastly refused to move, the girl flounced away muttering something that definitely contained 'bitch.' Becca closed her eyes again, her eyeballs rattling behind the lids soothing with every breath.

It was dark. Walking to the toilet, the eerie stillness chilled her. The vitality of dance had stopped. Looking around, it was like a film effect where time had stopped and she was able to walk unnoticed through the crowd.

Peering into faces they all stared at the same thing. Following their gaze, Becca tried to decipher what she saw. How was everyone in the toilet? Why was the toilet in the middle of a night club? Nothing made sense. Becca felt her legs, relieved to confirm she was wearing trousers.

Flicking the light switch, nothing happened and she resisted moving it up and down. Electricity was obviously part of the stopped time warp the party-goers were in.

Two bodies lay on the floor next to a toilet. Clinging to one-another, their eyes stared from wide black pupils, mouths, red in translucent paleness, gaped like unconvincing waxwork dummies in a chamber of horrors.

A hand of someone in the crowd reached out nearly touching one of the girls. As Becca forced herself to look at them she squinted. There was something familiar about them. Despite their pallid complexions and gauntness, she knew them. Where did she know them from? Come on, come on. Almost there, you know them.

"AArrggh!"

The scream woke her and she jolted her head from the back of the couch, the couples either side already up and stumbling towards the noise. More screams joined them along with cries of, "Oh, my god. Oh, my god!"

Pushing herself up from the couch, Becca craned to see what they were staring at. Everyone stood still and Becca swooned.

Oh, no. It was just like her dream.

Pushing through the crowd saying frantic "Excuse me's," she had to see, she had to find out, who the girls were.

People jostled but always seemed to move more in her way. They couldn't know why her need to see what was happening was greater than theirs.

The surroundings looked different and the stillness oddly more surreal than in her subconscious, and it wasn't a toilet they huddled on, but on a bed in one of the bedrooms on the lower floor of the HMO.

The eyes were just as she'd seen them. And the gaping mouths. And her recognition. But in the cold light of wakefulness she had no doubt.

Great wheezing breaths creaked their way into Becca's lungs as she stumbled back through the crowd. How? How can it have happened? Two girls she'd had an issue with less than an hour ago, and now both were dead!

It couldn't be coincidence, it couldn't. What were the chances the girl who trod on her foot and the other girl who had judged her pizza intake would be at the same party with her? Even if it could be explained; the party was near to the pizza restaurant so the occupants were likely regulars and so may have extended her an invitation, but the chance of them both being dead and in the exact manner she had just dreamed? That was impossible.

She had to get away, but she had to stay to see if there was any chance they might be all right. Breathing wasn't filling her lungs and she felt dizzy. Thumping at a pain in her chest she closed her eyes and opened them again with the next wheezing breath.

The room spun and she clutched her head as her brain scraped against the inside of her skull aching and pulsing with every tight inhalation. Blue lights lit the hallway through the tiny fan of glass in the front door.

"Someone let the ambulance crew in."

Becca stumbled forward and reached the door first, determined to help. Yanking it open, the little and large of paramedics stood in the porchway. The petite lady asked, "Young girls, suspected OD?"

Becca nodded. What had they taken and how had she dreamt about it? The open door was too much to resist and as soon as the crew were inside, Becca darted out onto the street and bolted for home. Edging the corner, once she left Park Place, her breathing slowed to a normal pace and the dizziness began to ease. Collapsing on a bench, head in her hands the nausea left and beating heart rattled in her chest.

Actively controlling her breaths, Becca knew she had to get back to see if they were alive. Steadying herself, when she reached the corner she could see down the street and the ambulance waiting outside the student accommodation.

As the first stretcher came out Becca gasped; not for what she saw, but for what she could not. White sheets covered both girls' faces; she didn't even know who had come out first. Slapping her forehead with an open palm, she wished it hurt more. What should she do now? She hadn't a clue. Nothing made sense. Her life didn't make sense.

Chapter Eighteen

Racing to her flat, she fumbled her key from her bag and wrestled it into the lock. Leaning against the door to close it, when it clicked into place, she slumped to the floor. Tiredness clawed at her, but she couldn't go to sleep. She couldn't ever go to sleep again, could she. Who else might die?

Standing, she jerked the door back open and scurried to the kitchen. Filling the kettle, she drummed her fingers to distract her mind while it boiled. As the frantic bubbling reached its climax, she annoyed herself that she should have found a cup in that time and got things ready.

Grabbing a large mug from the cupboard, she paused after scooping two heaped spoonfuls of instant coffee into it and debated a third. One more mountainous heap would do the trick. Pouring the hot water, she stirred it round and took the black gravy back to her room.

With the mug in her hand, she allowed herself the comfort of perching on the bed. Tipping back and forward, she jiggled for reprieve and took occasional sips of the bitter brew.

Why was she having these dreams? Her gran was ill, her cousin an accident waiting to happen, perhaps. But the girls tonight? She'd only just met them. The only thing they shared, up until their death, was that they'd both annoyed her. It seemed as though she met them purely to see them die.

How were her dreams so exact? Were they even dreams? They seemed to happen almost at the same time as the real events; like she was killing them in her mind and willing it true.

Eyes squinting, her head fell to one side. It wasn't possible. It had to be another coincidence. Her mind was susceptible at the moment because of the stress she was under. She must have seen the girls whilst falling asleep. Before they overdosed, they were probably really drunk and made her think they were at risk. And the crowd surrounding them, well that didn't take much imagination. And it wasn't exactly the same. Her dream was weirder.

Slugging back the rest of her coffee, Becca rested the empty mug on her bedside table. That had to be the explanation. She was reading too much into it, and who wouldn't? It was definitely strange.

Sitting on her bed, waves of exhaustion broke and she leaned back. Closing her eyes, images swirled, unrecognisable at first, but soon the blonde hair and blue eyes of a familiar face pulled into focus. "Sophie!" she screamed and leapt out of bed.

She often dreamed of her family. She missed them. But now, although she knew she couldn't possibly be responsible for those two poor girls dying, she wasn't convinced enough to be willing to take the risk.

Four scoops of coffee gave her a pain in her chest but kept her wide awake. Scrolling through Facebook, checking uni-mates' twitter feeds and levelling up on Candy Crush followed by boxset bingeing on Netflix, she almost fell asleep during series two of Stranger Things, but then the chorus of a million birds declared daytime and time to get up.

A shower. She needed one. How could she have gone to a party so grungy and filthy? Would what happened still have transpired if she hadn't been there? "Of course it would!" she scolded. "You didn't give them whatever they took. And you didn't wish them harm. You were just sensitive to the possibility and it happened, that's all. I bet you're not the only one who was worried about them before they did what they did."

Spinning the shower tap to even hotter than usual, Becca stepped under the vigorous flow. Leaning against the tiled wall as the steamy heat built, Becca felt the exhaustion of the most stressful and sleepless night being lulled by the warmth. Panicking, she twisted the tap the opposite way and what was probably still warm but icy to her boiling skin, she gasped and shook under the chilling torrent forcing herself wide awake. "Good. Time to get some great pictures."

Eyes wide, camera slung low and gripped in two hands, Becca was ready; a paparazzo to the world of juxtaposition. Snapping at anything and everything, she didn't have the presence of mind to think, and so opted for a scattergun approach and planned careful editing as her best bet for uncovering a gem. And she could afford to relax after Janet Barker's generous extension.

A bird on a wire. A postman swerving across the road in his red van as the very early birds set about catching their worms. It was what Becca loved about city life: whatever time you went out, there was always something happening; always life going on.

Her thoughts turned immediately to their potential demises. What would cause these good people to breathe their last breath? There were so many ways to die, and it was life's only certainty.

Forcing them onto a different track, her thoughts began to wonder about the more mundane, such as what she might eat today and what would the weather be like.

She hoped it would be nice on Thursday. Not that a funeral didn't suit the dreariest of rainy days, but she couldn't do with getting soaked through at the graveside.

Click, click, more pictures, more and more in a frenetic burst of mania that filled the camera's memory and probably with nothing useable for her project. Oh well, it had been a distraction.

Fumbling in her camera bag, she removed a memory stick which she connected and downloaded the contents of her camera so it was clear and ready for use.

Pausing for lunch she momentarily fancied a pizza, but the poor waitress's sunken eyes and gaping, lifeless mouth loomed into her attention and she lost her appetite altogether. "You have to eat or you'll make yourself really unwell!" she scolded deciding the aromas from Burger King smelled calorific if not incredibly tasty.

Queuing, the choices were too great and when she reached the front she blurted, "I'll have a quarter-pounder with cheese, please."

The young man behind the counter smiled with a puzzled look. "It's not quarter-pounder, we do Whoppers here."

Resisting the urge to say, 'Okay, just give me some McChicken nuggets then,' Becca handed over her debit card and said, "Yes, I'll have that, please."

"With cheese?"

Scowling, Becca nodded. "Yes. Of course. Why would I want my quarter-pounder with cheese, but my Whopper without? That makes no sense."

"Sorry. Did you say you wanted fries?" he asked timidly.

"Yes. And a coffee to drink. Can you put an extra shot in it? Actually, make it two. Cheers."

Becca stood aside to await her order and allow fellow queuers to place theirs. Soon she sat by the window, devouring food like a dainty savage.

Sipping at her coffee, she wondered what photo-opportunities she might find this afternoon. Smiling at the very idea, she sipped and sipped at her acerbic beverage.

"Finished with that?" a man collecting trays asked.

Becca nodded. "Not the drink though. I'm still sipping that."

The man juddered. "Ohh, I hate cold coffee unless it's supposed to be cold."

"Me too."

"Oh, but you've been nursing that one for nearly two hours."

Sitting back in her seat, she frowned. "No. Don't be silly."

He laughed. "I thought you looked lost in your own world. I do that, when I've got the time." Jolting his eyes and arching his brows, he smiled. "Would you like another? If you give me the money, I can go and get one for you, if you like?"

"Yes. Yes please." Handing over a ten-pound note, she gave instruction for its strength. Disappointed that late morning had become early afternoon with nothing more achieved, she hoped this coffee would do the trick; and that in her mindless daydreaming she hadn't killed anyone.

"Here we go. One black, extremely strong coffee, and your change." Hovering, most of the seats were empty now so with less to clear, he was able to be chatty. "Student, yeah?" Becca nodded over her hot cup. "Thought so. Busy time, I'm guessing. You look exhausted."

Tears pricked her eyes as she nodded again. The urge to spill and tell this stranger everything was strong, but she couldn't. He either wouldn't understand, or worse, he would and then what would he think?

"Photography, I'm guessing," he said, oblivious to the emotional wreck in front of him.

"Oh, my camera didn't give me away?" Becca grinned, batting away tears.

Throwing back his head, he laughed. "Yes. Exactly!" as though they'd shared a witticism. Perhaps they had. After no sleep, Becca didn't feel quite herself at all.

"I might stay here drinking coffee instead."

"Are you sure? You'll never sleep."

And the tears were back, this time he noticed and his own eyes wide, he wandered away muttering how sorry he was and that she should ask if she wanted anything. He would always help a struggling student.

Oh, she was struggling all right: struggling to hang onto her sanity.

Her camera hung around her neck like a burdensome pendant. When she arrived back at her flat, she couldn't remember if she'd taken any more photos or if she'd wandered aimlessly. All she did know was that she was wearied but wired. Walking was exhausting and she wanted to rest, but she already knew she wouldn't sleep.

Stopping at the kitchen to grab another super-strong coffee, she closed the door to her room. Sitting on her bed for a mere moment before the fingers of sleep prodded her to jolt up again. Dancing. That would keep her awake.

Scrolling through her collection, she jigged about to Rita Ora and Katy Perry and tried to be as upbeat as the music, but it didn't feel right. Dancing seemed disrespectful to two souls who had lost their way last night taking drugs to help them dance forever. And now caffeine was doing the same to her.

Slumping on her bed, she scrolled some more for more sombre music. Classical strings echoed around her room but they were too dramatic and sent shudders down her spine.

The perfect song arrived next. Jedd Neilson. She'd bought one of his albums after meeting the talented soft rock singer at Fishguard Folk festival. She'd never heard of him before, but her dad had introduced him as a celebrity who had topped the charts in the seventies. He had been very nice to her and she loved his music.

Settling down, she listened to a collection of song covers he'd performed at the festival, and Spotify provided access to some of his original hits from long before she was born. Early tracks had a different vibe to the easy-listening she was used to, but she supposed it was a different time. Nodding along brought back memories of home. As well as her dad, she could picture Sophie strumming along with her own guitar.

Thoughts of family skipped in her heart and she forced her eyes open with ever more violent head jerks. She had to stay awake. She had to.

Jedd's songs were becoming increasingly bizarre. One about cheating on his wife on the road with the band made her wince. Relationships were a touchy subject. She'd never be unfaithful. It wasn't the physical act so much as the duplicity. If she didn't want to be with someone, she'd tell them. Why lie about it?

The next song was worse. Black girls were this sort of tart and Chinese girls were that and white girls did things no-one else did. It was foul, and a letter of complaint to Spotify for allowing such filth formed in her head, but she was too tired to make it make sense. How could her dad have taken her to see such a misogynist? Had she heard these terrible lyrics as a child but not understood them? Shaking her head, memories were tainted now. At least she felt awake.

Music and dancing had lost its appeal so Netflix and Candy Crush did their best, but deciding what to watch and then getting stuck on a level frustrated her. Mindless scrolling through funny cat videos and her Facebook newsfeed brought distraction as the screen glare and the coffee combined to fight fatigue away.

'How to videos' and 'You'll never believe what this celebrity looks like now' click baits grabbed her attention and she scrolled though list after list of 'Thirty of the weirdest things caught on film' and 'The world's funniest place names.'

She even completed quizzes to determine which house of Hogwarts she would be in if it actually existed and she was really a wizard in the making, as well as finding out what she'd look like if she was a Barbie doll, or a dog.

Her thumb ached with the repetitive scrolling. Despite the simple information rebounding around her thoughts, it wasn't enough. The caffeine which had kept her awake for more than a day suddenly stalled and crashed her to oblivion before she could even think 'I should put this cup down and get my pyjamas on.'

As it fell to the floor splattering the final dark dregs onto a carpet that would up and leave if it had the capacity, Becca's head fell back to the downy dream world she'd fought to flee. Deep in her subconscious, she busily constructed the next nightmare that would shatter her life, but until she awoke, for now at least, she was blissfully unaware.

Chapter Nineteen

If she'd been in control of her dreams, she would have woken up straight away and rushed more coffee into her, but the caffeine crash had thrown her into catalepsy. Every aspect of her dream would have rung alarm bells and had her scurrying to the kitchen, especially who she saw, and where they were.

In the garden of her childhood home, they were all there: her mum, dad, Sophie, even her gran, all dressed nicely, not that they were ever not, but they were clearly going somewhere. It looked familiar but altered; a memory that had been edited.

They strolled as a slow-moving group along the road, nods and cheery greetings from neighbours were answered with equally friendly retorts as they made their way to wherever they were headed.

Through the town, lots of the pubs advertised 'Live Music' but despite Becca expressing desires to go inside, she was shuffled past.

"Come on, Becca. We can't listen to all of them, can we. That's why we all decided together who to see."

"And who's that?"

Rob grinned and shook his head knowing there was no possibility she would have forgotten and that she was obviously making a joke.

And he wasn't wrong. Although she didn't remember, had no clue where they were off to or who they were going to see, in a strange way she felt she did.

Certainly, as they strode downhill and into the harbour of Fishguard Old Town and the *bom, tiss, bom, tiss* of snare and hi-hat filled their ears, she wasn't surprised she recognised the song.

Another sandwich board propped outside The Harbour Inn told of 'Live Music' and this time they went inside.

The band on stage strummed and twanged guitars and bass and the drummer banged away in frenetic satisfaction, all with their eyes closed or so near to being closed they could be performing in their sleep and looked like they'd be just as happy without the smiling, clapping audience that jiggled about on chairs around tables filled with pints and pints of beer in various stages of consumption.

"You used to love this. I bought you their album and you listened to it all the time," Rob leaned into his daughter to explain, but there was no need. Becca had listened only minutes before in the different time and dimension of the real world and she didn't love it anymore.

The significance was beginning to prick at her psyche, but she was too far under to do anything about it. Eyes glazing as she stared at the scene, she tried to diagnose their health. Her dad looked fine, the old two-step and thigh-tap combined with a forced smile and eye-twinkle that accompanied any perceived enjoyment of music, especially when he was sure it was mutually gratifying to his company.

Donna performed the same movement but somehow appeared more of a dancer, adding the occasional shimmy and head toss, and Sophie wore the face of a disgruntled teen in disbelief she'd been dragged out somewhere so lame. They all looked healthy though.

Where was Gran? With an ethereal sigh of relief, the area of her mind that had become alert to the danger calmed a little. This wasn't one of *those* dreams, it was just part of the grieving process: her gran being there as full of life as ever then suddenly not there at all.

Announcing the final song of the set, Jedd performed an offensive ditty about killing puppies and having sex with their mothers and as the words echoed around the room and the audience jigged and smiled, Becca knew she wasn't hearing right.

Shaking her head, she hit her palm against her forehead in an attempt to bring sanity back. Accepting her dad's offer of a drink from the bar as the set came to half-time with the final strum of the song that didn't exist, Jedd Neilson announced time for a break. "And any members

162

of the band would love to have a pint with you. Mine's a *Doom Bar*, by the way!" and everyone laughed. It was exactly the same thing he had said when she'd met him years ago.

Whilst the band had a break, another chap with a guitar hopped onto the stage to entertain the crowd in their absence. Becca flinched at grotesqueness yet to come, but whilst his maudlin cries seemed more likely to depress than entertain as he shrieked banshee screams over minor chords, the lyrics were innocent.

The audience stared at one another and sipped their glasses of beer self-consciously. With a "Thank you very much," The lighting of the venue darkened and the guitarist removed the capo that had raised the pitch of his screeching songs and proceeded to strum a dour rendition in two-time sobriety of Chopin's funeral march.

A red ray of hazy light shone from the stage and all eyes followed it. The beam alighted on a drink. In a tankard, the contents of which bubbled and fizzed as green smoke spilling purple in the red light, wafted from the top.

The poisoned chalice was held by a hand of one particular person, and Becca was shocked then in turn unsurprised, and relieved who that person was.

As Jedd Neilson held his pint of death aloft, Becca was so relieved it wasn't her family, his heartfelt gratitude to the fans who had supported him since his early hits and through the post success wilderness where he'd always managed to make a living doing what he loves left her unmoved.

"So, this is for you. I knew I could rely on you to the end. I'm surprised the end has come so soon, but, none of us know do we? Well almost none." He directed his pint at Becca and stared into her eyes. "Cheers, or how do you say it here in Wales? Yucky da, or something? Well, yucky da, and toodle-pip. I bid you adieu."

Bringing the tankard to his lips, Becca leapt across the room. "Stop! You don't have to do this."

"Oh, but I do, and I have. Look." Tipping the pint upside down. "See? It's empty. Chopin's eerie composition echoed from the stage as the lights grew dimmer until Becca was aware of nothing but her hand in front of her.

A gasping wheeze brought her jolting up. Throwing back the covers she raced to the bathroom and threw up. Collapsing by the toilet, Becca shivered on the cold floor. "No, no, no!" she hugged her kicking legs to still them.

Staring at the ceiling, the patterns of the tiles made faces that glowered down at her. "I didn't know I was going to fall asleep. I tried so hard not to."

'You should have tried harder. You know what happens when you do! How many more must die?' The distaste for Jedd's earlier music tightened in her chest and she screwed her eyes tight. It was enough wasn't it. If the paranormal phenomenon was real, it was more than enough.

Head pushed against the cold wall, each tile had a different leering face and each one poured disgust from on high. She hid her head in her hands and rolled to the toilet again. Forehead creasing, it occurred to her that she didn't know for sure if Jedd Neilson had been killed in her dream. He might have died years ago for all she knew, or he might be vigorously still alive.

It wouldn't take much to find out, but in her fragile state of mind, she decided to avoid it, at least until after Mel's funeral tomorrow.

The funeral date and time throbbed in her head, but all other schedules had faded to a surreal sepia. Mrs Barker gave you time, she reminded herself, feigning off a stab of guilt that she hadn't replied to the dozens of people offering their help to model for her, but she couldn't bear to look at Facebook right now. All the posts about Mel and even her gran were raw. And What if there were 'R.I.P. Jedd' notifications that sent her into despair? No, she was sure they'd understand and wouldn't want to pressure her. When she was ready, they'd be willing to help out again.

She just had to keep herself busy today, and awake tonight and tomorrow, saying goodbye to her cousin with her family, she'd find closure.

Spinning in her chair, with a sigh she felt she had no choice. She should set up a photoshoot.

Distraction behind the camera was why she'd come back to Cardiff and she had done all she could walking around the city. Something with structure might prove a better distraction

Opening up her laptop, careful to avoid Facebook's newsfeed she opened only her messages.

> *'I'd love to support you. Just tell me the time and the place...'*
> *'Count me in, it would be an honour...'*
> *'Anything to help out a fellow student x'*

Messaging the group to meet outside city hall, her heart fluttered with a nervous excitement. This was the best decision she had made in a while. She had no idea what theme the shoot would take, but she wouldn't tell the models and so she could do whatever she wanted at the time.

With the idea she would come up with a plan en-route, she showered and dressed and headed out.

Clouds bubbled in the sky. Perhaps sunny weather activity might present well, or free movement in font of immobile structures; the constraints of government compared to the freedom of human will. She liked that. The human form was beautiful. Each line on every face told a unique story and so just as people never describe a mountain as ugly, despite the vast variety of shapes and sizes they came in, Becca felt the same about people. Each was a miracle of nature and she could always find beauty in that.

Humans, again, of all shapes and sizes, in movement fascinated her too. She favoured seeing less common shapes dancing over conventional beauty because rarity is beauty by definition.

As she strolled down the hill, pride filled her heart at the sizeable group who had arrived just for her artistic endeavour. As they looked up and saw her, some knowing her already, others only from her Facebook student persona, they recognised the artist, camera slung jauntily over her shoulder, confident swing to her step.

"Hello everyone. Thanks so much for coming. I don't have a set plan for you, and to be honest, I'm touched and overwhelmed at how many of you have shown up to help me... Thank you." Looking around them, she tapped her lips with a slender finger as her creative juices flowed. "I'll split you into groups and I'm going to ask you to express opposing emotion..."

Playing with various ideas utilising the different appearances and attire of the groups, she was sure she had some great shots, but it didn't even matter. She had succeeded in distracting herself and when they had finished and several suggested grabbing a pizza, she was thrilled for the company.

"Thanks for today. I'll put a few shots up on Facebook when I'm done so look out for those."

"Any time. We've loved it."

"Yeah. It's great to be part of art!"

"A real honour to be included in your work, Becca. Thanks."

When all the gratitude had passed both ways and there was nothing more to be eked from the conversation, Becca was tempted to invite them back to her flat to keep her awake. But as one by one they commented on how tired they were and how they would go to sleep as soon as they got home and wake early for morning lectures, their yawning set her off and she decided their company might be likely to send her to sleep instead.

When she arrived at the flat, she threw open her laptop intending to edit photos until it was time to get up, but what she saw had a sudden and profound effect of her capacity to stay awake.

In her Facebook newsfeed, a friend of her dad's had shared a post with a video from when she'd met the band Jedd and its now sadly deceased lead singer...

Wanting to close the screen, the video played automatically and the songs from last night's dream filled her ears.

'RIP, Jedd. You were a star...'

'Heaven gained another great musician. Rest in peace big man...'

'I can't believe he's gone. At least he went the way he would have wanted, doing what he loved...'

Becca typed in 'Jedd Neilson' into the search bar and the news headed the screen.

'Late last night, Jedd Neilson, lead singer of seventies rock band, Jedd, died of a suspected heart attack during the interval of their show at one of his favourite venues in South West Wales.

168

Jedd is survived by his two sons, Jack and Paul and loving wife, Maureen. He was 67 years old.'

Becca's fingernails rattled on the keyboard and she lifted them from typing random letters into the comments. How could this be? Another person she'd dreamt of who was now dead. Another person she'd turned her wrath on killed.

Sliding back her chair, Becca paced the room. If she dreamt about them because she was psychically tuned in, that was one thing. But why was it those she'd just been thinking about? Her gran and Mel, well it was natural they would be in her thoughts. But those two girls? She hadn't met them before, and within hours of doing so, they were both dead.

But Jedd had entered her head from the past. A random music choice bringing him to mind and random internet choices of his old songs showing her anger she may never have felt. It was clear, whether they were close family, or people she was cross with, or those she hadn't thought about for years suddenly popping into her head, no-one was safe.

Round and around her room she walked until she became aware of what she was doing and stopped herself. Stepping to the bathroom, she had no reason but hoped one might present itself when she got there, none did. She couldn't face a shower, couldn't bring forth the vanity to apply the creams and moisturisers she

169

sometimes used to feel pretty. Even peeing halted in her edginess.

Walking back to her bed, there was no way she was about to lie down and risk falling asleep, she strode to the bathroom again swapping circuiting the room for lengths instead.

Alternating the movements and occasionally adding a figure-of-eight when she became aware, she walked every square inch of her apartment until, exhausted, she fell to her knees. Great gulps of emotion creaked out of her in whale-song wails. Pulling at her hair, she screamed into the floor.

A knocking on her door pounded her heart into her chest. Who could it be at this time of night? Yanking it open half expecting the Grim Reaper to be waiting, scythe in hand, she didn't know what to say to the mousy round girl in front of her.

"Is everything okay? I heard through the ceiling you were really upset. I'm downstairs you see."

What could she say? No everything was not okay but she couldn't tell her why, could she? She would mark her as either completely crazy, or a murderer.

"I'm a night owl. I can sit with you if you'd like some company? We don't have to talk. We can just sit. Or, I am a good listener if you want."

Becca shook her head. "That's no to the talking. But, thanks, I could do with your company. Please, come in."

Stepping over the threshold, the girl looked for a seat then realising the bed was it, perched awkwardly on the edge.

"Would you like a drink? I don't mind getting you a tea or coffee?"

"Kitchen's closed. They lock them at night in case drunken students do drunken cooking and cause drunken fires!"

Nodding, Becca sighed, "That makes sense. I think I feel a lot safer now you've told me that. How come you know, but I didn't know?"

"Well, maybe you haven't tried to make a snack at four in the morning. I've got a kettle and toaster in my room now. We're not supposed to so I keep them hidden under my bed when I'm not there. You know, in case of a random inspection."

"Do they actually do those? It seems like a terrible invasion of privacy."

"I don't know. Maybe. I don't want to risk being caught anyway."

"Fair enough. I'm Becca," she held out a hand.

"Amy."

"Pleased to meet you, Amy," she smiled, but then it dropped. What if this girl had come into her life, not as a comfort, but to have her end dictated by one of her dreams?

"What is it? You look as though you've seen a ghost!"

Becca stared at her. She looked healthy enough. "Are you okay? You don't have any underlying health conditions? You're not accident prone? You don't stick forks into that toaster of yours?"

"No! What, are you some morbid germaphobe? Are you worried if I was it might rub off on you?" She grinned.

"No. I'm not scared of what *you'll* do to *me*..."

Amy sidled away from her new acquaintance. "Wha... What do you mean?"

With a shake of the head, Becca said, "I'm not some serial killer. I won't hurt you or anything. Not on purpose anyway."

Edging still further, Amy frowned. "You're an *accidental* serial killer?" her face concaved to the sourness of the suggestion.

Arms limp, Becca sighed. "I was determined not to say to you because I don't know you, but yes, I think that's exactly what I am."

Chapter Twenty

"Wow," Amy nodded along to Becca's confessions. "I can see why you think that, but it's not possible."

"Who's to say what is and isn't possible? Only God understands."

"Yes. That's one way to look at it. Another way; my way, is to use a scientific approach. That is to say it only needs a supernatural explanation when no other explanation is available."

"But it's so unlikely. How can it be possibly be just a coincidence?"

"Listen, Becca. I'm studying criminology. I don't want to be a lawyer or police woman, but crime fascinates me. And so, I deal in hard facts. One hard fact is just how many people die every day! In Britain, it's over a thousand. You've had dreams about a few of them and it is remarkable, I'll grant you, but to conclude you're somehow influencing this figure," she chuckled, "Well, it's nonsense."

Becca wanted to believe her. "I know the facts as well as anyone else. I'm not in the habit of jumping to conclusions. But I'm telling you, I don't feel safe. Every time I fall asleep, I wake up and someone is dead."

"But the only odd thing is that you know them. Can't you see? Your gran was expected to die. You said you missed going to see her but all your family were gathered at her death bed? I'm sorry for your loss, but dreaming about it can't have been much of a surprise. And your cousin? Mel?"

"Yeah. Her funeral's today."

"Well, if she turned up drunk to your gran's funeral, wrapping her sports car around a tree doesn't seem the unlikeliest of ways for her to leave this mortal coil."

"But I dreamt it. Exactly!"

"Did you? Really? She was sloshed, and you'd seen her car, but are you sure looking back on the dream you aren't just interpreting it as exact now you know the facts?"

Becca shook her head. "No. I *saw* it!"

Amy shrugged. "And as for the two girls at a party? Unfortunately, that sort of thing happens all the time; especially in a young, university city like this."

"But I'd met them both, and again I saw it."

"You were drunk; asleep at a party. By the time you woke up, you said the crowd were already staring at what had happened. It's much more likely that you had become aware of what was going on whilst still unconscious, isn't it? You have to agree it's more probable than you being some weird angel of death who dreams people to their downfall?"

"I hope I don't dream of you."

"Do what you like. I'll be perfectly safe, I have no doubt."

Drumming her knee with fingers she had just removed from a chewing, Becca stared at the coffee stain on the carpet. Of course, it made sense, but she couldn't shake the feeling. There was too much at stake.

"After losing two family members, particularly having dreamt about them, it's no wonder you've become confused. You shouldn't feel bad."

"Thanks! But what about Jedd Neilson?"

"I would guess you listened to his music because you'd heard he was sick, and then you probably read it before falling asleep, or at least expected it on some subconscious level."

"No! I haven't heard his music for years. And the lewd songs; I'd never heard them before in my life!"

"I understand. I'm saying that maybe reading, perhaps not even remembering at the time who he was, that he was ill made you play the music without knowing why." Holding her hands up to Becca's forming objection. "I know you don't believe it, but it's the only thing that makes sense. And in my experience, the explanations that make sense have to take precedence over the ones that sound insane!"

Your experience, Becca scowled. You're only what... eighteen? There's a lot more in the world than you understand. She didn't bother saying it wasn't that she hadn't thought of these logical explanations for herself, but in her own experience, coincidences that added up meant something and she wasn't about to risk dreaming about anyone else.

"Thanks, Amy. You've been a big help. Sorted me out. I was just being crazy." Standing up and holding open the door, she smiled. "I suppose I should get some rest before my cousin's funeral tomorrow," then remembering the lateness, she corrected, "Today, actually."

"Okay. Sweet dreams. Dream about me dying if it'll make you feel any better!" Amy snorted.

"Will do."

As soon as the door closed behind her, Becca rushed and re-opened her laptop. *'How to disrupt dreams.'* The advice came, unsurprisingly, from the opposite perspective: how to get a good night's sleep. Becca knew she couldn't stay awake forever, but if she could survive on fragmented, dreamless sleep, then maybe she could keep everyone safe.

It was already time to wake up and get ready for the day's sombre activity anyway, so she wouldn't have to risk failing to establish a broken pattern yet. With relief, she headed to the bathroom and turned on the shower that was still set to tepid from her last wakeful wash.

Rubbing vigorously with a scratchy towel on exiting, she felt wide awake and ready to pay her last respects. If Amy was right, and she would love her to be, then today could give her closure and hopefully return things to normal. But she would read through her notes on good sleep practice and implement the opposite of all its advice before she ever closed her eyes again.

Distraction was advantageous. Walking to the station because this time she was travelling light, Becca didn't even have her camera. She didn't want to focus on anyone for fear they'd turn up dead in a dream.

Hunkered in a shop doorway, the same homeless man slumped over his meagre belongings but she didn't have time for him today.

Shielding her eyes, the dazzling spring sunshine shone surprisingly hot and all the more uncomfortable for wearing black. Waiting on the platform, she took off her jacket and kept her focus on her phone, despite the screen being indecipherable in the brightness.

When her train rumbled into the station, Becca took her time so she could choose a seat as far away from passengers likely to talk to her as possible.

One or two tables to the front of the carriage that were still empty and whilst she was sure they would collect people on the way, at Llanelli perhaps, she hoped if she gave a show of aloofness people would leave her alone. She didn't want to talk; today would be difficult enough. And she certainly didn't want to make any new acquaintances.

The first station left her unapproached. As the doors swished open and flush-faced trippers boarded, they took any seat in preference to sitting with the miserable girl at the front.

The journey skirting the coast, Becca let her attention be drawn by the cresting white horses of Carmarthen Bay. When the train stopped at the village of Ferryside, the ruins of Llansteffan Castle atop its hill on the opposite side of the estuary caught her eye, as it always did, and she wished she had her camera after all.

Her phone had a reasonable offering, but not for a seasoned photographer. Snapping a few shots still gave her pleasure but abandoning her aloofness soon proved a mistake; she desperately hoped not a fatal one.

"Is it okay if I sit here?" Becca would have loved to have said 'No,' but on what grounds? Because she was sick of being hit on on every use of public transport? By the time she'd looked away from the scenery to notice who was asking, the young man had already unloaded his rucksack onto the chair opposite and slumped down with a sigh.

"Beautiful, isn't it. You never tire of a view like that."

He meant *he* never tired of it. His insistence of using *you* was presumptive. He had no idea what Becca tired of. Ignoring him, she allowed herself a surreptitious glance. Heart stopping, she screeched, "Oh my God, Callum?" But when he turned to face her, he looked nothing like him.

"Afraid not," he laughed. "But I can be if you want?" he smiled with a wink.

Becca went back to snubbing him. Even joking about being her ex-boyfriend was far from funny.

"Okay, I guess not!"

Becca saw, in her peripheral vision, him remove his phone from his pocket so they ignored one-another as only young people from this generation could.

He coughed as the train came into Swansea Grand Station, but Becca didn't know if he was trying to get her attention or clearing his throat; until he spoke.

"Off to a funeral, or do you just like to wear black?" Grinning, it was clear he thought the answer was the second choice. Disgusted at the insensitivity at either suggestion, Becca averted her eyes. Now he'd annoyed her, did that put him at more risk from her deadly dreams?

"Sorry if I've caused offence. Here, let me get you a cab."

Becca screwed her fist into her leg to resist letting rip. Was this moron some type of test? Racing to a waiting taxi, before her table companion could reach it, she yapped at the driver, "Oystermouth Cemetery, please."

"Is that man with you?"

He'd reached the window and was mouthing something to her. Checking she had her phone and purse, there was nothing else she might have left behind so she was happy to snap, "No, he bloody isn't. Just some freak who wouldn't leave me alone on the train."

"Do you want me to sort him out for you?" Looking at the driver, he looked the rough type who might enjoy a scrap. Rescued once again by a chivalrous older stranger. What was wrong with her generation? "Thanks, but if you can just get me to the cemetery, that'll be great."

Driving away with a brief glare at the peeved creepy man, the driver acted surprisingly sensitively and didn't ask any stupid questions.

Along the coast, childhood memories of time spent on this beach with her cousins lumped in her throat. As the land train took tourists from the city to the Victorian resort of Mumbles, their jollity looked out of place and fuelled the reminiscence. How many times had the family ridden on the same train a decade ago? Ice-cream on the pier or from the kiosk shaped like an apple at the carpark.

She would never understand how her uncle and aunt could leave such a beautiful place to go to the other side of the world. Their empty nest must have rattled with Mel so busy with her career, but Becca couldn't imagine her own parents doing the same when her and Sophie left home for good. The thought of it hurt in her chest, but she was being foolish. It would never happen.

Passing the castle ruins, large houses overlooking the green nestled in their private worlds behind immaculate hedgerows and Becca envied them. As the taxi pulled into the gateway of the cemetery, there were a few other cars there but not as many as she expected. "What time is it?"

"Oh, er, a quarter to twelve."

She was early, but not too early. The train being more reliable than the roads, she supposed, longing for her family.

Cars with people she didn't recognise pulled in behind the taxi as she handed over her money. "Will you need collecting afterwards?" he asked. "No, thank you, I'll get a lift. Plus, we're going to a hotel for the wake."

"I thought you would, but I didn't want to assume and leave a damsel in distress."

"Thank you, you're very kind."

"Especially with weirdos like that boy at the station hanging about!"

Becca nodded and smiled. She couldn't have the conversation go on forever.

Watching as the cars pulled in, some more Porsches and a couple of Mercedes, she deduced they belonged to Mel's former work colleagues, although, where she lived in Mumbles, everyone drove something expensive so they could quite easily be neighbours. *Ex*-neighbours, she corrected. It still seemed surreal. Even seeing similar cars didn't make it real.

At last, her mum and dad's VW pulled up and she waved as they took one of the last spaces. The rest of the guests would be parking on the street. Mel's mum, dad, and sister would be coming from Mel's house, which was odd because none of them had ever seen it before except in photos on Facebook, and very soon it would be returned to the mortgage company.

Becca frowned thinking that while a family came to terms with their tragic loss, faceless financiers waited to pounce and reclaim their pound of flesh before what few true assets Mel left would be distributed among her debtors as it turned out her good-fortune selling houses had been exaggerated and everything she had was from loans.

Her estranged husband, Stephen; who was he to her? Cousin-in-law? Second cousin? She had neither known nor cared before, but he would presumably attend. Would he ride in the same car as his in-laws who had always despised him, and now truly hated him? Who was even paying for the funeral?

There must have been family discussions within her own household that being away in Cardiff she hadn't been privy to. Maybe they were giving her credit cards one last fraudulent bash.

Seeing everyone gathered, she wondered with a guilty sigh how the other deaths were affecting the other families.

The loss of the girls her age hit her more than the others. It was so easy to-identify with them. And their parents must be a similar age to her own. How would they survive if something happened to her or Sophie?

She could sense her mood plummeting and she knew to avoid that. A darkness deep within drilled from a surface that had no idea the depths of despair it might free. If she were a Texas tycoon, she'd be onto her next fortune, but this blackness could consume her.

"You okay?"

Becca nodded at her sister, her mum and dad's attention having been taken by people stopping them on her way to them.

"Are you okay?" she was asked again as Donna and Rob reached her and she carried on nodding. 'No. Not at all,' she wanted to scream.

Her questions of who would be in which car were soon answered as the funeral cortege pulled in, fronted by a bearded man holding a top hat in his hand while his head bowed in respect. Gulping down memories of her gran's funeral, Becca blinked away pooling tears

Uncle Clive and Auntie Lorraine stepped out as he held open the door, whilst a darting-eyed Stephen exited the other side of the limousine. A second black car behind carried sisters who hadn't seen her in ten years.

Red-eyed and blotchy-faced, they nodded recognition to the group Becca stood in. Did they really recognise her? She'd changed a lot since they'd seen her and for some reason, they always called her Callie.

Offended, she'd had it explained it was a family nickname and she'd assumed as a child she must have had trouble pronouncing 'Carrie,' as in Great Aunt Carrie, but never had it confirmed. It didn't make a lot of sense because she never saw much of Carrie either growing up, but her gran always spoke highly of her so she might have said her name wrong.

As they stood in head-down silence, pallbearers pulled the Mel-sized coffin from the hearse for them to walk behind. Seeing it, Becca's fingers flew to her mouth. Eyes searching, without words she rushed as discreetly as she could and threw up into a bush.

Hands shaking, she struggled to stand. What was she even doing here? What would she say to her grieving aunt and uncle and cousins? She wouldn't tell them she was responsible, that she was angry Mel had disrespected her gran's memory and then had been sick in her room.

She wouldn't mention how she'd dreamt about it happening at the exact same time it actually did.

It wouldn't help and they wouldn't believe her. She'd get through today and gain closure. That's what she needed

Brushing herself off, she could smell sick in her nostrils and tried to remove it with a hanky before making her way over to the graveside. Glances in her direction showed no care as to why she'd disappeared and come back, and even those who had seen her in the bushes paid no head. Grief affected everybody in its own way.

Her eyes met with Clive's and Lorraine's and Mel's sisters, Elizabeth and Catherine (Liz and Kate she'd seen them as on Facebook) and they stared back a glint of something in their stare she didn't understand. They didn't know, did they? They couldn't suspect her involvement?

The vicar's words floated over the congregation and they took what they could from their comfort, then when he'd said all he had, Kate cried at how she wished she'd seen more of her sister and how life is precious and ends in the blink of an eye. Or a dream, thought Becca.

Steadying herself as they lowered the coffin into the ground. Lorraine stepped forward and, as tradition dictates, threw soil on top; the woman who had given her life dotting the final full stop. Becca and her hid their faces

Sad expressions drifted back to cars ready to make their way to the Oystermouth hotel to send Mel off appropriately, or insensitively, with drinks, and stories of her life.

Becca sidled next to Sophie in the back of their parents' car and stared out of the window. Sophie reached across and squeezed her hand and when their moist eyes met no words were needed.

As the car pulled onto the gravel drive a few hundred yards from the graveyard they remained inside for a few minutes. They'd all seen what had become of her; in some ways that made it harder for them than for her close family, who for years had been anything but.

By the time they reached the bar the atmosphere had already turned from tragedy to celebration.

"Can I get you something?" Uncle Clive had everything raised: eyebrows, chin and nose all reaching for heaven in the exalted act of buying a round.

"I'll have a pint with you, Clive. What have they got?"

A discussion of the pros and cons of the various draught ales proceeded while the women stared at one-another. Donna broke the silence with an inane inquiry into their journey. "Good flight?"

"Tiring."

Nods all round as those who had been on the plane confirmed it had been, and those of the Tate family supposed it must have been. "You'll have to come out to us one day. It's lovely in Tasmania."

Well it would have to be to leave your daughter behind. No wonder she felt unsupported and turned to drink, no-one said because they all knew they could have done more.

"I wish Melanie had come with us. I never understood why she didn't." Eyes combed the room and fell on the same man: Stephen, then drifted back to the discomfort of their group.

"Clive's gone for a *Whisper of the Sea* and I'm having a *Mermaid's Curse!* Brewed just down the road, apparently. Mine's more of a dark malt and Clive's is quite hoppy, wouldn't you say, Clive?"

"MMmm mm. It's nice. Better than the lager back in Tasmania, I have to admit," he grinned.

I'm so pleased your daughter's funeral has some brighter moments, Becca seethed as she stared at the floor.

"And look at you two. Both gorgeous. No surprise with Sophie, but you've definitely bloomed surprisingly. And it's nice to see your tongue in your mouth!" he chuckled and everyone except Becca joined in.

Answering her frown, he grinned. "I can say now you're such a beautiful young woman, but boy were you an ugly kid. Well, more when you were a baby, I suppose. Kali, we used call you!"

"I'm glad you've said that. I never knew why. Did I have trouble saying Great Aunt Carrie's name?"

Clive shot his neck back like a tortoise taking its first bite of a lemon. "Great Aunt Carrie?"

Lorraine leaned in and explained it was his mother-in-law's sister and he nodded, the sour taste still in his mouth. "No, no. Nothing like that. You were always eloquent. Spoke lovely. No. You were a whiny little so-and-so and you never had your tongue in!"

"I don't understand?"

"Like Kali."

"Who's Kali?"

Shaking his head, his mouth rose sideways on one side pointing to his ear. "Cor, blimey. You haven't learned much about your heritage, have you. My lot are mad for it. Always on the internet finding stuff out about the Indian side of the family. You do know your Great Gran was Indian, right?"

"Of course."

"You wouldn't think it to look at your gran." A nudge from Lorraine prompted a "God rest her soul." Face filled with fitting sobriety, he croaked. "Real shame we couldn't make it over for the old girl's send off. Maybe if we had we might have... you know?"

What? Seen how unwell your daughter was and given her some support before it killed her? It would be cruel to say, but the absence of sympathy cut deep enough.

"That's who you look like! Blimey, doesn't she, Lorraine? The spitting image of Christine when she was younger. You'll have to find some old photos. You are, you're your gran's double, I'm telling you."

Becca had seen photos, of course, and this pleased her; her gran had been beautiful. "But who's Kali? You said you called me Kali?"

"Oh, yeah. Well she's that Hindu goddess, isn't she. You know, the one with all the arms and that?"

"I thought that was the god, Shiva?"

"Kali was Shiva's wife," Donna leaned in.

"Only the bad side of her. She killed a load of blokes, or something. You see her in pictures, a necklace of skulls and a skirt of bones."

"And you thought I resembled this... this... goddess for some reason?"

"Well, you always looked like you were ready to kill someone. I said, didn't I Lorraine. If looks could kill, eh?" He stared as the surrounding faces regarded him blankly and he still seemed misunderstood. "Well, she always has her bloody tongue sticking out doesn't she?" He lolled his tongue out and made a grotesque moaning noise. "Oh well, you're a proper beauty now. Really cute."

Becca smiled her sickliest smile. "You'll have to excuse me," she said, turning away and not explaining for what. "God help you if you end up in my dreams," she muttered under her breath.

At the bar, other cousins were chatting. Joining their conversations was uplifting and sad all at once as funny stories of Mel's exploits were tempered by the sure knowledge they were over.

Her eyes rose just as Uncle Clive was waddling across the floor towards her. What did he want now?

"Becca, can I have a word?"

Her heart sank, and she gulped. "Er, okay." Standing, she followed him into the corner where he perched on a stool.

"Listen," what was he about to say? "Your mum's been telling me how stressed you've been lately. Sorry about the whole Kali thing, and your boyfriend. I didn't know. Anyway, what I'm trying to say is you're welcome to come back with us... To Taz."

"What? Why would I want to do that?"

"I think you need a break; a complete change of scene."

"No. Thank you. I need to stay here, I am in the middle of a degree course. I'm surprised Mum didn't mention that."

"Take a year out. There's more to life than exams. Look at me. Left school when I was fifteen, and I haven't done too badly, have I?"

Becca didn't want to hear what possible achievements he could have made that would make her think ditching her education would be the best next step.

"Your sister's coming."

"Sophie?"

"You don't have any other sisters, do ya? Yes Sophie. And she wants you to come too."

"Sophie's going to Australia? Why?"

"It's a beautiful place. Tasmania is God's country, for sure. Come on, you'll love it!"

"No. I need to stay here. I want to stay."

"Okay. Well, we're flying out day after tomorrow if you change your mind."

"Okay, thanks." Can I go now? Holding his stare, she melted him into submission.

"You haven't forgiven me for the Kali thing, I reckon."

"I'm not thrilled. You've been calling me after a Hindu goddess of death since I was a baby. With my Indian blood, you don't understand what you've done. You don't understand the powers you're messing with."

"Powers? What, you're gonna dance on the graves of your enemies! Ha!"

Dance on the graves of your enemies

"I have to go. I'm sorry for your loss, I must go."

"Steady on, Bex, I was only kidding!"

But Becca couldn't stay another second. Her enemies? Her gran wasn't her enemy, and Jedd Neilson? And Mel and the girls weren't either.

190

She was a little peeved for a short time, that was all. What was happening?

Racing from the hotel, she ran down the street, over the road, past the amusements and ice-cream parlours, through the trees and down the steep ramp onto the sand.

She remembered playing on the same spot with all her cousins a lifetime ago. Shaking her head, it really had been a lifetime for Mel. Ten years. Ten years, and so much had changed.

Digging her hands into the ground, she brought them up with fistfuls of sand which she let pour out before scooping it back up to pulverise in her grip. Amy was right. It was all logical, wasn't it? She was nothing to do with the goddess, Kali. She had nothing to do with all the people who had died around her, other than the coincidence of noticing them.

Watching the ocean as ebb turned to flow and the tide raced toward her, the temptation to let it wash over her, to let it wash her and all her pain away was short lived. Pushing herself up to her feet, she brushed sandy hands onto her black trousers and walked along the esplanade. It was four miles or so back to the station. It would do her good.

Step after step drummed it into her. Just get back to normal. Stop obsessing with death and everything will be all right. Get home, go to bed, go to sleep and it'll be okay. Uncle Clive's slimy face loomed into her mind. He'd be fine. She didn't have the power to kill people in her nightmares, how could she. And even if she did, she wouldn't. She wasn't that sort of person.

Chapter Twenty-one

Riding the lift to her apartment, she presented her key card, stumbled inside and fought her clothes off and her nightdress on. Part of her may have feared she was headed to a nightmare from where she'd never recover, but that part had been rationalised into submission.

Adopting her sleep position: one arm resting between her thighs, the other under her pillow, worries surfaced but plunged beneath wave after wave of shattered sleep, drowning in her exhaustion until the world of dreams and nightmares became her inescapable destination.

She was in the aeroplane again. The masks were down and they were banking steeply. Looking around at the other people on the plane, terror blazed in their eyes.

In front, a stewardess was reminding passengers of the crash procedure. In her hand the mask shook as she struggled to place it over her mouth, her legs bowing as she placed her head in her lap.

Cries of 'Please don't panic,' as the surety of the growing catastrophe rippled through the seats like a wave of despair. Some stabbed at phone screens desperate to hear loved ones one last time; loved ones who had no idea waving them goodbye for a wonderful shopping trip to New York would be the final time they'd ever see them again.

Gripping the armrest, bracing herself seemed preposterous against the force of over three-hundred tons of metal and flesh hitting the ground, but she knew that even in the worst crashes, some people survived and if she were to be one of them, she would take all the advice she could get.

Passengers sitting next to her weren't leaning forwards into the seat as the stewardess demonstrated. "It seems stupid," Becca called from bended waist, "but it might work. We could make it out of this alive." Turning her head, to see if they had heard, the rotund bulk of the gentleman showed the reason, other than defeat, why he wasn't bracing himself because his stomach simply wouldn't allow him to lean forward. His wife sat, legs towards him, 'If we go, we go together.'

Sitting up for a moment to see if she could help, she gasped. The owner of the round stomach was Uncle Clive. Lorraine cuddled into him and Kate and Liz sat across the aisle, arms stretched to make physical contact.

"We won't make it, Sophie. We won't make it alive so I'm not going to spend the last few minutes of my life hunched over a plane seat. I'm going to go out holding the love of my life. It's not such a bad way to go."

Sophie? *Sophie?* Couldn't they ever get her name right? But then, looking at her hand, it was fleshier than her own, and the nails more manicured and glitzy. Touching her body and her face, it was all so familiar yet so alien. Squinting at her reflection, her mouth fell open. They were right. She was Sophie.

Jolting awake, spit in her lungs gurgled as her body conspired to murder her whilst she slept. Creaking oxygen between the pools of liquid, life flooded back into her and with each croaking breath she grew stronger until, at last, she coughed the fluid obstruction out.

Swinging her legs around, she leaned forwards and allowed herself to recover. What was the time? Her phone screen said nine fifty-seven a.m. She'd slept for eleven hours. Panicking, she dialled her mum's number.

"Hello, sweetheart. Are you okay? You worried me when you left in such a hurry. Auntie Carrie was upset to have missed you so I wanted to run off and find you, but Sophie said to leave you; that you needed a bit of space."

"Oh. I'm sorry I missed Great Aunt Carrie. I didn't even see her."

"Your sister said you were stressed. Particularly after spending time with Lorraine and Clive."

"They haven't left for the airport yet, have they?"

"What? No. They're not leaving until tomorrow. Flight's at eleven. Sophie's very excited, but we'll

195

miss her. Are you sure you couldn't do with a break, yourself? It's expensive. It might be the only chance you get to go and Lorraine and Clive are paying."

"Tell them they can't. The plane is going to crash!"

A sigh followed a pause. "Oh, don't be ridiculous. They fly on the best airlines. It'll be fine."

"Mum, listen. I dreamt about Gran dying at the exact time she did. And then Mel. I saw it happen. It's when I'm cross with someone, my anger manifests in some weird way and I dream about them and then they die. I was really angry with Uncle Clive, yesterday, and last night I dreamt about their plane crashing. I'm really scared he's going to die and take Sophie with him!"

Donna made no sound from the line.

"Mum? Did you hear me? I know it sounds crazy, but it keeps happening. You have to believe me. Two girls at a party; one had been my waitress at a pizza place and the other bumped into me drunk. I fell asleep and dreamt about them and when I woke up, they both were dead!"

Another sigh.

"Then Jedd Neilson. Did you know he died? Well I dreamt about him too. I listened to his songs, I don't know why, I haven't done for years. Some of his old ones are really rude. Hearing them, I got angry and the next thing I'm dreaming about him dying at a gig and that's exactly what happened! You must see? I didn't just dream they died, I dreamt *how* they died. And It's not a precognition, I'm dreaming it whilst it happens, and I'm sure somehow I'm the link. Clive telling me about the goddess Kali yesterday. It all made sense."

"And you were angry with my mum too, I suppose?"

"Well no. Never. But maybe. I was probably cross she was dying. I've never thought of life without her. You know how close we were. I couldn't bring myself to come and see her. I couldn't watch her fade away; that strong, wonderful woman..." Becca paused to swallow down her grief. "And I can't lose Sophie because I'm cross with Uncle Clive so you have to stop them getting on that plane. Take a different one."

"What difference would that make? Did you dream about a specific flight? A particular day? Or are you just assuming? It seems they're doomed whenever they go."

"That's a very flippant remark."

"Yes. Because you're talking nonsense. I know you're under a lot of pressure. I've said come home and take a year out, but you've been determined to push on, and I get it. But I really think you should reconsider: spend some time at home just relaxing. It's Easter in two weeks. You're coming back then, I presume. If three weeks at home doesn't sort you out, please say you'll at least consider taking more time?"

"Okay, okay. But about the plane crash. You might be right. I didn't see where or when they were flying, I don't know the flight number or anything." Hand trembling, short nails drifted their way to her mouth as tears stung her eyes. With a jolt, a plan hit her. "What flight are they on?"

"I don't know. They're flying from Cardiff, that's all. Phone Sophie, she'll know. She's off to Newport today to get her visas and passport up to date. You could meet up with her on the way back? That might do you good."

"Okay. I'll phone Sophie. Thanks, Mum. Love you."

"I Love you, too…" faded into telecommunications space as Becca dialled her sister before Donna realised she'd gone.

The number you are calling is unavailable. Please try again later.

Taking a deep breath, she sighed, "Don't panic. They're not flying until tomorrow. You can speak to Sophie before then."

Drumming her hand against the bed frame, she jumped up, not from enthusiasm for the day ahead but because she needed distraction. Showering would give four minutes, but she could extend that with a hair treatment, and maybe a face mask. Why not? She'd had a long night's sleep and no-one had died. Dreaming of the plane crash could even be seen as good news. Forewarned was forearmed.

By the time she finished pampering herself, lunchtime had arrived. Alarmed she hadn't heard from her sister, she phoned again but still the 'unavailable' tone assaulted her ear. She remembered going to Newport passport office herself and it took hours, so she was sure Sophie was stuck without phone signal in the secure building.

So, she'd follow on from her pamper morning by drying her hair and choosing something nice to wear and going into the city for lunch. Screwing up yesterday's black ensemble for the wash, or probably more inconveniently, the dry cleaners, Becca ran her slender fingers through the rest of her wardrobe.

At this time of year it might go from cool, almost chilly to warm or blazing hot. Choosing a summery dress with a shrug to slip on and off, Becca slid on sandals and headed out.

Checking her phone as she walked, poor Sophie must still be stuck in that building. Halfway through the day and she didn't yet know the flight details. She decided on a positive outlook; halfway through the day meant she must finish soon.

So many places to eat. She'd walked quite a distance in the sunshine; past the student's union, past Capitol shopping centre, and then she paused and nodded. Sushi. That was pretty healthy, wasn't it?

Striding over to the chain sushi restaurant, Becca sat at the conveyor and watched the little bowls whir round the room. It was difficult to see what was what until it arrived in front of her, but she felt affronted; if people before her hadn't wanted it, why would she?

Browsing the menu, different colours meant different prices. Don't pick up a grey bowl, she resolved on seeing the cost.

Picking one bowl, she popped it open and bit down on avocado but as the dishes went round and round, she couldn't resist the salmon and then the beef in purple bowls which cost twice as much.

"Would you like something to drink?" a pretty Japanese girl inquired. She pointed to the menu and indicated a fruity sake. "And hot food?" to which inquiry Becca ended up with dumplings and a Katsu Curry.

Her head swirled. Everything was delicious and she overate again. Washed down with wine, it proved just the distraction she needed. In future, if she felt more sociable, she could eat out more. There were always things going on with uni, but her student friends had become bored asking her and her saying she didn't want to come time after time. She just didn't feel very convivial most of the time. And when she did, the only person she'd wanted to spend her time with was Callum.

Maybe the next invitation, she'd make herself say yes. A great social-life was one of the expectations of being a student after all.

Lunch took so long, it lasted her almost to dinner but eating anything more was absurd. If she still had her old phone she could have scrolled down her contacts to see if anyone was free. She could go back and see who was around the dormitory. Amy, probably, but did she want to listen to the logic of someone she just met right now? No. She needed to find out about their flight and couldn't risk diversion.

Walking around the city, she glanced at her phone every five minutes, then every four. It was six o'clock. The passport office must be closed by now. Pressing send call on her phone, it rang four, five, six...

"Hey, sis! What a day. Hours and hours, but it's worth it, Tasmania here I come."

Becca offered silent thanks her sister had finally answered. "Mum told me. Why?"

"Well, I've finished school and I'd like a year out before getting my head down like you. I know you've been through a lot, but I reckon it's sensible, don't you?"

Becca gulped down a tear. "I guess. Things might have worked out better for me if I'd done that."

"Come now then. Take a year off. Auntie Lorraine and Uncle Clive are paying."

"No. I don't think I can. I don't want to. I need to stay here."

Sophie sighed. "Okay, have it your way but it'll be much more fun if you come."

"I'll miss you. I was looking forward to you coming to stay with me."

"When I get back, I'll visit."

"Okay. I have to tell you..."

"I know. You had a dream. I'm still going."

"Okay. I wish you wouldn't."

"I expected more of an argument. You don't believe it so much then?"

"Oh, I do. But I think I can keep you safe. I *know* I can," she corrected.

"Ooookaaay," Sophie agreed sarcastically. "Weirdo."

"I need the flight number though."

"Don't tell me you're going to pray for it?"

"Not exactly. Just tell me."

"I don't know. Have you met me? Is that the sort of information I retain?"

"You must do!"

"Clive and Lorraine have the tickets. I'm meeting them in the morning. Flight's at eleven. Google it."

Of course. After all that anxious waiting! The airport would have the flights listed. She could have put her mind at rest ages ago and not waited on Sophie all day. "Well, have a brilliant time. I'll miss you. See you when you get back. Buy me a boomerang or some thongs or something... That's what they call flip-flops. Don't get the wrong idea about your big sister."

"There's nothing wrong with thongs; of either type. I'm wearing them now."

"Eww. Too much information. And don't tell me which sort."

Sophie laughed through the earpiece. "Is that it? End of dire warnings?"

"Well, if you get a strange feeling not to get on the plane then listen to that feeling, but otherwise, you'll be fine."

202

"I'm gonna have that feeling now, aren't I? Now you've said. Maybe you should pray for us."

"Be careful. And I don't just mean the aeroplane. Don't get bitten by a spider or snake or eaten by a crocodile or shark or... Please, be careful."

"Has anyone ever told you you're a pessimist? I could stay in Wales and be hit by a bus. I mean, look at cousin Mel."

The heartless remark hung in the air. "You're right. See you when you get back."

Clicking goodbye, she knew what she had to do. Striding towards home, head down, she knew it would be okay.

Chapter Twenty-two

British Airways flight BA555 would whisk her family off to Australia from 11.00am and take twenty-two hours. It was a long time to stay awake, but there were periods of rest and she'd done it before. Knowing they were safely on the ground now meant she could sleep without worry until eleven tomorrow if needed. If she set an alarm for nine, she'd get another good night's rest and stay awake no problem.

Setting the alarm on her phone, she wasn't worried when it said, *'This alarm is set to go off in eleven hours'* knowing she'd wake naturally after seven or eight, or definitely nine anyway.

Opening her Kindle, she read a few chapters of a monster tale about a Bigfoot in the woods of South Pembrokeshire, pleased it was able to hold her attention. That was a step in the right direction.

After an hour's reading, she could have gone on, but sensibly closed the Kindle and popped it back in her bedside draw. Smiling, knowing she would be awake a long time tomorrow, it would be the ideal opportunity to complete lots of her Uni work. Photographing all day and night, the same shots at different times; or photos during the day and writing it up through the night should see her catching up.

Closing her eyes and tucking one arm under the cold side of the pillow with her other hand between her thighs, she took one last deep breath and settled for sleep.

Straight into dreams, they washed over her unmemorable and innocent. Memories revisited and replayed, pleasant at first then recollections of all that had happened in the last few weeks. Grimacing, head tossing from side to side, she rode the storm and woke half-an-hour before the alarm at half-past eight.

Allowing herself to snooze. There was no hurry. Leaning over, she set another alarm for ten-fifty just in case she dropped off deciding a lie-in in preparation of the long day was sensible.

When she turned the nine-a.m. alarm off, she rolled over and waited for the next. Sitting up and stretching, she picked up the Kindle again and read until she felt herself drifting back to sleep. Why did too much sleep make her even more tired?

Throwing back the covers, she headed for the shower. Keeping it at the tepid 'wake-me-up' temperature she'd become accustomed to, she turned it down two more degrees and squealed at the cold, laughing at what she was putting herself through.

A brisk rub-down with her faithful scratchy towel, that as she dried her hair she admitted could do with a wash, she was dry, invigorated, and ready to get out.

Camera, spare battery, different lenses, jacket in case it got chilly, purse, mobile phone. Good.

Closing the door, the familiar cries from the builders, now too high on their scaffolding for words to reach her, sufficed with wolf-whistles and cat calls. This time, Becca took it in her stride. Maintaining control was the way forward in every aspect of her life. Nothing could hurt her if she refused to let it and what was worse? She thought the day workmen didn't tell her how pretty she was would be a sadder one than today.

Striding to the city centre, pausing frequently to click dozens of photos; satisfied, she moved on to the next location.

The castle dominating the view entering the city made her smile. The mediaeval structure, largely intact, had been around through a lot of history. Back when Cardiff was the world's busiest port in the height of the industrial revolution its roots could be traced to the valleys in the distance with the iron and coal that existed in such abundance a hundred years ago. Now it played host to social and music events and acted as a museum attracting thousands of visitors every day.

Clicking away, sunlight was too bright on the screen so she used the viewfinder instead. Closing one eye and squinting through the little window, she felt like a photographer from days past and she liked it. The architecture and the people frequenting the castle walls today provided countless opportunities and took hours of the day, just as she'd wanted.

Opting for a lighter lunch, she relaxed over a TGI's. Attracting attention eating alone, it wasn't long before invitations extended her way.

"What's a babe like you doing on her own?"

"Well, obviously because I want to be," she laughed. "If I'm such a babe."

"Fair play. But the question is, do you still want to be on your own, now you've met me?"

Leaning on a thin but strong arm, tattoos covered a good proportion, some hidden at the wrist by a wad of leather bracelets. "I'm Robbie, by the way." He extended a robust hand and Becca took it.

"Becca."

"Nice to meet you, Becca. Care to join us?"

The last awful occasion she'd joined a party pulsed in her head. And this guy was memorable. If he annoyed her later, he was at risk of her killing him. She couldn't gamble at being persuaded to drink and falling asleep like before. "Not tonight, I'm afraid. I'll be looking after my sister and catching up with loads of Uni work."

"Why d'you come here then? If you've got so much work on?"

Declining had been the right choice. He was irritating her already. "Because I wanted to. Now be a good boy and go back to your friends. See, they're missing you."

Faces grinned as shoulders nudged each other as they watched with approval as their friend, Robbie, crashed and burned. Giving up, he turned with a shrug and mouthed 'Lesbian,' as he skulked to his table.

Caesar salad followed a hot brownie interweaved with a couple of mocktails kept her perky despite her finishing neither. Leaving to stroll through a new land of early evening photo opportunities, she shrugged on her jacket and paid her bill, glad of her student grant up after Easter; she must be dangerously close to running out of funds.

The castle looked beautiful, and very different illuminated in the moonlight, almost unrecognisable from the gothic splendour the daylight had shown. It had a make-believe, theatre quality that put Becca in mind of a theatre set. Camera out, she clicked through the viewfinder capturing plenty of wonderful shots until... "Damn!" How long ago did the battery run out?

Grabbing the spare from her bag, she clicked it into place and the camera screen that had been dull in the sunlight now shone in the dark. *Battery level low* the display warned. What? It had been on charge. Sighing relief, there was enough power to scroll through the photos and see the ones before breaking for food were still there, she pressed her lips together and snorted through her nose realising her desire to get the same shots at night was thwarted.

Knuckles whitening, determined to do what she set out to, she pointed her phone and snapped away. 'The camera's not too bad,' the phone shop assistant had said. She hoped he was right. Some useable shots might be good enough for inclusion, but she suspected she would need to come back another night.

Sauntering home, dejected but with more important things on her mind, she rubbed her eyes hoping her writing would keep her as awake as she planned.

Reaching the door, she slipped her shoes off without bending and left them where they lay. Stifling a yawn, she knew too well she couldn't rest; she still had ten more hours to stay awake.

Flipping open her laptop, before loading her Uni files, she checked the airport website. Sophie's flight was in the air and expected to terminate at 0900hrs.

She began writing. It was okay, but she kept having to cross-reference other photographers whilst not plagiarising their work, or any from all the universities offering the same course. Warnings popped up as she uploaded content forcing her over and over to find new ways to say the same bloody thing.

Fighting not to punch the screen, she channelled the anger into more typing and at last it was going well. Two pages of and eight-hundred words into a six thousand-word dissertation. It felt like an achievement.

But, one thousand would be better.

Eyes struggling, she found nonsense flowing from her fingertips and her typing becoming slower and slower yet more frequent.

Reading back what she'd just written, it made no sense. Cutting the gibberish took it down to seven hundred and sixty words. Clenching her fists, she growled through gritted teeth, "No! I've cut too much!"

Clicking 'undo' returned the eight-hundred and seventy-eight, the last seventy needed to go, but she decided to have a break before risking ruining the whole thing. Saving to the laptop and onto the university cloud, she slumped over her desk.

Jerking upright, panic in her eyes, had she fallen asleep? What was the time? How long had she slept for?

She recalled no nightmares, but to ease her mind she re-opened her computer. No news of a plane crash and the airport website still boasted British Airways flight BA555 in the air.

Connecting to her Bluetooth speaker, she blasted music through. Her usual taste wasn't cheery enough to keep her awake so she clicked on 'upbeat pop' on her app's playlist suggestions. Not to her liking, her leg still jigged under the table as her body awakened to the party vibe.

Cranking the volume up, Becca stood from her chair and danced around the room less in gay abandon more in desperation to stay awake. Another eight hours to go.

Leaning over the basin, she splashed cold water in her face and jogged back into the bedroom leaping into star-jumps and squats. Out of breath, she leaned on the wall.

Knock, knock.

Frowning, Becca opened the door. Amy stood with a smile, a cheap bottle of wine and two glasses clutched in her fingers. "Well, Miss Becca Tate. I'm still here! Could you not bear to dream about killing me? Or did you do it and my being here is the proof you needed?"

Becca raised her eyebrows wishing she had dreamt of her so seeing her now could be the indisputable confirmation she was being ridiculous. "Ha, ha, don't be silly," even she didn't know what she meant.

"I could hear you were awake and thought you could probably use some company?"

"Oh, sorry. Was my music too loud?" Seeing Amy may be a godsend, but she didn't have the mental capacity to argue with her again.

"Well, it might have been if I were asleep, but you know how it is, work when you can."

Becca nodded. She had no trouble working in normal waking hours when she wasn't trying to save a plane full of people.

"What are you doing up so late anyway?" Amy feigned not asking directly if her new acquaintance had flipped again.

"Same as you: working on my dissertation. I was doing well but started to flag. I thought the music might help, but I think I'll give it a miss and pick it up when I'm more refreshed."

"Oh, I'm not stopping you going to bed, am I?"

Yes. But that's just what I want. "No, not yet. I'll probably stay up tonight now."

Amy looked suspicious and slumped on the bed.

"I'm not sure I have a bottle opener, I'm afraid."

"Ah ha!" Amy produced one from a pocket in her dress that Becca wasn't convinced wasn't a nightie. "Amy thinks of everything."

Proving her point, as she opened the bottle and poured two glasses, she began assimilating evidence of her housemate's craziness. "Going on holiday?"

"No, why?" Becca followed her gaze to the computer screen with Cardiff airport flight tracker displayed brightly. Sighing, she had to admit "Some of my family are flying back to Tasmania. My cousin, Mel, remember I told you she died."

Amy nodded and tilted her glass in extra confirmation. "It was pretty unforgettable, and you said the funeral was the next day."

Becca paused to regain her composure. "Well her parents and sisters came over from Australia for the service and they're going back tomorrow. And my sister, Sophie, is travelling with them for an extended holiday."

"And you were finding out about flights for her?"

Should she lie? Perhaps a row would be the best thing to keep her awake. "Not exactly."

"Oh, my god, you had a dream, didn't you?"

Becca nodded, the gravity of her sister's plight prying at the corners of her mouth, crumpling them down.

"I knew you hadn't listened to me the other night, but, I promise you, Becca: the logical way is the true way. You're struggling because you're having a rough time and I can help you see more clearly." Patting the bed beside her, she smiled. "Come on. Tell Auntie Amy all about it."

I've met you once, you freak, 'Auntie Amy?' "There's not much to tell. My sister's on a plane and I dreamt about a plane crash; specifically one where her and my uncle, aunt and cousins were passengers. It was weird. In the dream, I was my sister, Sophie."

"All perfectly normal if you ask me. Why wouldn't you worry? It's natural for anyone to be concerned, and for you, after losing people like you have, I'd say dreaming about it should be expected."

Who made you the expert? "I do understand, but I'm not going to risk it."

"What do you mean? How can you escape risking it?"

Becca shuffled in her seat. "By not going to sleep, of course. What do you think?"

"But you've already had the dream."

"I didn't see them dying! I woke up before."

Amy's mouth curved into a crinkled self-satisfied smirk. "Oh. Like a warning, I suppose. A precognition."

"Yeah, probably."

"So, while you've been determined the other dreams weren't precognitions and that they were real-time events you were influencing, this dream is completely different because...?"

"Oh, I don't know. What if this was just a normal dream because I'm worried? It's made me fear I'll have one of *those* dreams."

"You are silly. But I like you."

Becca didn't follow up with, 'I like you, too.'

"Probably the best thing you can do is get a good night's rest. I'm sure it would horrify your family to know you're going through all this."

"I am sure they think I'm crazy. But I'm going to stay awake. I've only got..." she looked at her phone, "six hours left and I feel reasonably awake. I don't see what harm me staying awake will have but if I slept and something happened to them, I'd never get over it."

"Yeah, I suppose." Pouring more wine, she grinned. "Well I can keep you company at least. Got any boardgames?"

Becca took the refilled glass. "No, sorry. How about cards?" Standing, she rummaged through her bedside draws. When she turned with them in her hand, Amy was holding a silver frame.

"Your picture fell over. Who's that? Please tell me he's your brother and looking to settle down with a mousy girl from Portsmouth."

"Put it down!"

Amy placed the photo on the chest of draws, Callum and Becca smiled out into the room. Becca raced across and shoved it into a draw. "Ex-boyfriend."

"And you're not over him. I can't say I blame you, he's got it all."

"Shut up. Just shut up."

"Sorry. I didn't mean anything. You shouldn't have the picture if you're so bloody sensitive about it."

"Look, Amy. I can't be doing with this. I think you should go."

"Oh, come on, Becca. Don't be like that. We can play cards, I'll help you stay awake."

Becca weighed up her chances. Riled up now, she'd have no trouble keeping conscious. "No, thank you, Amy. I'd rather be on my own."

Standing, eyes moist, she stomped to the door. "Suit yourself."

"Are you crying? All I've told you I've been through and *you're* crying. Just fuck off, Amy. Take your fucking wine and your fucking whin*ing* and fuck off!"

Amy's lips trembled as she picked up the empty glasses. "Sorry," she mumbled as she scurried through the door. "I'm sure you don't mean to be so horrible. I'll check on you tomorrow."

Becca clenched her fists and screwed them into her thighs as she held back the tirade from shattering this girl. And she was right, she probably didn't mean it but she had more important things on her mind.

A minute passed as Amy scurried down the stairs to her apartment below, then Becca heard the slam as her front door bore the brunt of her frustration and she winced. "Bloody hell."

Cards still in her hand, she opened the box and proceeded to shuffle them. Holding the pack, she laid them out for solitaire. Losing again and again, she didn't care. She was awake and that's all that mattered. Three hours to go. Flagging, she had another shower and jogged around the room before deciding she should go outside for fresh air and exercise.

Cursing she hadn't charged either of her camera batteries, the early hour was unusual and photogenic; and once again the morning golden hour had eluded her. Tilting her head, she soothed her disappointment acknowledging she'd be too distracted anyway. Today, being wide-awake was enough.

Taking the stairs to start her heart pumping before she even reached outside, she padded down the hallway half-expecting Amy to pull open her door thinking she was on her way to apologise, so she was relieved to reach the street without seeing her again.

A million birds tweeted their morning song. The misty brightness had lulled her with a promise of warmth it didn't deliver. Eyeing a lamppost on the corner, she decided a circuit to that and back would wake her sufficiently for the rest of her watch.

Scurrying in trainer-clad feet, her slouchy joggers and t-shirt were no match for the cold and reaching the streetlamp grew into a feat of endurance. With a victorious fist clench, she circled it and scurried back. Taking the stairs two at a time, she ran inside her apartment and banged the door closed.

Slowing her heavy breathing, she tried to relax. Settling in front of her computer, she squinted at the screen. Her eyes struggled to focus and she sighed knowing there was no way she could do any more of her dissertation. Flipping onto the flight tracker, her eyes grew large and she smiled. Hands behind her head, she leaned back. Wow. They were early. British Airways flight 555 was now on the ground. Thank goodness.

Leaving her joggers and t-shirt on, Becca pulled back the covers and dived gratefully inside. Time for a well-deserved sleep.

Chapter Twenty-three

It was a different view this time. The plane was in front of her and it was dark. It took a moment to recognise what she was seeing, dozens of little rounded off rectangles lit up against the scudding clouds. Faces peered out and then she noticed the wings and she was sure.

Her own wings spread either side of her but when she looked at them, they weren't wings at all but four arms: two on each side.

Eyes drawn downwards, she rode the sky on a carpet of all those she had seen die. Her feet planted on a man's chest; his pallid skin scarcely recognisable as the well-known seventies' music icon. He lay on the pale remains of two overdosed teenagers, who, in turn sprawled on the mangled remnants of what used to be her cousin, and she on her gran, thankfully mainly hidden by the others, only a wry smile poking out. Beneath her, another figure could be glimpsed and, like her, it also had more than the usual number of limbs, this time with six arms. Who was it?

Becca could taste the air, swallowing, she realised her tongue was long and lolling to one side. Kali astride her enemies. Except, how could she describe any of these beloved souls as her enemy?

Suddenly, she was on the ground. With a throng of other people, her eyes grainy, she couldn't see; was it smoke?

The aeroplane wobbled in front of her. Impossible through the whine of the jet engines and the roar of the flames to be certain, but screaming escaped into the air; the agonising screams of hundreds of passengers as they burnt to their deaths.

Vomiting where she stood, no-one took any notice as, from behind cameras, they never removed their eyes from the tragedy unfolding before them.

Whisked to a different viewpoint, she watched the same distant plane as it came into land, as though through a rewound video-clip. She stared as only two of the landing wheels dropped down, the asymmetry gave it an ungainly deportment.

Striking the tarmac at two hundred miles an hour, it bent and shook, distorting as flames of friction burst into life. Fire engulfed the rear of the aircraft as sirens and red and blue lights flashed in the distance.

Then she was back with the original crew, behind her own camera, watching detached as firefighters directed their canons of water over the fuselage and wings as they roared like the fifth of November.

Throwing it to the floor, glass from the lens shattered into a million rainbow pieces as she raced for the wreckage. Strong arms wrapped around her. "Stand back. You can't go any closer. Stand back!"

Fingers outstretched, just her two normal arms now, her long fingers strained to reach the flames. "Sophie! *SOPHIE!*"

Heart throbbing, Becca rolled over in her bed and piled puke on top of the coffee stain. Dashing to the bathroom, wine acid burned her throat and nose as she brought more of the foul distaste to the world.

Shaking, tears flooded from her eyes and she banged the toilet seat with her clenched fist, snapping it into two sharp pieces.

Grabbing one, she wrenched it from the hinge, swinging it side to side, splitting it away from its constraint and thrusting it towards her neck.

For a slow-motion second, she considered helping it on its trajectory; plunging it into her jugular and ending this torment.

At the back of the class, her mind raised its hand; 'Sophie's plane landed safely. You checked before you went to sleep.'

Dropping the sharp shard of plastic, Becca slumped onto the bathroom floor, her palm falling in a pool of her own acid juice as she stopped herself toppling into the bowl.

Of course. She'd checked. It was a nightmare, that was all. The plane hadn't really crashed.

Wiping the foul liquid on a towel, she sniffed her fingers, head wrenching back from the stench. Pushing herself up, she lay the already dirty towel on the mess and washed her hands. Scooping water from the tap, she sloshed it around her mouth and spat the carrot cubes into the basin, prodded them down the plug hole and re-washed her hands.

Dabbing at her t-shirt as she hobbled back into the bedroom, it seemed to be unscathed. The stench as the puddle by the bed wafted to her, almost drove her to re-fill the toilet. There was no way she could clean it up now so she tossed more of her laundry over the top of it.

Remote in her hand, she aimed it at the tv but couldn't press the button that would allow the world of pictures into her room. "Don't be afraid. Sophie's fine. It was only a dream. You checked. Remember, you checked."

Pressing firmly, Katy Perry danced around singing how much she'd enjoyed kissing a girl in an MTV all-noughties countdown. Pushing the arrows on the keypad until she selected a news channel, when it flickered onto the screen, she didn't have to wait. Straight back into her nightmare, Breaking News was shown on all channels.

A British Airways aeroplane crash-landed in Tasmania. Amount dead: unknown.

Becca's knees had no hope of holding her up. Collapsing to the floor, her head bounced from the carpet and she stared, glassy-eyed at the ceiling.

Chapter Twenty-four

The world ended at that moment. For Becca it was more than she could endure. Details wafted into the room but she couldn't take them in anymore.

What she'd seen on the screen was exactly what she'd witnessed in her dream. Once again, she had seen it happen whilst it happened. She'd tried so hard. She'd trusted it was safe, but like all inevitabilities, her evil will would not be denied.

When would it end? How many more people would she murder? How many more of those she loved would she lose?

'So do we have a confirmed number of dead, yet, Steve?'

'Not, yet, Sarah. The emergency services were quick to respond so we're hopeful that there will be some survivors.'

'Do we have an estimate?'

'No. Not yet. And it could be days before the wreckage is clear...'

Becca forced herself up. Pulling the door, the handle caught in her watch strap. Yanking away, it fell to the floor. Wrestling through tears, not of grief, but of blind panic, she knew she had to get away. She had to get away from herself.

Flying open, the door banged against the wall and swung closed but Becca was the other side before it did. Pacing along the corridor, she took the stairs three at a time and lunged for the front door.

"I prefer your usual look, I'm not gonna lie, but you look good grungy. I mean, I still would..."

Becca didn't even glance at the workman. A cry warbling in her throat, she hurried along the street, without looking, she jumped headlong into the road. Squealing brakes and angry horns sounded like the opening to hell as cars dodged the crazy girl streaking into the road.

The other side seemed further away and the busy traffic gave distance from the televisual torture in her bedroom.

Head down, she stormed through the city looking at nothing and no-one with no notion of where she was heading. She'd have to hide. Keep away from people. But wouldn't that leave everyone she already knew in more danger?

Halting, she leaned against a wall. The knot of grief in her stomach refused to loosen; somewhere deep inside, every particle of her body feared letting out the pain for where it might take her.

Molecules in her brain scurried to find a way for their personality to battle on. Rattling around like change in a charity tin, Becca ignored them and for the same reason. She liked control; of where she spent her money, and of what thoughts she listened to.

But as she raced past, the crowd's logic rose like a life-jacket in a storm and Becca stopped dead. Pulling her hood down and her phone from her pocket, she stared as the slab of black plastic and glass conspired to keep her distraught by refusing to switch on. Like her camera, she hadn't got around to charging it.

She could turn back; return to her flat. The bulletins, whilst torturous, may yet prove to be her saviour if she heard the news she yearned for.

Hearing the blare of a report as she passed a bar, Becca stepped inside and stared. Nothing had changed. The same grainy footage, the same people interviewed and the same vague predictions about survivors.

But there only needed to be five for her family to be intact. The other families would be destroyed too, but there couldn't be many who had lost as much as she had recently. She deserved a break. But if she was responsible, what did she deserve then?

That's why she'd assumed as soon as she heard that if anyone were killed in the tragedy, Uncle Clive would be one of them which would mean Lorraine, Kate and Liz and worst of all her beloved Sophie would be massacred with him.

But it was possible, wasn't it, that Sophie had heeded her warning and hadn't gone after all? Goodness, it was possible for all of them to have abandoned their trip in light of Becca's dream;

unlikely, but thinkable. And right now, she'd take that.

If her family were safe, she'd grieve for the others lost, but she would sacrifice every one of them if it meant Sophie could be okay. She flinched at the callous truth. Rushing away from the pub tv's lack of information, she left for her apartment again. Quickening her pace, she had to charge her phone and call her parents, or phone a survivor hotline or something. Someone must be able to tell her her sister was all right.

Reaching the top of the stairs, she could see her door was still open, and for a moment she wondered if anything might be missing. As she stepped inside, she knew her belongings were safe.

"I hoped you wouldn't be long. I didn't want to close the door in case you didn't have a key."

She smiled to see Amy despite last night's expletives. Someone to check what she was too anxious to do and put her world back together again.

When she stood and held out her arms, Becca allowed her to comfort her. "I can't believe you were right. Oh my god, Becca. I don't know how you knew." Pulling away to look into her face, she stared into her eyes. "Have you heard? Do you know if your family are...?"

Becca shook her head. "Can you help me?"

"Of course. We'll look at your laptop shall we."

Amy sat at the desk while Becca lay back on her bed.

"There's a helpline, but they're saying it's likely to be busy. We'll still call though, eh? Where's your phone?"

"Here. The battery is flat."

"Charger?"

Becca rummaged in her bedside draw and tossed the cable to Amy.

"Right. Yes, it's completely dead." Regretting the choice of words, she brightened saying, "We'll use mine." Calling the number on the screen led to an unsurprising busy tone so she re-dialled again and again. "What do your folks say?"

"I don't know. I haven't spoken to them?"

"Blimey, Becca! They might have good news."

"Yeah. And they might not."

"You have to know. There's no point clinging to false hope. And if it is good news, you've got nothing to worry about."

"Except my dreams have killed hundreds of people."

For once Amy didn't have an answer. Instead, she busied checking the charge on Becca's phone. "Leave it plugged in, but I think you have enough power to call them."

Becca didn't move.

"Unless, you want me to phone them for you?"

Convinced she would, Becca knew it was a simple choice of biting the bullet or subjecting her devastated parents to her suffocating friend. Slouching from the bed, this call could be her redeemer or it could send her into a chasm she may never crawl out of.

"Oh, Becca! I've been trying to phone you. Have you heard from your sister?"

"No."

"You've seen the news?"

"Yes."

"I wish we'd listened to you. How did you predict this?"

"I don't know, Mum. Are you saying Sophie went with Auntie Lorraine and you haven't heard from her since, and that the plane that crashed is their plane?"

"Yes!" she wailed down the phone and then it went dead.

"Hi, Becca. Your mum's not in a good place right now."

You don't say. "My friend, Amy is constantly calling the hotline. She might be one of the survivors."

"Do you want to come home?"

Picturing her mum crying and her dad supporting her. It would be too real. There would be no comfort there. What could they do? Cuddle each other and say it'll be all right? She'd be better off with Amy. At least she could tell her to f off if she needed. "I'll stay here, Dad. Work might keep me sane."

"And we'll drive you mad? Come on girl, your mum needs you."

"No, she needs Sophie. That's what we all need, and until that happens being together will be worse for all of us."

"Well, I can't make you come home, but it'd be great if you could."

"I'll think about it. That's all I can say. I love you, Dad, but I'm gonna go now, okay?"

"Tell me if there's news."

"Of course." Why on earth wouldn't I? "Bye." She turned to Amy who shook her head and pursed her lips. Still no connection.

"Thank you, Amy. Thanks for coming back when I was so rude to you."

"But you were right. I still don't think you're responsible. That's just a weird step too far, but coincidences are stacking up."

"Why am I not to blame? I don't just see stuff, I live them at the same time they're happening; and it's always people I'm cross with."

"Cross? Barely. Only when you look back. I mean, why were you cross with your uncle? Because he used to call you a silly name? And your sister? Because she was leaving you behind?"

"I don't want to talk about it."

"You're right. I'm being insensitive. Regarding coming back even though you were rude? That's what friends do. I like you, Becca. If you'd dreamt of me and I'd ended up dead you would have thought it was because you were angry with me, but now you're not. I don't think these minor grudges could lead to you killing anyone."

"Oh, I know it's not rational. And if you'd died in my dream, I absolutely would have thought it was because I was upset with you, and it would have been. It may only be because a more painful nightmare diverted me that you are still here."

Amy twisted a ring around her middle finger.

"I don't have any control. This weird power seems to take any excuse."

"Well test it then. If you're so sure!"

"Deliberately kill someone you mean?"

"Why not?"

"Because I don't want to. I wouldn't hurt anyone. That's why I'm so afraid."

"But there are plenty of people who deserve to die. Trust me. The crime reports I've read. I could provide loads of candidates."

"I think you need to shut up before we fall out again. Keep phoning the hotline, I'm going to clear up these sicky clothes."

"Is that what that smell is. I thought it was last night's wine."

"Well, it is in a way." Becca scooped up the clothing and popped it into her IKEA laundry bag before scraping the one from the bathroom floor. Kicking the broken toilet seat to one side, blood drained from her face as she recalled how she'd been willing to attack herself earlier. Leaning against the wall, she re-balanced. "I'll take this straight down to the launderette. See you in a bit."

"What if I get through? They might not talk to me if I can't provide dates of birth or whatever."

Anxious for the mundane diversion, Becca could see no other way. "Okay. There's a tenner in my jacket, will you take them for me?"

"Sure. What are friends for?"

Becca took her phone from Amy's hand as she stood and hauled the bag across the room. It

229

looked much bigger and more cumbersome in Amy's short arms.

As the door closed behind, a voice pierced her ear and she was thankful she hadn't left. "British Airways flight 555 hotline."

Becca's mouth opened and closed but she couldn't speak.

"Hello? I'll have to end the call if you don't say anything. The lines are extremely busy."

"Sophie Tate!" she blurted. "She's my little sister."

"Hold on." Becca could hear tapping on a keyboard. "Her name is on the boarding list, yes. Travelling with the Smiths?"

Becca had to think for a minute. Her mum's maiden name was Austin, but of course, Uncle Clive was Clive Smith. "Yes. That's right."

"The best I can tell you is that none of the party have been identified as any of the deceased. They may be in hospital. Injuries are being treated as priority over identification, which I'm sure even in your distraught position you can appreciate."

Becca nodded and forced out a rasped, "Yes."

"Hang in. Try to be optimistic. If the news is bad, you don't want to be living it a moment sooner than you have to, and if it's good, your family will need you. I can take your number and call you as soon as I get something definite to report."

"Thank you."

Becca gave her phone number, then as soon as she clicked *END*, she dialled her parents.

"Dad. It's a case of no news is good news. Of the bodies they've identified, none of them are any of our family. Not the news we were hoping for but not the news we're dreading either."

"Okay, thank you."

"Try to stay positive, Dad. Hopefully, Sophie's going to need us soon."

"Okay. Bye for now."

Lowering the phone, the call was over before she even pressed the red button. Was he sulking because she wasn't going home as ordered? No, her mum was distraught and he was bearing the brunt. Well, it's his job to look after them. Becca knew she didn't have the strength to prop them up, then recognising her agitation at the pair of them, she gasped. "No! I can't be cross with anyone else!"

Chapter Twenty-five

That's why my idea is crucial."

"Explain again why deliberately trying to kill someone is such a good plan?"

"Because if you're killing them, you're not killing your mum, dad, sister, or me!"

Becca sat on her hands. "So, you believe me now?"

"I'm not saying that. But you believe it and it's driving you crazy. If you try to take out horrible people; and I mean murderers and child molesters, you'll either find out you don't have the power you think you do, which is what I believe will happen, or you'll rid the world of some disgusting scum. Win-win."

"I don't approve of killing anyone. No matter who they are."

"Yeah, but if you had to choose to kill your parents or..."

"Well, obviously."

"And at the very least, you can get some rest knowing that the worst that can happen is that shitheads get what's coming to them and maybe you'll find nothing happens. Either way you can rest."

Eyes widening and her face relaxing, she sighed, "I guess. I mean, I can't stay awake forever, and even when I do it doesn't help. I checked that flight had landed before going to sleep, but it must have been wrong."

"So completely changing your focus seems like a good idea, doesn't it?"

"Why are you so keen for me to kill someone?"

"I'm not. I'm keen to prove to you that you can't in what I reckon is a risk-free way."

"How do I control what I dream about?"

"You seem pretty suggestible. Like the last thing you focus on before going to sleep is what you dream. Don't you reckon?"

"I suppose."

"So, if I log into my Uni files on your computer, you can pick one of the vile pieces of shit I've been reading about and you can read about them until you fall asleep."

"You know what, Amy? You might be right."

"Thank you! Now. Go and shower, I'll buy you lunch," then looking at her watch, "Late lunch, early dinner… 'Linner.'"

"Okay. You can buy me linner. Thanks."

"Keep you occupied until you hear about your sister."

"Yeah, I know. So best not talk about her, yeah?"

"Sorry. See you in twenty minutes. I'm just going to chuck something different on."

"Make it half an hour. I'm going to have a bit of a soak."

"In the shower?"

Becca grinned. "See you soon."

Chapter Twenty-six

The pizza in front of her was as sad and flat as anything she had ever seen. When she'd ordered, it was because that's what she normally ate rather from any desire for food, and when it arrived it skulked on the plate knowing it wasn't welcome. How could she think of eating when her sister was missing?

"Eat up. It'll go cold."

"I can't. I've lost my appetite."

Amy nodded. "That's fine. I should have known trying to treat you when you're so upset was a long shot. Don't worry, we can ask them to box it up and take it home. I'll eat it tomorrow if you don't want it."

Becca's eyes squeezed tears down her cheeks. Her new friend could have moaned that she'd just wasted twelve pounds, which wasn't an insignificant amount of her student budget, but she'd done nothing but try to make her feel better.

"But you may need your strength, so trying to eat even a little bit might not be a bad idea."

Becca offered a corner to her lips. Eating for sustenance made sense. This wasn't a treat to be enjoyed despite whatever her sister was going through, it was necessary nutrition presented in her favourite form to try to get her to eat it. Biting with a new determination, she forced it down her throat, grateful the gooey cheese was hot enough to aid chewing in her arid mouth.

Once she'd consumed half of it, the chewing and the taste became a methodical solace. She knew people ate for comfort and then had to diet in between to control their waistline, but it had never appealed. She'd always had her favourite foods, but the rest of the time she ate enough to keep alive. The rarity of eating heartily happened so infrequently her weight was unaffected. She knew she was too thin, so eating like this was probably a good thing.

"Oh. I guess I'll be having Pot Noodle for lunch tomorrow after all," Amy grinned as Becca mopped up salt, pepper, and chilli flakes with the last of the soft cheese.

"Thank you. I needed that. I hope I do need the strength to comfort my sister and not deal with my grief." Frowning, she shook her head at stating the obvious.

"What shall we do now? More leisure distraction, or some work?"

"I don't want to stop you doing your Uni-work, Amy. If there's stuff you need to get done, I could sit with you so I don't fall asleep."

"I don't know if that'll work. I fall asleep writing it. I can't imagine how dull it would be to watch me!" With a wave indicating to the waitress to come over, she asked Becca, "More drinks? A pudding? They're great here."

They were, but whilst sustenance might be justifiable, oohing over a chocolate cake seemed unseemly and just thinking about it brought a lump to her throat. "No, thank you."

"Can we have the bill, please?" Amy asked and the waitress scurried off to print it.

As they walked from the restaurant, Amy slipped her arm around Becca's. "Right. How about a museum? Distracting and free, and arguably work."

Becca nodded. "Okay, which? We're kind of in the middle here so we could go modern at Techni quest, or arty at the National Museum or the castle?"

"I reckon you're more of an arty girl, so The National? Where is that?"

"I'll show you."

The building siting the museum was a magnificent colonial styled dome and pillars in white presenting a sense of stepping back in time even before stepping inside.

Becca enjoyed the past. It was safe and predictable; the stories there already concluded. The most shocking plights can be dismissed with a frown with no need to invest emotion. Suits of armour from Roman to modern displayed in one room. War was always upsetting, but the ones on display here were in the past. All over now. There, there, it'll be all right.

One day, her own life and everyone she knew would be past too, and she hoped future museum patrons would not be gasping at how terrible a time it had been, cooing over an example of Becca's student flat. 'This is how students used to live. This girl was famous for killing people in her dreams. A descendant of the Hindu goddess, Kali who killed her husband when he tried to stop her dancing on her enemies' corpses...'

Shaking herself from her negative reverie, Becca put herself firmly back in the past with old masters on display in one room and dinosaur bones in another.

"I like this old stuff. I like piecing together peoples' lives from the evidence; imagining what their times were like," Amy stood over a cabinet of Bronze Age spearheads. "There's a Basking Shark in the other room," she added. "Have you seen it?"

"I've been before, yes. I like it, but the gaping gills make me feel peculiar." Her mind fell back to her missing sister. Each time she wasn't directly focussed on something else, it chipped away at her, sweeping the sand from beneath her feet and threatening to tip her into an ocean of despair.

"You okay?"

Becca stared at her phone, willing it to ring with news they'd found her family alive and well. The longer time went on the unlikelier it seemed.

"You've got signal? Your ringtone's turned up? You need to keep distracted or you'll drive yourself mad. You probably won't hear anything today."

"Really? That must mean she's in a bad way or worse."

"Why?"

"Because she'd know how frantic we'd be and make sure she contacted us otherwise." Dialling, she held the phone to her ear.

"Who are you calling?"

"I've got a new number. Sophie won't remember it, and what if the woman I spoke to wrote it down wrong? Hey, Dad. Any news?" Tears stinging her eyes, she lowered the phone. Pressing *End* she wailed, "I can't do this!"

Striding from the exhibition, Becca stormed to the stairs and scampered down. She knew Amy would follow and she was grateful, but she had to get away. Suffocating, she pulled at her collar. Running through the doors and back out onto the street, she fell to her knees. She wanted to scream at the sky, but no sound came, just the echo of her breaking heart as her crumpled mouth groaned in sorrow.

Arms wrapped around her head as Amy stood above her and held her. Stroking her hair, phrases came and drifted away as comforting words seemed an insult. Instead, she embraced her friend and caressed and kissed her hair and prayed she'd get good news.

Chapter Twenty-seven

Slumped on the bed, Becca let Amy take her shoes off and rummage through her drawers for nightwear. Holding up an old t-shirt, Becca nodded and when Amy threw it to her, she covered herself with the duvet, pulled on the t-shirt and tossed her clothes on the floor.

"Want me to hang those up?" Amy picked and folded the garments without confirmation. "I'm going to pass your laptop so you can have a read through some of the horror stories, so if you kill anyone in your sleep, they'll deserve it."

"Thank you. Can you read them to me? I don't think I can make myself understand."

"Sure. Budge up."

Shuffling in the bed, Amy slid in beside, still holding the laptop. "Right. There's this guy." Becca glanced at the photo. "Collin Fitzgerald. Murdered six girls in Dublin." She filled in some details but her friend's motionless expression seemed unmoved Then this one... killed prostitutes in Suffolk." Skimming through the report, she gasped. "No! This one. Oh, this one's gotta go... Serially raped and murdered children as young as six!"

Becca glared at the screen with disgust, her mouth crinkling in sour repulsion. "Let me see him. What's his name?"

"Wayne Bridges."

"Well, I'll never forget that evil face. For the first time, I hope I do fall asleep and dream the most horrific death for him."

"You look terrifying when you're angry."

"Do I?"

"I wouldn't want to upset you."

"Well, if your plan works, it won't matter if you do because I'll be too busy disposing of the worst scum in society."

"I hope it works too." She was about to add, 'And that your family are found safe and well,' but recognised Becca was keeping them from her mind deliberately.

"You want me to stay?"

"Yes. Please. I find you comforting."

Amy beamed. "My pleasure."

Laying side by side, Becca felt part of a team. Whatever happened, she had someone who would help her through. She just prayed she wouldn't need it.

"No, no!"

Amy watched her friend sleep. Heart racing, she wondered, should she wake her? If she was dreaming about Wayne Bridges dying, she wouldn't expect her to act agitated. Not unless the bastard was escaping. "Becca," she cooed with a gentle shake.

Grunting and moaning, Becca threw a hand up. "No, no, no!"

"Becca!" Amy called tapping her arm.

"Wha... what is it? It's going to close and I need to pay for all this stuff..."

Amy rolled her eyes. She may as well let her carry on sleeping. Wide awake now, she decided to call the British Airways number and see if there was any news. Taking her phone into the bathroom so Becca could sleep, she thought that late at night might be a better time to call for the time difference, and because a lot of other people would be trying to sleep.

The line was busy. She wasn't the only one having the same idea. Remaining on hold, she pulled the toilet paper down and rolled it up over and over in distraction before they answered her call. With dates of birth and names all recallable in her head, she posed as Becca and the person on the other end of the phone was happy to disclose what she knew, but there was no information to give.

"I have to say, at this stage, the chance of finding any more survivors is becoming increasingly unlikely."

"Ok. Thank you."

Shit.

Perched on the seat-less loo, she tapped her lips, and then her nails found their way between her teeth. Ripping at a jagged edge, Amy rubbed the catching nail on her zip to file it down, but it only made it worse. Opting for taking ever bigger bites, her nail ended up too short, the plump new flesh beneath smarting from exposure like a newly hatched chick.

Far more trimmed than the rest of her nails, she considered chewing the others to match, but managed to resist until she had better tools than her teeth. What should she say to Becca? She could dress it up. Just because it was unlikely, didn't mean it wouldn't happen; that her sister, aunt, uncle and cousins wouldn't be okay. And if they weren't, it would be hard enough to deal with without pre-empting the grief. She'd say she spoke to them, and whilst they couldn't confirm they were being cared for in hospital, they were not named as dead, and that had to be positive. And she'd stop her phoning for herself.

"Amy!"

Amy pushed open the bathroom door and stood silhouetted in the light. "Oh good. I thought you'd gone."

"Not without saying goodbye. And no. I'm not planning to leave you. Uni work can wait."

"Thank you. I remembered you tapping my arm, unless I dreamt it."

"You were having a nightmare. I was worried and started to wake you but it was just about shopping!"

"Oh, yes. I missed the bus and got to IKEA just as they were closing. Callum and I were racing through the end bit, you know? With all the little knick-knacks in. And they called out they were closing. Nightmare."

"Yes. It must have been awful. You nutcase!" they laughed. "Who's Callum?" Amy suspected she knew already.

"That's who's with me in the photo. He, er, left me a while ago. I don't want to talk about him."

"You really loved him, then?"

Becca just raised an eyebrow.

"I'm surprised I haven't seen him around. But I guess I've only been here less than two terms. I haven't really seen anyone!" Seeing Becca's eyebrows raise further and her eyes bulge, she put up placatory palms, "Okay, sorry. You don't want to talk about it. You mentioned him, though. And if you want my opinion, anyone who leaves you wants their head examining." Amy flushed bright red.

"Thank you. Now drop it." Leaning over her bedside table, Becca scowled at her phone. "Still nothing." Looking at the ceiling, she barked, "Come on, Sophie! I need to know you're safe."

"I phoned them. Early this morning. Still no news, but it's heartening they haven't been identified amongst those who've died."

"You phoned again? Thank you. I suppose it is good news, but I'd give anything to hear her voice."

"I'm sure. Come on. We need to do something to distract you again." Amy turned and smiled. "My dream distraction technique worked then?"

"What? Wayne Bridges untimely demise has been reported?"

"Oh, I don't know. I just meant you haven't woken up panicking about killing someone. That's an improvement."

"I don't think I dreamt anything. Apart from the IKEA dream. Maybe things are returning to normal? I just need my sister back. Please, God. Let her be okay."

The second museum in two days struggled to keep Becca's attention. Amy waited across the landing of Cardiff Bay's Techni quest Centre for Becca to shoot a bomb of air at her as she aimed the air canon as per the light-up instructions. Amy laughed as her hair tousled in the breeze created by a simple channelled contraction of a diaphragm at the bottom of the canon/tube despite being fifty feet away. Becca struggled to raise a smile.

Where was Sophie? If she was critically ill, surely staff at the hospital could have ascertained her identification by now. And if not her, someone in the family. What could have happened to all of them?

Presumably they sat together, and if they hadn't then it was even less explainable how there could be no news of any of them. Unless...

Amy walked towards her. "You have a turn. It is good. Go on. It's fun."

"What did they really say this morning? When you phoned the airline, what did they say?"

Amy's shoulders slumped. "Nothing different to what I told you already, I promise. Just, they weren't perhaps as optimistic as I indicated ..."

"What do you mean? Tell me!"

"Like I say, nothing. They did suggest it was surprising they hadn't turned up as alive or dead yet... And that the longer time went on, the unlikelier them being found safe became." Amy plastered on a grin, "But, nothing we didn't know already."

"You said they were optimistic."

"What would you prefer? That they'd said, 'Yes we found them all dead this morning?' Would you? No, of course not. So, I reckon, them not being found dead is reason to be hopeful."

"You're right. Sorry. Come on. Hit me with a big ball of air!"

Mooching in the gift shop, they bought pencils with Techni quest written along their length and Amy bought a notepad. They had no use for either and had intended to buy more interesting souvenirs, but everything they admired Amy described as, 'Cost Prohibitive.'

With money they hadn't wasted gift shopping, they had a coffee. "What do you want to do next? I could help you with your dissertation?"

"There's no way I'll be able to focus."

"No. I don't suppose."

"But don't let me keep you from your work."

"Don't be silly. Sophie will be found soon and there'll be plenty of time then. And I'm only in my second term. How behind can I get in a few days?"

Raising her skinny-latte cup, Becca tilted it to her friend. "Thank you, Amy. I don't know how I'd manage right now if it wasn't for you."

Bingeing on Netflix was all they could think to do for the rest of the afternoon and evening, and when it came time to consider going to bed, Amy flipped open the laptop again. "Wayne, again? Or some other scumbag?"

"Scumbag sounds mild for what he did. How about Devil Incarnate?"

"I agree. So, you want to stick with him for dream distraction?"

"There can't be many who deserve to die more. No. I'll try to dream of him and I hope tonight I actually do and we wake up to news of his agonising death. He should have done to him what he did to his victims."

"Well, read it before going to sleep, and maybe he will."

"Okay. Give it here." Becca scrolled down the reports the university had prepared in their criminology curriculum.

Bridges sexually abused females, some of whom were as young six years old. His eldest victim was twenty-six. He is unusual in this regard, finding gratification in mature females yet seeking younger victims, it is thought he is an opportunist psychopath. Not clever enough to plan his attacks, he acted on a whim when he found his victims in vulnerable situations.

He didn't pick random targets, instead, attacking people he knew, suggesting a growing uncontrollable desire which culminated in his necessitating having them sexually.

He had said murdering the women and young girls wasn't his intention, but he had to do that so they wouldn't tell. That was also the reason he provided for meticulously disposing of their bodies. Again, the diverse methods of disposal, as with the varied appearance and ages of his victims showed him to be opportunistic hiding one in the foundations of an extension to the offices he worked knowing concrete would be poured the next morning, and other times burying them. His last victim, six-year-old Hayley Morris, he chopped up into tiny pieces and dispersed them into food waste bins of his neighbour's caddies because it happened to be collection day.

It was this last devious act that led to his capture when seagulls emptied one of the bins onto the road and a human finger belonging to Hayley, who no-one had even noticed was missing at that time, was discovered on the street.

All bins were seized and examined and the only one found not to contain human remains was that of Bridges house; which instead of making him appear innocent, further incriminated him. He buckled under questioning and provided a full confession pleading guilty without trial.

He is currently serving six consecutive life sentences in Durham 'Category A' prison and will never leave.

The attacks had happened before Becca was born, but reading what he'd done, death seemed too good for him. Rotting in jail forever was a worse punishment, and surely the other inmates made his life a living hell.

"You know what, Amy. I think I'd prefer it if this shithead stayed alive and faced his entire life being abused by other prisoners. You got anyone else in mind?"

It surprised Becca the difficulty she was having. Even presented with the horror stories Amy showed her, killing on purpose wasn't in her nature and she couldn't help but believe the justice system had got it right.

Those who had done less and were expected to come out, who was she to decide they were wrong and they deserved to die? And those she thought she would happily kill, she now, having read their heinous crimes for herself, considered death would almost be a relief for them.

"Don't intend to kill them then. Just use them like you used Wayne Bridges last night: to focus your mind so you don't worry about having dreams that you later attribute to killing someone else."

Becca noted Amy's dismissive tone. One night not slaying a vicious killer and she'd decided it was all in her head. Well, maybe she was right.

She had been terrified when she'd acted tetchy with her dad that he would fall foul of her subconscious, and trying to dream of murderers resulted in the most normal nightmare she'd endured in months.

"Well, they're all firmly in my mind, so anyone else would struggle to displace them, which means the world is safe from me tonight."

"Good. You want me to stay with you again?"

Becca nodded. "Until I hear about Sophie, I could do with the company."

Amy slid in beside her friend and cuddled her to sleep.

The cacophony seemed so alien when it wasn't expected. Becca pitched Amy from her grasp and rushed her hand to her phone. Not recognising the number she swiped the green 'answer call' button but it confounded her addled sleepy head. Petrified she'd miss whoever it was, at last the little telephone icon slid to the side and she could hear a voice as she thrust the handset to her ear.

"Oh, my god, Becca. It's been so awful."

"Sophie! Oh, Sophie!" Amy sat up beside her, heart pounding. "I was so worried about you. Do Mum and Dad know you're safe?"

"No. I tried phoning lots of times but there isn't much signal and they haven't answered."

Becca's heart sank. Why? What has happened to them?

"We never made it to Australia."

"What do you mean?"

"It's awful, so awful. Auntie Lorraine is beside herself and our cousins are hysterical."

"What about Uncle Clive?"

"Oh, my god. I can't believe you don't know but how could you? He's dead!"

"He died in the crash? How did the rest of you survive?"

Sophie sighed. "No, we didn't crash. The plane had to land in Vietnam because... because Uncle Clive died on the plane! He was sitting next to me, well Lorraine sat between us, but, Becca, it was so awful."

"What time?"

"What time did you land in Vietnam?"

"I don't know. About nine, I guess. We had to circle for a bit, the plane was having trouble with its landing gear or something. Anyway, they tried resuscitating him, everyone knew what was going on and in the end he passed away. It looked like he was in agony. The weird thing was, his last words weren't anything about his heart or loving Auntie Lorraine or Kate and Liz, it was about you! He kept repeating, we used to call her Kali. She's beautiful now, but we used to call her Kali! It was bizarre."

Becca fell silent. Her head spun. Clive was dead and his last words were about her.

"They tried to move him but he was too big and heavy and there was no room anywhere else on the plane. The crew literally covered him with a sheet and strapped him in but some of the other passengers kept screaming. That's when they decided they couldn't carry on the whole flight with him so they abandoned us in Vietnam. I've only got your number because I wrote it down. I'm flying back to Cardiff tomorrow. Mum's going to be in a right state so I'd love it if you could share the train with me?"

Becca was still in shock. Clive was dead, and that's why the aircraft showed as landed when she checked and went to bed. And then she dreamt of it as it continued its journey and now hundreds of people were dead.

The carpet by the bed could never be saved as Becca retched onto what had become the usual patch.

Wiping her mouth on the back of her hand, she said, "You don't know about the crash do you?"

"What crash?"

"The plane that you were on crashed on landing in Australia. We thought you were on it and have been phoning for news of whether you're in hospital, or if you'd all been killed."

"What? Uncle Clive dying saved my life!"

"Mmm hmm," Becca agreed, but that's not what she meant at all. No-one was safe, and if she couldn't get her mum and dad to answer the phone, she was going to leave right now. She had to check she hadn't dreamed them to death too.

Pulling on her trousers, Amy frowned. "That's good news then. Why do you seem so panicked?"

"I killed Clive, and because I didn't know, hundreds more have died. Sophie can't get my parents to answer their phone."

"Well, it is late."

"They'd have answered."

"You think you've killed them too, don't you? But you didn't dream about them last night. You dreamt about shopping."

Biting hard on her lip, Becca gulped. "I only remember the IKEA dream, but I might have dreamt before that. Anyway, they need to know Sophie's safe. I promised I'd tell them."

"Okay. But it's two in the morning. There's no public transport and we don't drive."

Looking up from her phone as her mum and dad failed to answer her call either, she said, "We can hitch. There's people whizzing past at all hours. Goodness knows where they're going. We just need a lorry driver catching the Fishguard ferry to Ireland and we'll be there in no time. And what lorry driver wouldn't want to give us a lift?"

"They'd want to give you a lift, but thanks for including me."

"Don't you want to come? Of course, why would you?"

"That's not what I meant. Never mind. I'm coming. There's no way I'm letting you thumb a lift on your own."

"Right. Thanks. Let's go."

Throwing some clothes in a duffle bag, they stopped off at Amy's flat and she did the same. It seemed a foolish plan, but a taxi outside a nightclub took them to the motorway services, and from there a lorry heading west seemed likely.

"Are you sure you're doing the right thing, Becca? They're probably just asleep and your sister will want to meet you at the airport."

"Dad can drive."

"What? Hitch all the way to Fishguard to get driven straight back?"

"Well, we'll find out what time Sophie's flight home is and then go. And we can sleep on the way. You don't have to come if you don't want."

"And what? Spend the night here? I'm coming. I was just checking you were sure."

"Bit late now. Hey, excuse me…"

The Nolan's Transport Lorry had an address in Dublin. "See, Amy I told you."

"What if he's staying here overnight? They're not allowed to drive over a certain amount of hours."

"I know that. Excuse me," she called out again.

"Now, what can I do for you two ladies at dis time o' night?"

"I was really banking on you giving us a lift to Fishguard. I saw your Irish address and thought you might be catching the ferry."

"What if I just got off the ferry? You didn't tink o' dat, now dija?"

"Well? Have you?"

"No. I'm on my way to catch it at five o'clock in da mornin'. Da ting is, tis the one in Pembroke Dock, not Fishguard. But you're more than welcome to tag along. I'd love the company, so I would."

"Thanks so much. I'm Becca and this is Amy."

"Pleased to meet you. Shay. Now climb aboard, you just caught me."

Landmarks were eaten up and spat out at reassuring rapidity: Bridgend, Port Talbot with the steelworks spitting and fizzing beside the great lake and behind that the Bristol Channel. Past Swansea and Llanelli they were soon heading to a roundabout and leaving the motorway.

Sitting in silence for mile upon mile, as the lorry pulled into the services, he asked, "Want anything, ladies? Chocolate? Sweeties or crisps or a drink? Or do you need the ladies room at all?"

"I guess we should squeeze something out." Becca and Amy clambered back down the steps and headed for the toilets at the back of the shop that served late night visitors to the end-of-motorway-services.

"That was a stroke of luck. How did you know we'd find an Irish lorry driver?"

"I didn't. It was just lucky."

Drying their hands in the gentle waft of cold air, both girls opted for wiping the residue on their clothes.

"Hey! Isn't that our lorry?"

A Nolan's artic pulled out and as it swung around, Shay was unmistakable in the drivers seat. Rushing outside, they watched in disbelief as he drove through the exit and disappeared out of sight.

"Why did he do that?"

Becca shrugged.

Stones on the tarmac crunched underfoot. "You two must be Becca and Amy, am I right?"

Turning, the owner of the voice was smiling at them. "I'm going to Fishguard. Shay tells me you're headed that way."

"Yes. That's right. Are you offering us a lift?"

"Well, I'd have to be cruel not to now, wouldn't I? Of course. You're welcome."

Strolling beside their new driver towards a bank of lorries, Amy commented, "You're not Irish are you?"

The driver shook his head. "No. Norwegian. Pol, at your service."

Once inside the lorry which was bigger and plusher than their transport so far, Pol asked, "Why are you on your way from the capital to dead-end Fishguard at this time of night? Shouldn't you be out partying?"

"My sister has just been found. She was missing after that plane crash in Australia and I need to tell my parents."

"Wow! That's lucky. It's a real bad crash. You don't expect it from a big airline, do you? It goes to show you never know when the hand of fate might intervene in your life."

Or the dream of Becca Tate, Becca sucked in a sharp breath.

"Couldn't you phone them instead of travelling all this way?"

"No answer. But they need to know."

"Yes. I have daughters, about your age and I cannot bear to think how distraught I would be if I did not know where they were. You are a good daughter."

Becca nodded. What else could she add?

The lorry crawled up hills, but they passed familiar towns quick enough and when they reached Pembrokeshire's county town of Haverfordwest, Becca knew they were nearly there.

Dawn began coaxing the sun from hiding, and it raised a sleepy eyebrow to the morning. Shadows cast on mountains as the ocean glistened in the first light made the land look caught mid-yawn. 'You're early. I'm not quite ready for you yet,' it beseeched, but Becca disagreed. This was a beautiful part of the day.

So many charming photos could be hers if only she'd charged and brought her camera. But she had no time for interruption.

As the long vehicle dropped into the valley into Fishguard, Pol asked them where they needed to go.

"Stop at the little shop just here. We can walk up the hill from there."

"Okay, ladies. Your folks will be so happy you came. Good luck."

They thanked him in unison and waved as he drove on to the ferry terminal half a mile away, the dawn sunshine enough to light their way up the hill. "It's not much further now, Amy," Becca assured as they rounded the corner to a small estate of similar houses.

The Tate household stood in sombre blackness. Ringing the doorbell, despite hearing it in the background, and pressing over and over, the door remained resolutely shut.

"Are they deep sleepers?"

Becca shook her head, then bent down and retrieved a key from under a gnome. "Come on." Stepping inside, the silence echoed.

"Have they gone somewhere; do you think? Maybe Sophie got through and they're already on their way to Cardiff?"

"The car's in the drive. Wait here."

Becca padded up the staircase, heart pounding louder with every step. Treading down the landing, reaching her mum and dad's bedroom, she gripped the handle. Her hand shook as she turned it and pushed open the door. The latch loose, it swung free.

On the bed, motionless, lay her mother; beside her, a space where her dad should have been.

Hand shaking, she reached across and patted her mum's arm. "Mum? Mum, wake up. Patting harder and harder her mum didn't move.

The screaming was loud enough to hurt Amy's ears from the hallway. Racing up the stairs, she mis-stepped the last one and landed in a heap on the landing. Seeing light from one of the doors, she knew that must have been where the scream had come from so she ran past three other doors and burst in.

Silhouetted in the light of the en-suite bathroom, a man Amy presumed to be Becca's dad tugged a towel around his nether-regions. "What's the matter, Becca? What's happened?"

Becca stood up. "Nothing. I couldn't wake Mum, and then my dad opened the bathroom and we were shocked to see one-another."

"Why you're surprised I was in my own bedroom at whatever bloody time it is, I can't imagine."

Becca laughed. "He's given my mum sleeping pills and I panicked when I couldn't wake her."

"Of course," Amy's eyes bulged.

"And you are...?"

"This is my friend, Amy."

"Hi. Yes, Becca. Your mum's not slept since Sophie went missing and I was worried about her. You look exhausted. Do you want to get some shut-eye?"

"No!" Becca cried. "Aren't you going to ask me why I'm here? Sophie phoned. She's fine and flying home tomorrow."

Rob flopped onto the edge of the bed. "Oh, Becca, that's wonderful news."

Donna's psyche jabbed into her artificial chemical slumber and she opened her eyes and her mouth. "What's happening?"

"Great news darling! Fantastic news. Sophie phoned. They're all okay!"

Becca winced.

"They are all okay, aren't they, sweetheart?"

"Oh no. Not Lorraine? Not the girls?"

"Uncle Clive died on the plane. It's why they had to land in Vietnam, and why Sophie hadn't phoned. No service, and she didn't even know about the crash!"

"Clive? Dead?" Tears of grief combined with relief as she cried, "Poor Lorraine."

"Sounds like they all would have died if it wasn't for him. The lord sure does move in mysterious ways," Rob whistled.

"When's your sister's flight home?"

"I don't know. I guess she'll phone."

"Did she not want to travel up with you, Becca?" Donna asked.

"She did, but we couldn't get hold of you and I, er, I knew you'd want to be told as soon as possible."

Donna shot Rob a stern look. "Thank you. You're a very lovely daughter and big sister. Oh, who's this?"

"This is Amy."

Amy smiled again, awkward cheeks flushing.

"Hi, Amy. I'm mortified you should meet me in my nightie, half asleep, but I am pleased to meet you. Thank you for keeping Becca company. How did you get here?"

The girls glanced at one-another and Amy nodded in confirmation when Becca lied, "A friend was catching the ferry and we tagged along."

"Oh, that was lucky."

"Yeah," they both smiled.

"Well," Rob clapped his hands together. "I may as well make a pot of tea. Do you want me to bring yours up?" They agreed that after the sedatives, Donna might be better staying upstairs so the others left her in peace and headed for the kitchen.

Conversation over late night tea flowed easily with the pair able to fill gaps with amusing university idiosyncrasy anecdotes sparing Becca the need to confess about her dreams.

She had already decided what her plan would be. No more family would be sacrificed to her subconscious whim. She had to take control; stay awake and sleep for brief moments of her own choosing. Then she'd find out once and for all what she was capable of so she could take whatever action necessary to keep them all safe. Forever.

Chapter Twenty-eight

I t was over breakfast Sophie phoned again. "The flight's due into Cardiff at four o'clock. Will you meet me? We can go and see Mum and Dad then. Have you told them?"

"Uh-huh. I'm sitting with them right now. Got a lift last night so we'll all meet you at the airport."

"And, Uncle Clive?"

"Yes. I gave them the bad news, too. Mum's cut up for Lorraine mainly. She only knew Clive when I was a baby and hadn't seen him for years."

"Yes, sweetie," she called so Sophie could hear. "Poor Lorraine and the girls."

"But you're safe. That's the main thing. Sometimes the worst things can be a blessing. Clive saved the lives of his family by passing when he did," Rob nodded to his own point again.

"Can't wait to see you."

"Love you, Sophie. See you at four."

"Get some rest before we go, cariad," Rob scrutinised his daughter. "You look shattered.

Becca smiled. "I'll try. I might be a bit too excited about seeing my sister again though."

Grabbing Amy's hand, she disappeared into the conservatory.

"You must be feeling better if you're going to sleep."

"I'm not. No chance. Not until Sophie is safely home. I just didn't want them worrying."

"Okay. So what will we do?"

Standing, Becca pushed open the back door. "We'll go for a walk. You can stay and rest if you want."

"No. I'll come. We don't want you falling asleep leaning against a tree and blaming me if... Well, do we? No. I'm coming. I bet it looks better in the daylight."

Skirting out of the back gate and round the house, they were soon at the road and trekking towards the secret valley.

"Wow. You can see the sea so clearly from up here! I didn't know what it was like here and it's really beautiful. I can't imagine why your sister wanted to leave anyway."

"Adventure."

"Well, I bet she's had enough of that now."

"I bloody hope so."

Straining against the steepness of their descent, they rounded the corner, the tree that killed her cousin now wore its own scars in memory of her suffering. Becca gulped. If seeing what she'd done didn't keep her awake, nothing would.

"Come on! We'll be late for Sophie!"

Becca and Amy scurried back into the house and then out again to jump into the revving car.

They travelled in silence for minutes before Donna cleared her throat. Glancing in the rear-view mirror from the passenger seat, her moist eyes met Becca's. "She will be okay, won't she, Becca? I mean, you haven't had another nightmare have you?"

Being believed twisted the knife. There was nothing else to think other than she was responsible, but now wasn't the time to dwell on that. She'd know for certain soon. Today she could rejoice that despite hundreds of others suffering devastating loss, including her own aunt and cousins, she and her mum and dad were lucky.

"You okay?" Amy reached across and clutched her friend's hand. Becca had no words that would fit her jagged throat so said nothing. "Only, you've been pinching your leg pretty hard." Becca looked down. Material screwed into a gnarled ball between her fingers contained flesh within its folds and now aware, Becca felt the pain. Brushing at her thigh, she opted for chewing her nails.

Leaning to her ear, Amy hissed, "Are you sure you haven't had another dream? You seem tense."

"How? I haven't slept, have I."

Amy tilted her head from side to side. "Good. If you're sure."

Becca closed her eyes; Roman blinds giving her privacy from those so keen to pry into her mind. As the car sped south and east, the roads grew wider until they reached the eight lanes of the M4 motorway. *Barry Island/Cardiff Airport* directed the sign as Becca's eyes allowed in a sliver of light for the first time in an hour. Good. Soon she'd see her sister. They irritated one-another; they always had, but she'd never want to be without her.

Flights arrivals and departures displayed on illuminated boards around the terminal. The flight from Tan Son Nhat International, Vietnam was expected on time.

Sitting around a small table with exorbitantly priced soft drinks, they stared at the board. As the announcement changed from *Arriving* to *Landed* they breathed a collective sigh.

Staring at the announcement notices was soon replaced with scrutinising the arrivals gate. There were so many young girls who irritatingly were not Sophie they wondered why she hadn't been one of the first.

After the throng of travellers came isolated groups looking more business-like, strolling through like they did this every day.

Then, nothing.

No-one came through the gate. Eyes turned to Becca, but before the interrogation could recommence, Rob nudged his wife. "Look!"

Hugging one-another, Kate and Liz's gaunt faces mirrored their mother's. Beside them, a sorrowful yet grateful-to-be-alive glow to her cheeks, walked Sophie.

Running over to them, Sophie was clutched in a group embrace before, out of duty, attention turned to the others.

"Lorraine, I can't believe it."

"But him, you know, well... It saved your lives," Rob piped up yet again, his notion seemingly still under-appreciated.

Lorraine nodded and smiled at the brother-in-law she scarcely saw who despite his tactless remark seemed to, from the softening of her features, have hit the mark of comfort. "I know. I think he did it to save us. My angel."

The sisters clung tighter whilst Becca held onto Sophie. On the outskirts, fiddling with her hem, Amy pressed a line smile to her lips and looked away.

"I didn't expect you were coming back to Wales."

"Well, Clive always said he wanted to be laid to rest here." Lorraine paused to swallow and dab at her eyes. "He was born in Haverfordwest and he said he wanted to be scattered at the top of the Preseli's so he could always see where he grew up... Sorry," she clutched a tissue to her mouth, her shoulders trembling.

The Tates and Amy shared a glance. That meant Clive was here too.

Reading their collective minds, Lorraine composed herself enough to say, "He's in the hold."

Wide-eyed, they imagined for one horrific moment, his coffin tracking around the baggage conveyer for them to collect.

"The funeral directors will come and take him," she sniffed. "The service is planned for next week."

How many more were being shipped around the world to their country-of-origin from the BA 555 disaster? Becca's knees buckled and she fell to the floor.

"Oh, my goodness. Becca!"

Responding quickly to pats on her face, Becca flopped in their arms as Rob and Sophie lifted her to a chair. Staring up at them, she smiled. "I'm just tired I think... Haven't... slept..."

"Are you coming back to Fishguard with us?"

Becca shook her head which roused her brain cells enough to answer. "I can't. I've got some important stuff to finish off here. But I'll be home the week after for Easter, and hopefully I will feel a lot less stressed by then."

Donna fought the urge to argue, a happier Becca would be good, and at least she was safe. Both her girls were safe. "I don't know how we'll all fit in the car to give you a lift. I suppose you could sit on your cousin's lap. There's scarcely anything of you. And it's only a few miles."

"Oh, no thanks. If Auntie Lorraine, Liz and Kate are going with you, then Amy and I can sort something out, I'm sure."

"No, Becca. You just fainted."

"I'm tired and seeing my family got to me, that's all. I'll take it easy here, make sure I eat from all this choice," she wafted an arm, "And then go to sleep."

Donna weighed it up. Becca seemed fine now. She'd probably get food and rest quicker if she stayed here than if she fought the lunchtime traffic. "Well, we'll see you next week, then, I guess."

"Okay." Giving Sophie one more huge squeeze, she stroked her hair. "See you soon, you."

More gentle hugs came from the rest of the family as they prepared to depart. Watching them walk away; the broken and the free, the lump in Becca's throat stopped her calling out after them and she was glad. She had a mission.

"How are we going to get back?" Amy raised her eyebrows.

"There must be so many buses to the city centre from here. Time to use the might of the student card discount."

"We could go to the island. Get an ice-cream."

"No. I really do need to get back and sleep." Sleep was the last thing she would do, but she didn't want anything to interfere with her plan. "But I could murder a sandwich or something first."

"Where from?"

Seeing a huge queue at *Pret A Manger*, Becca nodded towards it. "Could you grab me something while I wait here?"

Amy shuffled from foot to foot. "Okay. What do you want?"

"Just anything in a baguette. But freshly prepared. I don't want one that's been sitting around."

Amy rose and shuffled to the back of the queue. Becca waved from across the food court and rummaged in her bag. When Amy stood close enough to the menu to begin making choices, Becca got up and ambled towards the toilets catching Amy's nervous eye as she tried to mouth sandwich fillings at a distance. Becca mimed back, 'Whatever,' and shrugged, disappearing into the wash rooms.

Peeping out, sure Amy was occupied ordering their food, Becca darted into the crowd. Skirting around the room, weaving in and out of the crowd, when she reached the doors, she busied through. Several buses lined up, two of which declared *City Centre* to be their destination. Hopping on the closest one, Becca showed her student ID, paid and slunk into a seat.

Shuffling down, she hid her face with her hands, but she needn't have worried. The bus revved and pulled away before Amy had even paid. How long would she wait for her to return from the toilet? Reddening, she felt mean, and she really could do with food, but something else was more important.

As the bus whizzed on winding roads from the airport to the city, she hoped she was doing the right thing. The fact she'd ditched her new friend in case she stopped her made her wonder, but no-one understood what she was going through. She had to know. How could she go on otherwise?

Buildings rose higher and higher until the streets were dominated by high rise. When it stopped at the student flats, Becca didn't get out. She didn't go to the door stagger inside and slump on the bed for much needed rest. She stayed on the bus to the railway station and that's where she alighted. The bank wasn't far from here.

Of course, he might not be there. Homeless meant you went where you wanted. She was putting some faith in fate. She didn't know what she'd do if he wasn't there, but if she saw him, perched in the doorway as before? Well, that would definitely be a sign.

As she retraced her steps, her heart quickened. What she was about to suggest questioned every ethical bone in her body but she couldn't think of another way.

She'd tried Amy's suggestion and it hadn't worked, and in many ways, she hoped this wouldn't work either. Trying to force a dream about murderers she'd never met brought nothing and perhaps that was why. She hadn't met them. Everyone else who had been taken in her nightmares, she had. The hundreds of victims from the plane crash were the exception, but the person in her sights had been someone she knew, she just got the method wrong and everyone else suffered.

People who she hated easily; vile dregs of humanity who preyed upon the vulnerable, she could do nothing about. But her uncle who moderately offended her couldn't escape.

She knew it sounded crazy, that's why she had to be sure once and for all. Find the homeless man who said he wanted to die... And kill him.

Chapter Twenty-nine

Heart pounding, she rounded the corner. Where was he? But she should have been more patient because there on the street in front of the bank he crouched. He may only use the shelter of the doorway in the chill of night

She had rehearsed in her head a hundred times what she might say, carefully broaching the subject of his serious intent and introducing him to her conceivable capabilities.

Instead, when she approached, she would later suppose that hunger, tiredness and stress conspired a different approach and she blurted, "You're still here. You told me you wanted to die!"

Glaring, he let his scowl fall and bowed his head once more. Becca sat beside him. "Sorry. Only, if you were serious, I might have a proposition for you."

The man didn't move.

"I can understand you ignoring me so I'll just tell you my plan and you tell me if it's something you'd be interested in." Becca took a deep breath. "I have a peculiar supernatural ability. The thing is... I could dream you to death. I know that makes absolutely no sense, but every time I fall asleep, I dream of someone dying and when I wake, it's manifested. I've lost my gran and my cousin and my uncle and I nearly lost my little sister, and along the way there have been so many casualties I can't count them. I haven't slept for days and I thought if I could dream about someone who wants to die I'll be able to rest knowing I'm doing a good thing."

"Suicide is a good thing, is it? Because if I let you kill me, that's what it is."

"I suppose. And, no. I think it's a terrible, awful waste of life. But if you were going to do it anyway, I thought... Oh, it's coming out all wrong. Out loud, it sounds crazy and I'm sure I couldn't bring myself to do it anyway."

"I want you to."

Becca gasped. "Really? You were serious?"

"Yes. And as I told you before, I'm scared. The idea of someone doing it for me seems an easy way out."

"So you believe me?"

"I don't know, I want to. I want to trust you're the angel of death come for me, and that I've OD'd. And I'm pretty sure I'm hallucinating and that's what's happening, but it doesn't matter; if you can get me out of this shit hell of a life, then I don't care who you are."

"You're high now then? Because I need to be sure you're making a choice you understand."

"I'm never high; fucked up, but not high. I used to get high. Now all I ever do is peep my head above the parapet and wait to be shot down again."

"You're quite poetic. I didn't expect that. I suppose you haven't always been homeless."

The man gritted his jaw. "No."

"So what did you do before?"

"I'll tell you, and when I do, you'll know I'm serious about wanting to die."

Becca brought her knees up to her chest and listened.

"I used to be happy. I've been miserable too, you know life. Stressed about school, finding a job, girls but all that changes. You're too young to get it, but one day you'll meet *the one* and all those other worries disappear. For a while at least. They get replaced by others: Am I good enough? Can I pay the bills? That sort of thing."

"Doesn't sound so bad. But I guess the answer was no, or you wouldn't be here."

"Oh, I paid the bills. We had everything. Everything." Punching the pavement, striking again and again, the man stopped as tears streamed down his cheeks. "And now I have nothing."

"What happened?"

Lifting his fist to punch the ground again, instead, he flattened his palm and dragged it over his face. "I destroyed everything I ever loved. Literally. I haven't talked about this with anyone so you'd better be a bloody hallucination and you better kill me like you promised."

"I didn't promise. Not until I've heard your story."

"Oh, you'll promise. I guarantee it." Shuffling where he sat released fetid urine and alcohol

273

stench and Becca pulled a face. "I met her in my late twenties. Virtually given up. Thought I should settle before it was too late. I was already losing my hair.

"I had a good job in advertising and had money which I thought might make me a worthwhile prospect, you know, despite my lack of prowess."

If he was fishing for complements, he'd picked the wrong pond with Becca. "Go on," she sighed.

"I don't think that's why Beth fell for me, in fact I'm certain it wasn't, but it gave me the confidence to approach the most beautiful goddess of a woman I'd ever seen.

"She had a son, Jacob, who was two. She'd dumped the father before he was even born. It didn't seem ideal, but it was to me. Jacob called me 'Daddy' very quickly and then along came Annabel. I tried to love both the children the same, but I couldn't help myself. I adored my little princess."

Rocking back and forth, the man stayed silent for over a minute. Then, at last, voice croaking, he spoke again. "Beth had asked me to do it. One simple job and she asked me and I didn't do it. Not only that, I lied about doing it. All so I could go fucking fishing!" Balling his hands into fists, he hit his legs. "Fucking fishing."

"What didn't you do?" Becca leaned towards him hoping the words would arc across the gap.

"She said they'd all had headaches and I said it was a bug. 'Why haven't you had it then?' she'd pointed out. Because I'm stronger, I don't get ill. I didn't say that but I thought it. I certainly didn't believe there was anything wrong with the boiler, I'd just had it serviced.

"But I didn't consider it might have become damaged since. I even pointed out how the carbon-monoxide detectors would have picked up on a problem, and Beth said she thought they weren't working; that maybe they'd been turned off when they serviced the boiler and not put back on again, or not checked. I'd argued but promised to look into it.

"Her headaches continued and I really thought it was stress. Jacob and Annie had been playing her up. It wasn't the best of times. I was working late and I felt I needed to go fishing with my friends to get relief from the week.

So when Beth made me promise to check the alarms with a circuit-tester and reminded me again as I was about to leave, I had a choice: stop and take fifteen minutes to do what she asked, or lie. I lied and told her I'd done it the day before. I would have promised too, but saying I had was enough for Beth. That's because she didn't know what a worthless selfish piece of crap I am.

"Two days later, I came home pissed off no-one was up in the middle of the afternoon. Taking their bug a bit seriously, I thought, and I hate people pitying themselves. Ironic now.

"I stormed up the stairs. I mean, I'd caught four carp and a pike and driven home from our expedition and my wife hadn't even struggled out of bed and got the kids up. I actually had those thoughts. Stupid, so stupid.

"As soon as I saw her; saw the colour of her, a babe in each of her arms equally green, I knew I'd killed them. My beautiful girls and my little boy. I'd murdered them with my lies." He punched himself hard in the face. "And now I don't even have the guts to do the decent thing. If I kill myself and go to hell, I might never see my beautiful angels again. If you do it, maybe I'll go to heaven. No. Who am I kidding? I'm going to the burning mouth of hell. And it's what I deserve."

"You made a mistake. We all do. I've left my friend at the airport. I ducked into the toilet and she probably thinks I'm still there. If she gets hit by an airport bus, I'm going to feel responsible. What you did was terrible. Of course you shouldn't have lied to your wife, but you couldn't know what would happen."

"That's not the point. If I'd told the truth, she would have insisted I check, or even left the house until I did. Not doing it was bad. Lying about it was unforgivable. Every day I wish I hadn't. But I can't turn back time. All I can do is receive my punishment. It won't make me feel better, but it's what I deserve."

Becca wasn't sure deserve was the right word, but she understood why he wanted out. Struggling with her own guilt, the same thoughts had assailed her. Leaning forward, Becca spoke rapidly before she could change her mind. "Okay. I'll do it. Can you tell me your name?"

"Greg. Greg Davies."

"Okay, Greg Davies. I'll do it. I'll dream of you tonight. Goodbye. I don't suppose I'll see you ever again." Cheeks puckering, Becca offered a hand to shake.

Taking it, he gripped it as he stared into Becca's eyes. "Don't let me down. You've made me talk and brought it all screaming to my mind so you better do what you promised."

As she walked away, Becca worried for the first time that her dream wouldn't do what she expected. Greg Davies had suffered enough.

Chapter Thirty

The feeling of being wide awake Greg's terrible tale had given left her with each step. With a pricking heart, she wondered about Amy. She'd understand, probably, but she knew she'd been unkind. She might even have supported her, but she hadn't been brave enough to risk it.

And she was sure now. There was no coming back from what Greg had gone through. Losing your family was one thing, being responsible was another altogether. The guilt he must live through every day; the *'What ifs?'*

Her own guilt rested on the results of her experiment. And then she would know what she had to do.

Struggling up the last steps of the hill back to her apartment, she paused and slapped her cheeks. "Don't waste this, Becca," she ordered. "Get home, focus on Greg and then you can go to sleep."

Her inner self listened to her outer voice and perked her up enough to keep going and not collapse unconscious in the street. As she reached home, she was pleased there was no sign of Amy. A row was inescapable, but she didn't want that disruption now.

Key in the door, she shuffled inside. Turning her nose towards an offensive odour, she realised it was her. She smelled. She'd been in the same clothes for over a day and a night, but nothing could be less important to her. Despite the early hour, she pulled back the covers, squeezed between the sheets and closed her eyes.

Picturing Greg was easy. Reflecting, he'd never left her thoughts since she'd met him. This was fate. The anger borne on their first meeting at his selfishness to consider wanting to die when life was so precious, now replaced with an understanding. What did he have to live for?

So much rested on the results of tonight's dream that, despite exhaustion, she was shocked to be struggling to fall asleep.

Sitting up, she clenched her fists but she knew from many sleepless nights that sleep couldn't be fought. It had to be wooed, romanced into compliance. With a sigh, she got out of bed and ripping the sheets off, she balled the pillow cases and the duvet cover with them and added them to her laundry pile. Yanking open the draw under her bed, she selected another set still in its packaging and proceeded to deftly make up the bed. It looked more inviting than the crumpled mess she'd laid in minutes before.

A glance at the time and she was sure Domino's would be open. Her stomach had given up sending messages, so often had they been ignored, but she was listening now. Confirming an individual meat-feast with extra olives and

279

anchovies, and soft drinks, she declined the offer of half-price cookie dough. She worked out she had twenty minutes to shower.

Emerging from the hot steam, she wasn't sure if she didn't feel even more alert; like she'd gone past sleep. All the times in the last month she'd desperately wanted to stay awake, and now this. She shook her head.

Something about the rap on the door alerted her. Padding softly she reached it and peeped through the spyhole she was now extremely grateful to Cardiff University for providing. She would pretend not to be in.

Knock, knock! Louder this time.

"Becca. I know you're in there."

But, how could she? And even if she had worked out she'd been abandoned at the airport and rushed back and seen her come home, she couldn't be sure she wasn't asleep, or in the shower.

She heard him before she saw his face, warped by the fish-eye lens. Shit! What lousy timing.

"There's no-one home, apparently," Amy's muffled sneer reached her as the delivery guy raised his hand to knock on the door.

Grabbing the handle, she'd have to face her friend now. Damn! The door creaked open.

"Domino's delivery for Becca Tate?"

"Thank you," she said, reaching out to take the boxes and bottle.

Amy glared, eyes moist, lips trembling. "Why? Why, Becca? Haven't I been a good friend to you?"

"Come in. I'll try to explain." But she didn't want her in. She'd explain tomorrow. Now she had an ever more difficult date with her bed and her dreams to keep.

"No. You enjoy your pizza. I know when I'm not wanted."

"Sorry. Look. Come inside and I'll explain."

"Go to hell!"

As Amy stormed down the hallway, Becca felt a mixture of shame and relief. If she was a true friend, and it was too early to tell, then she'd understand. If not, best to find out. She had too much going on to worry about other people's feelings.

Fully awake now, pizza tasted like heaven. Guilt pricked as she didn't manage to eat all of it. Maybe it could be a peace-offering. Or perhaps it would be breakfast.

Glugging the diet cola, she wiped her mouth and stowed the pizza box under the bed. Deciding she needed to wash her face and hands again before getting into her clean sheets, she popped back into the bathroom, squeezing out a wee so the soft drink wouldn't wake her.

Clean, sated and sleepy, she got back into bed. "Greg, Greg, Greg," she said his name over and over. She pictured his dishevelled, defeated body slumped in the doorway of the bank and tried to imagine him coming home to discover his devastation. She had no notion of how he would die, but she could let her dreams decide that.

Keeping the images of him and a wife and children dead under covers, over and over she repeated his name until 'Greg' stopped at Gr...' and she fell unconscious.

Her eyes pinged open. What was the time? She felt wired, refreshed, like she'd had the best night's sleep ever. Eight o'clock. Which meant she had slept for fifteen hours. No wonder she felt good.

Hauling the pizza from under the bed, she ripped a slice off and bit into it. Not as nice cold, but still good. With a frown, she tried to remember her dreams but turning her head this way and that, and squinting into different corners of the room, she couldn't recall a thing. Was this good news? Was it all in her imagination after all?

A walk into the city centre would tell her. If Greg sat large as life outside the bank, she was blameless for it all, wasn't she? She would scour her brain for explanations for the other dreams, but at least she could be confident they were precognitions, nothing more.

Unless she just couldn't bring herself to do it. The only other times she'd tried deliberately to dream someone to death, it had failed and she'd thought it was because she hadn't met them. But it might be something else. Her fear, channelling through to the universe and creating what she dreaded most.

But what if she hadn't failed? What if prisoners had died but it didn't make the news? A homeless man dying in the city was unlikely to be deemed newsworthy either.

Flipping open her now fully-charged lap top, guilt that it was Amy who had looked after her was swept away with her research. It didn't take long to find Wayne Bridges. Along with a description of his crimes, Google confirmed he was serving his time and mentioned nothing of him dying in prison. Was it because she'd shown ambivalence? That killing him was too good for him? It couldn't be, because she harboured no doubt about not killing her cousin and uncle and hundreds of other innocent people, but that still happened.

Maybe she'd been too tired. With the good sleep she had last night, she could get through some college work and then try again tonight. She noticed a reluctance to go out with her camera and knew she was unwilling to find something had happened to Greg Davies in the night. Giving herself a break, she opted to edit the photos she'd already taken. Then she could be sure what she needed to complete the project.

Mindlessly scrolling through hundreds of photographs from her camera's memory stick, she picked her favourites and then begun tinkering with them to make them even better.

Her preferences were all the ones with people's faces. The expressions she managed to capture were works of art, even if she did say so herself. Men sitting outside café's; an old couple on a park bench. If she could track them down, they'd all be delighted to pay for such gifted portraiture.

And then the ones from a couple of weeks ago. The homeless man she now knew as Greg juxtaposed on the steps of a mighty financial institution.

Most shots his face wasn't visible. Her focus had been on his possessions wondering what made some so precious you would keep them with you even though you had no home. The food wrappers were obvious. And the jumper and bottle of water. But that silver frame. Surely that had to have a photo of his wife and children. Why hadn't he shown it to her? And what was that? Zooming in three hundred percent, grateful for her camera's superior definition, it was a small trophy. What was that for? Fishing? It couldn't be. Losing his family to carbon-monoxide poisoning because he'd lied and gone fishing and treasuring an angling trophy?

Perhaps it was a punishment. He might stare at the photo and the cup, from one to the other, stirring up the raw emotion, helping it fester and rot so he could feel just as bad as he deserved to. Clicking print, confident her own photographic skills would provide the key, she would stare at this image before going to sleep and she would dream of Greg Davies and she would be successful. She could feel it.

Chapter Thirty-one

Hundreds of photo edits later, Becca ate the last of the pizza and declared herself tired enough for bed. Staring at the picture of Greg and the zoomed in image of his silver frame and trophy, she sipped at what was left of the diet cola until heading for the bathroom to put her pyjamas back on.

Hopping under her duvet, she surrounded herself with printouts of Greg Davies. Close-ups of his face, his unusual belongings, his hunched over body, letting her eyes fall on each one in turn.

Filling her senses with each photo until it etched in her mind, she took a deep breath and moved onto the next. Head falling back with fatigue, she kept on, staring, breathing, staring, breathing. Bringing her nodding head up for the last time, she fell into sleep confident her course was set fair to complete her mission.

Walking from her flat, her high heels echoing eerily in the night, the only sound. No cars, buses, nobody talking, just her shoes clippity-clopping along the cobblestone.

She knew where she was going and she smiled, her grin aching in her cheeks. Why was she happy? Because someone was about to die who actually wanted to? Wouldn't success send her into turmoil about all the other times?

Her heels clicked the pavement faster and faster, running at first, and then in a tapping frenzy. Legs buzzing as they moved so fast, the tapping stopped as she floated into the air.

Higher and higher, the city opening up beneath her: there was the colonial city hall and the museum she'd been to with Amy. There were the university buildings with the different colleges and campuses. And then the main street with its shops and cafés leading to arcades and malls.

Far below, the homeless community congregated. She couldn't make out individuals from so high up, but she saw the Midland Bank building and knew the figure in front of that must be Greg.

A scruffy man in torn clothes walked up to him and bent over. Arms waving, he beckoned more to come, but Becca couldn't hear what they said. One by one, and then groups, rushed over, crowding over Greg, huddling and wriggling.

Had he died already and they had just discovered his corpse? Or were they attacking him, kicking at him after a disagreement. Maybe he told them what he'd told her and they hadn't taken it well.

She couldn't see, and as the crowd dispersed, when the last one left, all she glimpsed was a figure lying on the ground. Dizzy, colour drained from her as she crashed back to the floor. With the presence of mind to brace for the impending collision with the pavement, she shrunk into a ball, face screwed in anticipated agony. As her head hit the floor, it wasn't hard as she expected, but instead her pillow cushioned her and she stared with pounding heart at her ceiling.

Tears streaming down her cheeks, she turned to look at the clock. Six in the morning. She'd never get back to sleep now. Should she go and check; see if her dream was real? She knew she had to, but she was too afraid. Turning onto her front, she pulled the pillow over her head and sobbed.

Pummelling the mattress either side of her face, slit eyes closed and her taut cheeks fell, pulling her mouth into a quivering arch. Why did she have to have this power? She'd never asked for it. But, maybe she didn't have any paranormal ability at all. When she found the courage to check, Greg might still be alive and well and she could help him in other ways.

She'd been selfish because she needed his permission to test her theory. But she knew, if he was dead, then she had done more than dream about him, she had virtually persuaded him that for him, ending it all was the only way out.

Struggling with mixed motivation, Becca threw on clothes scattered on her floor and ran out of the door, along the corridor and down the stairs, through the lower corridor and into the outside world.

"Please, God, let him be all right," she prayed as she jogged down the street. Lungs screaming, she rounded the corner. The bank was in sight.

Slowing to walking, Becca clutched a stich in her side. When she got closer, she gasped and sighed her relief. Greg was still there. It was all in her head. She was stressed and making weird stuff up, that was all.

But then Greg turned to face her and her world spun out of control once more.

The face staring suspiciously at her now was not Greg's, but instead, a girl about her own age. What tragedy had led her out here? Slight built with translucent skin. But neither that nor her piercing green eyes were the most striking thing about her appearance. Her most striking feature was that she wasn't Greg. There had to be an explanation. Her sanity depended on it.

As she rushed to her, the girl sat up ready to defend herself. "Where's Greg? He usually sits here. I saw him two nights ago so how come you're sleeping here?"

She shrugged and closed her eyes.

"Don't ignore me. Have you done something to him?"

"Hey, miss. Leave her alone."

Becca turned to three men walking towards her. "Where's Greg?"

"I don't know what you're talking about."

"Greg! He was here just two nights ago."

All three shrugged in unison. "You're making a scene. You need to leave us alone."

"What did you do to him? Did you find him dead? Did you kill him?"

One of the men lunged forwards and shoved Becca hard. Keeping her balance, she stood her ground. "You'd better watch yourself, saying shit like that. Ain't none of us killed no-one."

"But I saw..."

"Whatever you think you saw, you're wrong."

"That is well out of order," another in the group whined. As Becca's gaze fell to him, she gasped. The trophy was in front of his hotchpotch pile of stuff.

"That's Greg's!" In two steps she was there plucking it from the floor. "How did you get this?"

"You better put that back right now. I don't got much so I'm not going to let you take what little I do have."

"It's Greg's." Next to the man with the trophy, a girl sat. Poking from a bag was clearly the corner of a silver frame. And wasn't that Greg's coat on the guy sitting with her? "You've taken all his stuff. Where is he? What have you done with him?"

The three shared a smile and then in unison shrugged. They had a code and Becca had no hope of breaking it. They would never tell because they had nothing to lose.

And it didn't matter. It was just details. Whether Greg had died of natural causes, or an overdose, or if they'd beaten him for his belongings, she knew why it had happened. She'd made it happen. She was the killer,

289

anything or anyone else were merely playing their parts.

Blood drained from her head as she stumbled forward. Clutching at her face, she wanted to run, get away from herself, but there was nowhere to go. And tonight, she'd dream again and someone else would die; and the next night and the night after.

A bus sped past and at once she understood Greg's desire to end his life and his fear of doing so. For a split second, jumping in front of its speeding bulk seemed like the solution. If she'd been closer to the curb, she might have.

Hands shaking, feathered fingers drummed on her face as she hid from the rawness. She couldn't take any more. Death hung in the air and she smelt it. How many had died at her whim and how many more?

Dropping to her knees, sobs shook her body. "Help me, please! I can't do this anymore."

Her friend might know what to say. She was probably not talking to her, but she could tell her how sorry she was. At least it was somewhere to go; something to do; a different focus. Just having a plan, however small, could get her safely off the streets before she succumbed to something regrettable.

Head down, she bounded the pavement in long strides. She had to get indoors; she had to save herself from herself.

Plunging down the lever handle, the door creaked open and instead of heading all the way upstairs or to the lift, she ran to Amy's flat and knocked hard. "Amy! Amy, help me. I'm sorry I treated you badly but I really need you."

The door opened and Amy's puffy face peered out. Regarding her with slit eyes, she opened the door fully and waved her inside. Covering her yawn with a raggedy sleeve, Amy stared at the time. "Six fifty! What's happened?"

"I've killed someone else."

Amy slumped on the bed. "Really? Who was it this time? I suppose I should count my lucky stars it wasn't me; after yesterday."

"A homeless man called Greg. And, Amy. I did it deliberately."

Amy's mouth dropped and her eyes squeezed open, struggling against the morning light but wanting to take in everything.

"That's why I left you at the airport. I didn't always mean to do it, but I suddenly needed to. I worried you might stop me, and I had to finally understand. But now I do and I don't know what to do. I killed him. I deliberately killed him. I'm... I'm a murderer."

Amy frowned. "I don't know what to say. I can't believe it's true. I just can't."

"What! Then why did you give me those murderers to focus on? Why did you help keep me awake?"

"Because... Well, I have my moments, but mainly to help you. If you believed it, it was upsetting you and I just wanted you to feel okay. As your friend, I didn't think it mattered if I believed or understood, just that I tried to help."

Becca edged away. Her comrade lost to logic.

"And it did help. Those night's you dreamt of those scum, you didn't have any nightmares."

"But then I dreamt about the plane."

"If I'd just lost my gran and my cousin, and my sister—I don't have a sister—was going on a long flight, I'd probably have a nightmare about it crashing too. It's normal."

"And it's just coincidence that the plane did crash?"

"Exactly."

"No. You're wrong. But I can't make you understand."

"Like I said, I don't need to understand to be your friend. I can help you look into it. We can find out what's really going on so you can get help."

"You think I'm crazy."

"I think you're not making a lot of sense and some professional help might be a good idea."

Becca turned and bolted for the door.

"Becca! Come back. Let me help you!"

What could she do? Not sleep, that was the only certainty. What had her research suggested? Do the opposite of good sleep hygiene. Do non-sleep promoting activities before bed. Use her bedroom for anything other than sleeping. Exercise. Drink coffee, the list went on. Becca vowed to disobey every good sleep rule. And set alarms. One every hour so she'd never reach REM sleep and never dream again. What was the alternative?

Walking the street, she had no notion of where she was going. Each car and bus that passed, she had the same thought, 'I should end it all before someone else dies.'

Heart racing, Becca edged away from the road, weaving in and out of people who were grabbing their morning papers, or cleaning windows before the rush of the day, or environment-conscious commuters walking to work.

"Are you okay, miss? Has something happened? Do you want me to call someone? An ambulance? The police?"

Becca stared at the man poised with his hands up, resting on the crank handle as he opened the canopy to his shop.

The police. She'd killed hundreds of people, of course she should go to the police. They wouldn't believe her, but they could keep her safe. They could get her help.

Spinning on the spot, she struggled to recall the direction of the police station. It wasn't far. Just up past the trains. Scurrying away, Becca breathed hard. She was safe for now with her new purpose.

"Miss! Hey, miss, come back. Are you okay?!"

On she walked, breathing hard, the large grey building was soon in sight. With each step it grew until she reached the door. Panting, Becca slumped inside and collapsed against the desk.

"Are you okay? You look terrible."

Forcing up her gaze, she hissed, "I want to confess."

"Confess what?"

"I've killed people. Lots of people."

The lady behind the desk stiffened and Becca heard the click as doors locked around her.

"Wait there, I'll get someone."

Chapter Thirty-two

You've created quite the charge sheet, haven't you?" Dr Fenton's smile crinkles his lips. Her shocking revelation given details and context falls back into his areas of his expertise. He had heard a lot of craziness from a lot of patients in his time, and he is sure he understands Becca's condition perfectly. The trickier part is to get her to understand it too.

"Carrying the burden of all these people dying, I wouldn't want to do it. I think you're coping incredibly well. Now, it's been a very rough few weeks and it would turn the sanest of individuals round the bend," his eyes cross and he continues with a grin. "So, I don't want you to worry. You're not crazy. In my humble opinion." His palm rests on his chest and Becca is sure he believes his opinion is anything but humble.

"Even all this talk of Indian goddesses of death. I think you're more at risk of sickle cell anaemia than acquiring supernatural abilities to kill people in your sleep!" He chuckles at his own expertise. "Now, first of all, remember: you've lived twenty-one years *not* imagining you kill people in your sleep, and only a few weeks of this torment. What does that tell you?"

"That I've come of age?"

"Interesting," he nods, "I was suggesting more that it meant it wasn't likely, but I can see what we're going to need to do here. I think it will be helpful to examine each episode individually. Looking at them as a whole is a little overwhelming, and I want to make sure I'm understanding you. Does that make sense? Good," he says without confirmation from his patient. "So, your gran, I think we've covered that enough. And then there was..."

"My cousin, Mel."

"Crashed her car after everyone knew she was drinking. You say she even turned up late and proceeded to get drunk at your grandmother's funeral?" Becca nods, even though it isn't needed. "Well, the timing was unfortunate, but knowing the area as you do, what with growing-up there, you dreamt something that was pretty likely, and under normal circumstances would have provoked merely mild interest."

"Mild interest? I dreamt the exact circumstances at the exact time my cousin crashed her Porsche into a tree and died?"

"Okay, it is unusual. Not the event so much, but the fact you dreamt it. But I'll talk to you about that in a moment. I know a thing or two about dreams. Okay, after your cousin, Mel..."

"What do you know about dreams?"

Annoyed to be diverted, the doctor sighs. "Just that what we remember of a dream can often be altered to fit what happens. Memory is fallible at the best of times, remembering a dream is very unreliable."

"How do you know?"

Tilting his head, he sighs again. "Well, there's actually quite a lot of research on the subject. Do you mind if we get back to our discussion? I do think it's important. Remind me of the next dream."

"The two girls at the party, but before them there was the taxi driver and the family on the train expecting a baby who I don't think I killed, but I'm not sure."

"Let's stick to the ones you are sure of. Not muddy the waters, so to speak. So, the two girls: the only odd thing there is that you'd met them both before. Other than that, perfectly normal. You were drunk, you were tired, you half-asleep/half-awake saw what was happening, and after what you'd already seen with your gran and cousin, it was a natural conclusion. I can see that. But if it was the only thing, it wouldn't be that remarkable, in fact I don't think you would have seen it in the same way at all."

Folding her arms, Becca snorts. "I knew you hadn't been listening."

"I have listened. My advice is for you to listen to my take on it. Afterwards, we can discuss it further and iron it all out."

Becca relaxes her shoulders and unfolds her arms. Sighing, she resolves to hear him out.

"Then there was that singer? Well that's easily explained by you reading about it on social media just before you fell asleep. I know you don't remember, but it really is most likely. Then you say you worried about your dad dying after he irritated you on the phone? So, you tried to dream about murderers so that if you killed them, they'd deserve it. Is that right?"

Nodding again, Becca sits quietly awaiting her turn to discredit his explanations.

"But you didn't kill any murderers, and you didn't kill your dad."

"Because I managed to stay awake, and then my focus was on the aeroplane."

"I sympathise, I really do. And plane crashes are rare so that if you have a dream about one crashing and then it does, attributing meaning is natural. It happens all the time. Not remembering all the other weird dreams that bear no relation to the waking world, when something happens we can connect, we do. It's human nature."

Smiling his simpering smile he carries on. "But you didn't get the details? You didn't know your uncle had already died on the plane. If you really were influencing things, wouldn't you know that? Hmm?"

Becca shrugs.

"But there's one other death you're not telling me about, isn't there?"

Becca scowls at the doctor and shakes her head.

"I've read your files. I thought I best get up to speed when the police asked me to come in, so you might as well tell me."

Eyes fixed to the floor, Becca picks at the skin of her knee visible through a rip in her leggings.

"Come on, Becca. Who else died? Tell me, it's important. I think it's the key to why you feel you identify so well with that goddess, Kali."

The agitation grows and a wound on Becca's leg begins to bleed. Doctor Fenton knows it's time to strike with his ace card. "You know what I think? I think you blame yourself for your boyfriend's suicide."

Becca leaps up and the doctor flinches. "Don't talk about Callum. He has nothing to do with this. He left me, and I'll admit, I'm not over it, but it has nothing to do with these other deaths..."

"Other deaths? So, you are willing to admit what he did. But are you willing to at least accept the possibility that unexpressed feelings of responsibility have been projected onto these other events? Don't you see? You've tried to appear responsible for deaths you knew you couldn't credibly have any influence over because you can't face the one death you believe you did!"

Collapsing into her seat, Becca's mouth falls open and primeval groans creak out.

Fighting the urge to rush over and hug her, Doctor Fenton knows it's against protocol and, anyway, he doesn't want to stem the flow of grief now he's finally lanced it. He suffices with passing her a tissue from his dispensing box on the table.

"Grief is a terrible thing. It's going to take time to get over it. I'm sure you loved him very much." He squints his eyes. "I'll refer you for counselling and perhaps in the meantime I could prescribe something to ease your anxiety. What do you think? Would that help?"

Becca nods. "Why did he leave me?"

"Let's call it what it is."

"Why... Why did he take his life? We had everything. We were going to be together forever. I thought that's what he wanted. I thought he loved me."

"Oh, I'm sure he did. But when someone's in the dark place Callum was, they tend to see things differently. He would have felt worthless, and he would have been convinced you, and the rest of the world, would be better off without him."

"Why would he think that? He was so... everything. He was perfect."

"University can be a struggle for anyone. Not doing so well, especially when your bright-as-a-button photographer girlfriend is acing her course."

"Oh, my god. It *was* my fault. I put too much pressure on him to succeed."

"No. You can't blame yourself. If you'd known, you might have eased up. But how could you know? Callum played his cards very close to his chest. We can only work with the information we are given, and we can't look back and blame ourselves.

"Take me in my job. Most of the time I help people. They take my advice and they go on to lead fulfilling lives. But there will always be those, like Callum, who slip through the net. And I can't blame myself, any more than you should, for not seeing it coming."

Becca stares at the floor, but then jolts her head up as the doctor's last statement seeps in. "What? What do you mean, you didn't see it coming? You met Callum?"

Doctor Fenton joggles his head from side to side. "I'm not supposed to say, but under the circumstances, I think breaking protocol is a good idea. Yes. I was treating Callum for some time. I thought he was doing great, but even with twenty-three years psychiatry experience, I called it wrong. You see? I'm as much to blame as you."

Breath exploding from her, her eyes bulge and she pants as the doctor's words swirl in her head. As they come together and make sense, she screams. Flying across the room, her fist smashes into Doctor Fenton's flabby face; clawing at his flesh, his screams gratify her as she gouges at his skin.

With a bang, the door bursts open and two uniformed police men rush in. As they grab Becca, her arms go limp, the exertion taking all her strength.

"Come on. Back to the cells for you, young lady."

Stepping away, Doctor Fenton whistles as he dusts himself with flat palms. "No, no. That won't be necessary. Miss Tate just reacted to some very bad news." Dabbing at his cheek, he frowns at the sight of blood. His deliberation to send her on her way or keep her is clear on his face and rests on the side of being the bigger person. He could have done more for her boyfriend and it must be a shock for her to hear. "Other than that, I think we've reached an understanding. I don't believe being locked up is the right thing for her."

Scribbling on a pad, he rips it off and hands it to one of the officers to pass to her. "It's medication for anxiety with some rather good anti-depressant qualities. It's quite fast-acting so you might see an improvement right away."

Propped up between the two policemen, Becca pants and stares. Dragged from the room, she doesn't take her eyes from the doctor until the door closes and locks behind her.

"Well, miss. You're free to go. Don't let us see you behaving like that again, okay? Do we have a deal?"

Becca smiles and bows her head. "I won't behave like that anymore."

"Good girl."

Her fingers aren't crossed behind her back, she means it. She won't physically attack the good doctor. She has no need.

Chapter Thirty-three

With a lightness in her stride, Becca retraces her steps from the police station, past the railway, past the shops and the bank where she'd lost herself this morning. Calling into the pharmacy, she sits and awaits her prescription without thought.

Popping a pill as soon as she gets out, she knows she's ready to feel better. "Time to get some work done," she smiles to herself as she reaches her apartment. Pulling her files from under the bed, she admits it could be improved, but it's good enough. After Easter she could expect more projects and she won't want this one hanging over her. She should finish it off and hand it in tomorrow. She might even head home early because there would be no point starting anything else before next term.

Typing the last full stop, she gazes down at her work. She's seen others, some better, but most not as good at all. And considering what she's been through, she knows it's of a higher standard than anyone expected and pride swells in her chest.

Scrolling through her phone, Becca dials home. "Hi, Mum? I've finished my coursework sooner than I thought. I'm thinking about coming home tomorrow, if that's okay?" Tears flow from the other end hearing her daughter sound so much more like herself. "I've realised I need to grieve for Callum. And forgive myself."

"Oh, my baby. I'll help you. Any way I can. You're not to blame. You're a wonderful, beautiful person, cariad. Do you want us to come and pick you up?"

"From the station. Not from Cardiff. I'll be fine. Tell Sophie I'm on my way!"

Getting her washing together, Becca packs some outfits, rolling her eyes that she'll turn up home quite the quintessential student with more dirty clothes than clean.

Stretching and yawning, she pulls off her clothes and slips into a night shirt. Under the covers, she opens her bedside drawer and plucks the picture of her and Callum from its hiding place. Cushioning soft lips against his image, she smiles. "I am so sorry I didn't realise what you were going through, my love. You should have told me, not that idiot doctor. But at least I understand who's to blame now, don't I."

Placing the frame gently beside her, she closes her eyes and smiles. "And I know exactly who I'm going to dream about, just in case it's not all in my imagination. Don't you worry about that."

Waking refreshed, Becca is disappointed not to remember any dreams. Cocking her head, she hopes it doesn't mean she hasn't had one. With a sigh, she opens the click-lid on her bottle from the pharmacy and takes more of the little tablets before heading for the shower.

As the water drips after she turns off the taps, she emerges hot and steamy and wraps a bath towel around her whilst, with another smaller one, she scrunches her hair as she checks through her folder one more time. "Excellent! I'm pleased with that."

Looking at the bags of washing, she decides to call into the university and hand in her work, and come back for her stuff afterwards.

"How are you doing now, Becca?" Janet Barker asks as she flicks through her student's project. "I didn't expect you to hand anything in, let alone work of this quality. Good for you."

"I didn't think I was going to finish, but thanks for taking away the pressure. It really helped."

"Oh, it was absolutely my pleasure."

As the door clicks shut and she walks from her tutor room, Becca gazes across at the canteen. One last coffee before collecting her stuff would be nice. Finding a table, she runs a slender finger around the rim of her latte glass. The sound of a familiar voice stops her heart.

"I thought it was you! May I sit down?"

Her instinctive smile slips with equal horror and joy as the face she smiles into is none other than Greg Davies.

"Bet you don't recognise me clean and shaven?" he coughs. "Are you okay? You look faint. Thought you'd killed me, did you?" he chuckles.

"I went back to check and you weren't there. What are you doing here?"

Greg's smile straightens. "Delivering these. I've had thousands printed." He hands her a pamphlet. On the front is a photo of a woman and two children and behind, arms wrapped around them is Greg. "I thought my tragic story might stick with people more than a generic government effort."

Touching the faces in the photo, tears prick Becca's eyes.

"I believed you. And I waited for death to come. And that's when I knew it wasn't what I wanted, that I could have a purpose and if I didn't do something, my family's deaths were even more of a waste. It's what they would want, isn't it?"

A lump forms in Becca's throat as she wonders if Callum had that last second of regret where things could have turned around, but jumping from a bridge, it had been too late. "I'm sure they would, yes. You're doing a good thing. And you know what else it means? I don't have the power to kill people in my dreams. It was all just too many coincidences."

"I guess you're right. I'm living proof. Well, I'm glad I saw you today. Gives me a chance to thank you. You came into my life to end it, instead, you gave me the kick-start to save it."

"You're welcome, I think," she says. "How can you afford to get all this done?" she points a slender finger at the wads of pamphlets.

"I was wondering when you'd ask. When you saw me on the streets, I wasn't homeless. Not like some of the others. I have a house and money, I just couldn't face going to the home where I let my family down, so I left and didn't go back. Now, thanks to you, I have."

Blushing, Becca smiles. "I am so pleased for you, Greg. I know you'll do your family proud. Learn to forgive yourself." She knows it's advice she needs to take herself. Replacing her empty cup to the table, she stands. "I have a train to catch. I'm going home too."

"And I've got to get these out. I thought I'd start with student accommodation and go from there."

"Good idea. Oh, and happy Easter for next week."

Pain at Easters, Christmases and birthdays lost crease his face but he fights it. "Happy Easter for next week to you too."

Hauling her bags to the front of the building, the Uber arrives just in time to take her to the station. "Return ticket to Fishguard, please." Bundling her luggage onto the train, she is surprised to find a table to herself and she secures it by filling the other seats with her dirty laundry bags. She knows glares will come, but she doesn't care.

Ensconced on the train, bags surrounding her, Becca pulls out the novel about the Pembrokeshire sasquatch. It's good, but her eyes struggle to focus when she reads the same sentence for the fourth time with no meaning. Dropping it on the table, her page is lost. With a shake of her head, she replaces it to her bag.

Opening her purse, she stares at the photo of her and Callum produced in miniature for wallets and purses. "I love you, my darling," she says, touching a kiss from her fingers to his tiny celluloid lips. "*Main tumase pyaar karata hoon.* That's what my gran always used to say to me. It's Hindi for 'I love you.' I'm sure I've told you a thousand times, she was half-Indian. You'd never have guessed it with her thick red hair, and you'd never think I'm an eighth Indian with my auburn curls, either. I wish you'd seen more of her, cariad. But I suppose you can be together in heaven."

Eyes clouding, she is determined to release the blame and guilt she feels. She hadn't known about Callum's suffering. Being wrapped up in the fairy-tale, she never saw what was obvious. But then, she wasn't trained to see that, was she. Someone else was. Someone with, what did he say, twenty-three years psychiatry experience? Callum went to him for help and what did he do? It was clear now who was really responsible.

Becca sighs. Leaning back, her tongue lolls to one side, she stills her kicking feet and closes her eyes.

Chapter Thirty-four

"What happened to you?"

Collin Fenton's hand moves innately to the scratches on his face. "Oh, it's nothing. A patient didn't see eye to eye."

"Nearly ripped your eyeballth from their thockets more like. I hope you prethed charges."

Collin shakes his head. "She's been through enough, I think."

"Well, let me buy you a drink at lunchtime, you poor thing. Honethtly. The thingth we have to put up with." She shakes her head. "You'll have to choose thumewhere though. I don't really know thith thity yet."

"Thank you, Celia. That would be lovely. Of course. I thought I detected a West Country accent."

"Brithtol."

"Yeah." What's the difference, Collin wonders?

"I think it's close enough to lunch time, don't you?"

The tolerance that goes with the job was coming in handy. Collin was so pleased not to be judging her question by the behemoth size of his colleague.

Strolling out to Celia's car takes them forever as she struggles putting one straining plimsol in front of the other. "Is that your car?"

"Yeth," she lisps.

So many wrappers and greasy fingerprints are visible, Collin sniffs the air expecting to smell it from twenty paces. "I don't think we need to take it," he shakes his head. "There are plenty of places within walking distance."

As Celia's face flushes red, Collin Fenton realises they've already reached the limit of her mobility. "Or we could catch a *bus...*"

He says the word at the exact same time a bendy city bus clips the curb and ploughs into the only pedestrian close enough, propelling him with fatal force into the ground.

Screams screech from Celia's rubbery lips as her colleague and superior splats into the pavement like a swatted fly, blood and brains smearing on the asphalt as though a wiper blade would see him off.

Fifty miles west, speeding away from the city and onto the peace and beauty of the Pembrokeshire Coast National Park, Becca Tate stirs in her sleep, her legs tap under the table, and she smiles.

We hope you have enjoyed this book

If you would be happy to leave a few words on Amazon or Goodreads by way of a review, or even just a star rating, that will be invaluable in helping other readers to find it, as well as helping the author to be more discoverable.

If you're happy to help, please follow the link.

http://author.to/MCCarter

Thank you.

Remember the link to a free short story mentioned at the beginning of the book?

Join the author's reader group for updates on new releases etc. and receive *No1 hot new release in short stories*, '*Frankenstein's Hamster*' absolutely free.

https://www.michaelchristophercarter.co.uk/no-1-hot-new-release-free

May we draw your attention to the following book you may enjoy by Michael Christopher Carter which is featured as the book Becca is reading, "The Beast of Benfro" as well as another title dealing with nightmares in a different way, "The Nightmare of Eliot Armstrong".Thank you.

Read on for more titles from this author

About the Author

Michael grew up in the leafy suburbs of Hertfordshire in the eighties. His earliest school memories from his first parent's evening were being told "You have to be a writer"; advice Michael didn't take for another thirty-five years, despite a burning desire.

Instead, he forged a career in direct sales, travelling the length and breadth of Southern England selling fitted kitchens, bedrooms, double-glazing and conservatories, before running his own water-filter business (with an army of over four hundred water filter salesmen and women) and then a conservatory sales and building company.

All that came to an end when Michael became a carer for a family member and moved to Wales, where he finally found the time and inspiration to write.

Michael now indulges his passion in the beautiful Pembrokeshire Coast National Park where he lives, walks and works with his wife, four children and dogs.

If you'd like to contact Michael for any reason, he would be delighted to hear from you and endeavours to answer all messages whenever possible.

mailto:info@michaelchristophercarter.co.uk
https://www.facebook.com/michaelchristophercarter
https://twitter.com/MCCarterAuthor
https://www.michaelchristophercarter.co.uk

More books from Michael

Frankenstein's hamster

Monsters can be small... And furry

Harvey Collins is a seventeen year-old prodigy gifted with a scientific mind that even has Oxford University excited.
When his sister's Christmas present of an adorable hamster falls foul of their alcoholic rodent-phobic father, Harvey is the best person to give him a new lease of life.
Using what's left of the hamster and parts of a rat and even himself, Harvey soon develops a pet like no other.
Bestowed with remarkable intelligence and a thirst for revenge, Harvey's hamster is a monster in waiting.
Will anyone make it out alive?

http://getbook.at/FrankensteinKindle

Or get a copy absolutely free by joining Michael's Reader Group (where you'll also get news of new releases)
https://www.michaelchristophercarter.co.uk/no-1-hot-new-release-free

Blood is Thicker Than Water

What is wrong with the water in Goreston's Holy Well?

When the vicar of a small Welsh community disappears after two little girls are murdered, Reverend Bertie Brimble steps into the breach.
His family are horrified at the danger he's putting his own daughter in. Especially as she looks startlingly like the other victims.
They do everything they can to keep her safe until Bertie himself begins behaving strangely, battling the worst possible desires.

And he's not the only one...

A terrible fate awaits anyone who drinks from Goreston's Holy well
Can Bertie uncover the truth about what's in the water before it's too late?

"Still reeling from the twists...

"Kept me thinking long after I'd finished reading..."

"The epitome of a great writer..."

Blood is Thicker Than Water is a remarkably thought-provoking horror tale from Wales's master of the supernatural.
http://viewbook.at/BloodWater

The Beast of Benfro

Could the truth kill them all?
When struggling dad, David Webb, survives a vicious attack from an unknown creature in the woods, his fears swiftly turn to his flirty neighbour whom he believes might not have been so fortunate.
Calling the police only serves to place him firmly at the top of their list of suspects when she fails to turn up safe and well. Left to rot in jail, his only hope is his delinquent younger brother.

But as they get closer to uncovering the truth about the beast in the forest, they unleash a danger far darker: a menace which threatens everyone they hold dear.
Can anything save them from the Beast of Benfro?

http://viewbook.at/BeastBenfro

The Nightmare of Eliot Armstrong

Can you stop a nightmare coming true?

Eliot Armstrong, swarthy, handsome, head of history at Radcliff Comprehensive is jolted awake every morning; tortured by horrific, indecipherable images of a road accident.
Piecing the disturbing visions together day by day, he's horrified when he recognises one of the cars... his wife Imogen's.
Is it a precognition of his wife's fate?
Or is it a subconscious metaphor for the danger his marriage is in from his man-eating colleague, Uma Yazbeck?
He must do everything in his power to save his wife, and his marriage, But for Eliot, his nightmare is only just beginning...

Do you like thrillers with plenty of twists?
http://viewbook.at/nightmare

Destructive Interference
– *The Devastation of Matthew Morrissey*

Christmas will never be the same again...

When Matthew Morrissey takes an innocent stroll to his local convenience store to buy batteries for his daughter's Christmas present, he doesn't know it will ruin his life.
But, when he returns home, **everything has changed...** There are strangers in his home, his neighbours deny ever knowing him and he ends up attracting the attention of Bristol's finest.
Matthew has a theory about what is happening to him and who is to blame. But first, he has to escape.

Can he solve the mystery and save his family, or has he lost them forever?

Christmas will never be the same after reading this twisting thriller from
Wales's master of the supernatural
http://mybook.to/Destructive

An Extraordinary Haunting

The Christmas holidays can't come soon enough...

Swansea student, Neil Hedges is counting the days
until he can leave his terrifying student digs and go
home for Christmas.

For weeks he's suffered terrifying noises in the middle
of the night and things moving which shouldn't. It's
all becoming clear: someone or *something* wants him
out!

When at Christmas, a psychic friend of the family
confirms his worst fears, Neil and his fellow students
can't bear to go back.

But nothing is as it seems, and when beautiful former
housemate, Elin Treharne, is plagued by nightmares
of her one-time home; nightmares which reveal a
disturbing and life-threatening truth, even she doesn't
realise the peril she's in...

Only Neil can work it out and save her before it's too
late.

But Neil can't cope...

*If you're looking for a paranormal thriller beyond
the norm,*
you've found it.
http://getbook.at/Extraordinary

You don't have to be DEAD to work here... But it helps

You hear your name, but no-one is there...

Night after night after night, growing more and more gruesome in its demands, a voice from the darkness.

What would you do?

Angharad's simple life is about to take a sinister twist...

Since retiring from working in a care home, Angharad is very much self-sufficient: growing her own vegetables, eating eggs from her hens, drinking milk from her goat and even water from her own spring flowing at the bottom of her garden in rural South-West Wales. In many ways, it seems ideal.
But who is it calling out her name in the dark when no-one is there? And what could they possibly want? Angharad doesn't know, but she must find out.
Will she uncover the truth before it costs her, her life?

An intriguing and thought-provoking short novel from Wales's master of the paranormal.
http://viewbook.at/DEAD

The HUM

Just because you're paranoid,
it doesn't mean they're not coming to get you...

A strange humming noise, which seems to have no
source, is tormenting the villagers of Nuthampstead,
England, in 1989...
To the Ellis family, recently moved from the valleys
of Wales, it has a sinister significance. They don't like
to talk about it.
But Carys Ellis is only six, and she has to tell
someone about the terrifying visitors to her room in
the middle of the night when her family would not,
and could not be roused.
And that's only the beginning of Carys's plight. Her
mother is a long-term sufferer of a number of mental
health problems. Diagnosed with bipolar disorder,
manic depression, and borderline disorder, she's a
drugged up mess.
And Carys seems to be heading the same way . . .
Twelve years later, beautiful loner, Carys, is
pregnant.
She's never had a boyfriend; never had a one-night
stand; she's never had any intimate contact with
anyone to explain her condition.
Not anyone human anyway.
Plagued by the dreadful humming all her life, Carys is
convinced the noise precedes close encounters of the
fourth kind; and that the baby inside her is not of this
world.
She can't tell anyone. Her mum couldn't cope, and
her dad's been relocated from Cambridge

Constabulary to a quiet Welsh village after a nervous breakdown leaving Carys struggling with her own demons.

Can she protect her baby from its extra-terrestrial creators, or will they whisk him away for some unknown purpose?

Will the demons who torment her get to him first?

Or, is she just a little crazy...?

Michael Christopher Carter's stunning portrayal of one family's struggle against mental illness and other-worldly threats is a masterpiece.

Described as "Life changing," this thoroughly well-researched novel is a must read for anyone curious about what exists both out in the cosmos and within our own minds.

http://viewbook.at/TheHUM

Printed in Poland
by Amazon Fulfillment
Poland Sp. z o.o., Wrocław

58730098R00190